E. A. WHYTE

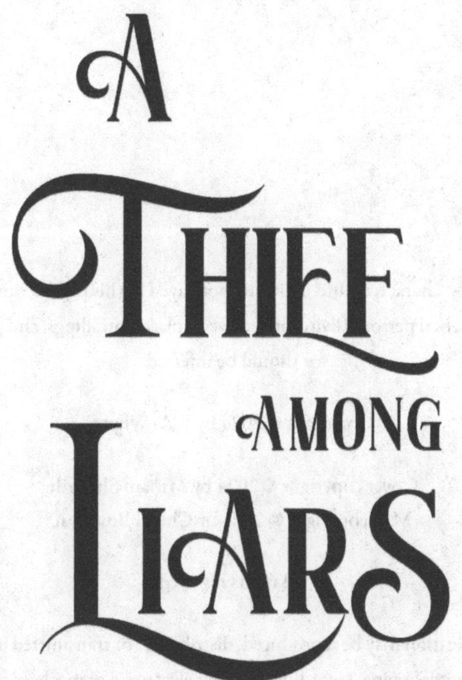

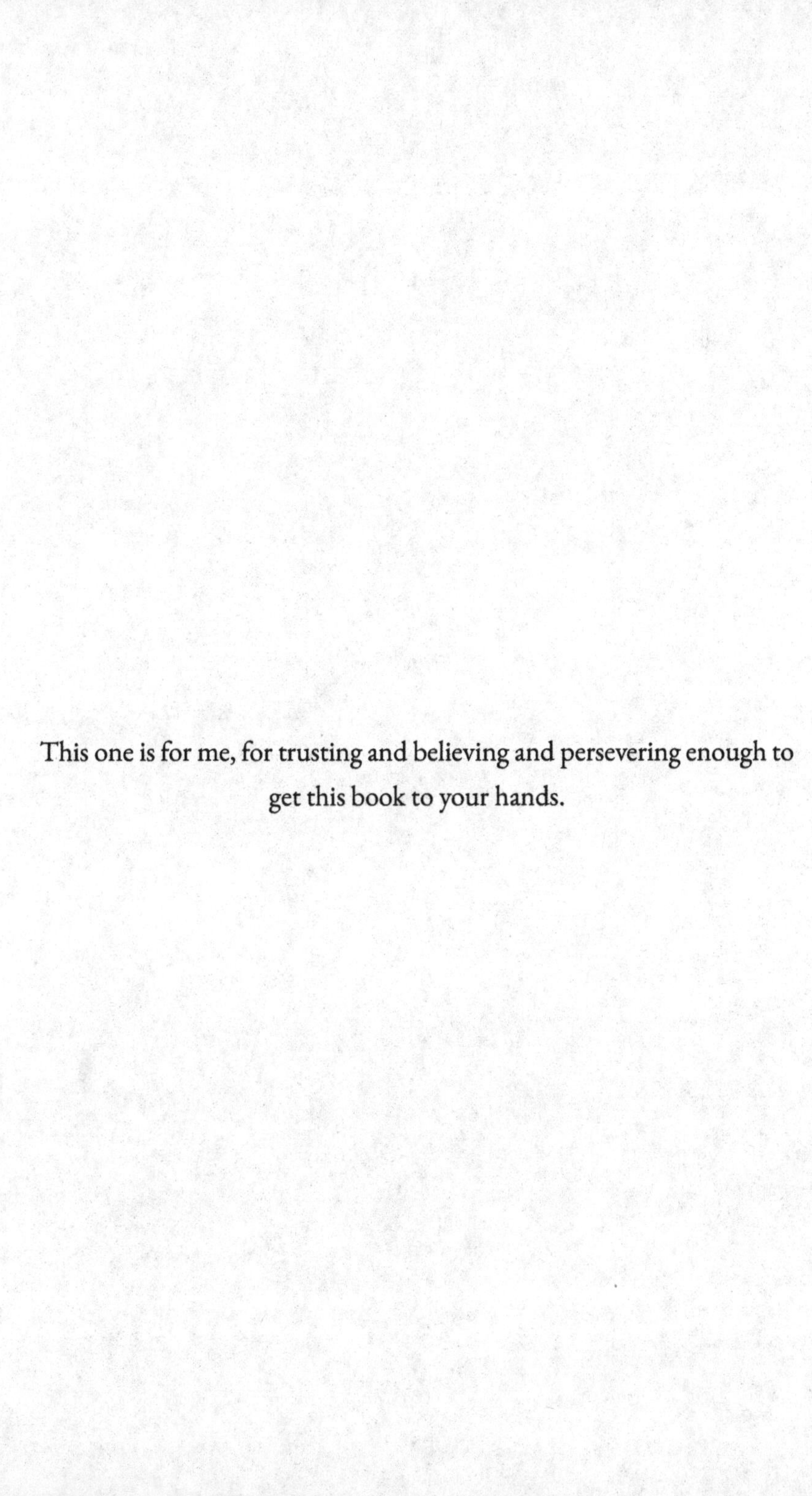

This one is for me, for trusting and believing and persevering enough to get this book to your hands.

Yvelle
The Citadel
New Town
Wellborn
Forsaken Hollow
Scourge Manor
The Underworld

ONE

Ceylon

A good heist is a simple thing. It has only two requirements: a target and an exit. Ceylon was hired to acquire the painting, and she had a clean exit. It was almost too easy.

She pressed her back to the rough stone wall, grateful for the cover of dark. A trickle of sweat beaded down her spine, and—though the night was pleasant—she suppressed a shiver. The ground-level window beckoned. Waiting was the worst part.

Six guards milled about the manor; she'd been watching for the past five days. They never followed the same pattern, but it didn't make a difference. She would be in and out with the painting in less than fifteen minutes.

Ceylon peered over the windowsill as a guard entered the cozy, ornate library. He gave the bookshelves a desultory scan before leaving again. With a centering breath, Ceylon slid the window open as quietly as she could. Checking once more that the guard had moved on, she threw her leg over the sill and slipped inside, pulling the window closed behind her.

She was fast, but there was no point leaving clues. Even these incompetent hired hands would notice an open window.

Ceylon inspected the room, scoffing at the unnecessary grandeur of the gaudy imported wallpaper and hand-carved molding. This manor was one of the oldest in Wellborn, the borough nestled in the northeastern quarter of Yvelle. There was a certain charm to it if she squinted enough.

A peek out the door revealed an empty hall. Ceylon waited a moment longer, craning her neck to see as far as she could. Her knowledge of the layout was imperfect. She'd tried to sneak in two days ago disguised as a laundry maid, but they had simply informed her the linens had been sent out for the week. A lesser thief would've panicked. Ceylon only adjusted her plans to account for the unknown. She'd had plenty of run-ins with guards like these before and always came out no worse for wear.

Her featherweight leather boots were silent on the hall's red carpet. She made her way past the sitting room and a spare study and a—

Ceylon's footsteps halted, backtracking to the study. The sculpture resting beside the fireplace—she knew of few like it. Cherry wood carved by hand and a speckled inlay of real turquoise melathanite. It had to be imported from Vydor or elsewhere on the Southern Continent, if only for the detail. She wouldn't come across a treasure like this even if she'd planned to.

But she hadn't been ordered to steal a sculpture. Her reputation was already crumbling; she couldn't let her father down again. Besides, she would never get the clunky thing out by herself.

With a sigh, Ceylon moved on, pausing at the corner to the main entry and pressing her back to the wall. The guards at the front door chatted, something about what they were going to do once their shift ended. Their plans undoubtedly involved the closest tavern and a couple of large mugs of ale. These fools could do anything with their personal time, and they wasted it intoxicated.

Ceylon didn't even have to create a diversion as she stepped around the corner. They were too immersed in their conversation to notice the girl scurrying across the marble hallway behind them and up the grand wooden stairs.

If she could choose any place to live, it would be similar to this manor. It was large enough to stand on one side and yell, and it wouldn't reach the other side. Her kind of place. Private. Quiet.

Although she would decorate differently.

At the top of the stairs, Ceylon paused, her heart beating a steady rhythm. She was out of view of the main entry, but there were three more guards up here, and she had no idea where they were.

She glanced down the hall that branched off from the upper landing. A short distance down, another hall led to the study she was seeking.

Footsteps sounded to her left, and her heart sped. She was exposed at the top of the stairs. There was the door across from her, but she wasn't sure where it led. It also meant passing in front of the oncoming guard.

To her right was a gold chandelier suspended from the ceiling about a foot or two from the railing of the stairs.

Ceylon hopped onto the banister, her feet light and balanced. A small stature was a benefit in times like these. She leaned over open air to reach the edge of the light fixture. It hadn't been lit for the night. Glancing down to the marble floor of the lobby far below, Ceylon thanked whatever Magus might be listening that she wasn't afraid of heights.

She was silent as she slipped her feet onto the limb of the chandelier. It swung but righted itself. Ceylon was young again, playing games of hide-and-seek in Scourge Manor, scurrying around the rafters and servants' halls. Back then, if she was caught, her father threw her in the dungeons for a day.

She didn't get caught anymore.

Footsteps grew louder. She gripped the chandelier loosely as she folded into the darkness, tucking the art tube in with her. A moment later, the guard appeared, obscured by crystals, the dim light from the wall sconces catching on his hand-me-down uniform.

"Oi, George. Is that you?" called one of the guards from the lower level. Rather loudly for a night shift.

The guard on the top level took a few steps down the stairs, moving closer to Ceylon. He cursed under his breath. Ceylon willed every muscle to stillness, observing.

"Course it's me, Benji. Who else is gunna be up 'ere? Now shut up before you wake Lord Granvilles."

The guard trudged back up the stairs. Ceylon let her shoulders sag just an inch. A few more steps down, and she would have been completely visible.

"Jimmy and me are going to Owl and Fox after this shift, want to come?"

The guard, George, paused. So did Ceylon's heart.

"You know what happened the last time I went with you. I'm not carrying Jimmy's sorry rump all the way home again."

Ceylon rolled her eyes. "Go or don't go. Just move along," she muttered.

George frowned. "What was that, Benji?"

She cringed but didn't move otherwise.

Another guard appeared from the upstairs hall. "Would you lot shut it? Lord Granvilles is going t'have a fit if he hears this. Get back t'work." He stalked off.

George shook his head and moved back to his hall. He continued to the right; the new guard went left. That meant there was only one unaccounted for. Ceylon might not know exactly where he was, but she could handle one guard if necessary. She let out her breath, shoulders dropping.

Luck was on her side tonight.

Ceylon removed herself from the chandelier, stepping lightly on the railing before bounding up the stairs. The painting was calling; she shouldn't leave it waiting.

There was nothing special about the third corridor. It looked like all the others, with closed doors and mounted candles burning away the darkness. The door to the study stared her down from the end of the hallway.

She moved quickly, lock picks in hand. There was no way of telling when that guard would show up, and she was standing in plain sight. Ceylon jiggled the knob, checking it was indeed locked, and set to work. There were few jobs in a heist she didn't excel at, but to her, lock-picking was an art.

With a click and a twist, the door popped open, and she slipped inside.

A large wingback chair faced the window, overlooking the street below. Why Granvilles wanted a view of the filthy thoroughfare, Ceylon would never understand. She would have placed the study toward the back of the manor with a view of the curated gardens. There was a desk with intricate carvings and a number of full bookshelves.

It was a picture of peace and success, built on the backs of those who could never afford such luxuries. But what really interested Ceylon was the painting that hung to her left—one of the few remaining genuine Louvels. She didn't care much for the piece herself. She had been told it was an abstract depiction of nature. To her, it looked like somebody had fallen on a canvas while covered in vibrant paints, but she wasn't hired to pass judgment.

The frame was the length of Ceylon's arm span. There was no way she could transport it subtly. She had been prepared for that and carefully removed the painting from the wall, resting it on the carpet. Slipping her knife underneath the corner of the frame, she applied gentle pressure.

"Come here often?"

She stumbled, dropping the frame facedown with a crash. She whirled on the uninvited guest, listening for footsteps.

After a single breath, the wingback chair spun around. Her blood boiled.

"Dark days...Malachi?" Ceylon cursed.

Malachi, the source of her declining reputation, had a habit of showing up at her private jobs. How he still got wind of them, she had no idea.

Malachi shrugged. "It's not my fault you failed to check the room."

"Get out." Ceylon turned her attention back to the painting. She flipped her dagger and continued popping the canvas from the back of the frame.

Malachi pushed off the chair, ambling over to where she stood. "Ah, but as it so happens, I have a buyer interested in a genuine Louvel." He shrugged again. "I can't leave without it now can I?"

Ceylon threw Malachi an exasperated look. "You're kidding. I let you take this, and my father kills me. I've been casing the place for a week and you want me to just hand over the painting?"

"Hardly—I'm going to take it from you." His pale green eyes sparkled in the dim light seeping through the window, whispering secrets just out of reach. It reminded her of another night, another hijacked heist.

Ceylon ground her teeth, and her hands stilled. "Tell me who the leader of the Forsaken is, and I might be convinced to give it to you."

Malachi tutted. "What, so you can tell Daddy, Lord of the Underworld? You know I can't do that."

Ceylon returned to the frame with a shrug. "Then get out."

She popped the last corner off and sheathed her dagger, preparing to roll the painting and stow it.

Light poured into the room as the door opened, momentarily blinding. A young guard—the one unaccounted for—froze. For a moment, no one moved.

Ceylon flew at the door. The guard shoved against it, his shouts waking the house.

"Would ya help?" she yelled to Malachi, who stood watching with amusement.

At her request, he ambled over to the door and leaned against it. His weight was enough to force it closed.

"Better?" he asked.

Ceylon breathed as she clicked the lock into place. She searched the room for anything that might barricade the door, opting for a small side table. Ceylon grabbed the legs and tugged. The table barely budged. She grunted with each heave, and although she didn't want his help, she had to admit she was grateful as Malachi took the other side and pushed.

With the table in place, Ceylon snatched the painting, rolled it, and slid it inside the protective tube slung across her back. Malachi watched her with careful eyes, as if he were waiting for something. But Ceylon didn't have the time to consider; she could hear more boots pounding down the hall.

They moved to the window. It was only the second floor, but with the guards alerted, they couldn't take the main road—too conspicuous. Maybe the roof...

Ceylon jammed open the window and poked her head out, checking every possible direction. There was a shadow below, a single guard on high alert. Bodies struck the office door.

Left and right revealed more windows with no sign of an easy escape. The only thing in reach was the drainpipe to the roof.

Up it was.

Ceylon shimmied herself outside. There were only a few inches of ledge for her to navigate.

Malachi staggered out beside her, his shoulders barely fitting through the window frame, and pressed his back against the upper glass. He wasn't solid muscle, but he was tall and strong. There wasn't much of a perch for him to stand on, especially in those stupid boots he insisted on wearing. How he moved about silently, she couldn't be sure. They were bulky and heavy, not the kind of stealthy attire she opted for.

With one hand clinging to the wall and one on the glass, Ceylon slid the window shut behind him. She inched to the right, where the drainpipe led up to the roof. Her fingers slipped around the pipe, toes pressing into the rough stone. She didn't wait for Malachi.

Even without rain, the rounded roof tiles were slick and shiny, and the steep slope threatened to send her tumbling to the cobbled road below. She straddled the ridge, taking refuge near the chimney stack.

She hoped the scout her father always sent wasn't watching her flounder. Just another reason to be thankful for the darkness. Now, to make her escape.

The gardens were a no-go. They were always lit with lanterns; she would be seen in a heartbeat. The way she had come in led to a side street; she could see the entry from her vantage point. But as the thought entered her mind it flooded with additional guards.

Not an option, then.

That left the east side.

There was an alley not far off, but there were no window ledges or drainpipes. Just a sheer drop.

Ceylon sighed. This heist was supposed to be an easy in-and-out. Leave it to Malachi to show up at the most inopportune times and put her on the run from average guards. She danced to the far chimney, balancing on the ridge like a tightrope walker from the circus. She turned back to the roof just as Malachi hauled himself over, huffing.

Ceylon attached her spidersilk thread to the chimney, clasping it with a device made for quick releases. She tested the tension, scanned the ground, attached her abseilers, and ensured Malachi wasn't going to get himself killed. To her delight, he had chosen the less dignified method of crawling across the shingles. He was a nuisance, but she didn't need him dead on her watch.

Their eyes met...and she tipped herself backward off the roof.

The wall loomed as she swung back towards the building, the thrill of falling in her stomach. Ceylon braced as she hit the wall before planting her feet and walking herself down. At the bottom, she twisted upright and dropped into the bushes, branches tangling in her dark auburn hair.

This side of the house was mostly dark. She would have to run to the alley. Thirty feet.

She looked up to see Malachi peering down and found a grin on her lips. The quick release snapped open; the cord coiled beside her leaving Malachi to find his own way.

Serves him right. Tucking the thread into her satchel, she rolled her shoulders and took a breath. The thrill of the chase fired through her veins.

She stood, gave Malachi a quick salute, and sprinted for the alley.

Shouts echoed off the nearby walls, voices drawing closer. Blood pounded in her ears. None of the guards would be catching her in their bulky getups, though.

Ceylon beamed as she crossed into the shadows, slowing. She knew her way around the overcrowded town like the back of her hand. Better, even. She didn't spend hours tracing her hand blindfolded. Instead, she strolled through the darkened back streets, the massive structures of Wellborn blurring into the tight-knit lanes of New Town—where the middle class lived and worked and died.

She side-stepped someone passed out on a trash pile. Pausing behind the Owl and Fox, she removed the bricks she knew were loose and tucked away the Louvel. Pride coursed through her, the thought of her father's approval warming her veins as she replaced the bricks. Let the pretty boy get caught. Malachi deserved to have his ego put in check.

It wasn't until she neared the river to cross to the Underworld that footsteps resonated off the stone walls behind her. If she were less trained, her shoulders would have hitched. But she was better than that, and her only reaction was a quickening of her heartbeat. In a single, imperceptible movement, she slipped a dagger into her hand. She kept on her way, pretending not to notice the stalker.

Ceylon listened carefully. Patient.

Then swept out with the knife. Fingers closed around her wrist, forcing her arm backward. She dropped the knife into her free hand and swiped again. The attacker leapt back. Ceylon crouched, ready, heart pumping.

"I must say, I'm rather offended you left me behind." Malachi smiled down at her.

She wanted to punch that smug look off his face. But as fast and cunning as she was, Malachi still had the height and strength on her. Under the right conditions, she would have no problem beating him to a pulp, only that she was expected elsewhere, and this alley didn't give her near enough space to do his beating justice.

"Not my fault you didn't make an exit strategy." Ceylon pulled her hand back but didn't sheath her dagger. "Do you want a prize for making it off the roof, or did you follow me for some other reason?"

"I told you; I have a party interested in a Louvel. The very Louvel you happen to be carrying." He extended his hand as if she would just give him the painting. Ceylon was set to make 500 rubit from this take; she wasn't about to offer it to him.

"Well, guess you're toast. Tell your buyer you couldn't come through because you're not getting this one from me." Ceylon spun on her heel.

Malachi shoved her against the wall, a silver blade pressing against her throat. His jaw was set, but there was a glint of mischief in his eyes.

"See, I was really hoping it wouldn't come to this. I know you're the Daughter of the Underworld and all, but I thought the past few years might have earned me a *little* respect."

There it was: Daughter of the Underworld, her unofficial title among the guilds. Her father, Bronn, was considered *Lord* of the Underworld. And she stood the slightest bit taller because of it.

Bronn ran nearly all the guilds in town. No one really knew where he came from or how he rose to power so fast. But in the years since the king and queen passed, royalty had stayed out of the Underworld, leaving the rabble to organize their own leadership. Bronn was the natural choice. Only the most foolish guilds—the Iron Clan and the Forsaken— still refused to kneel to Bronn.

A ferality descended upon Ceylon, and she tilted her head back to give him even better access to her throat. "You know what Bronn would do to you and The Forsaken if you hurt me. Do yourself a favor and put that silly little knife away."

Malachi feigned distress. "It's not silly. This knife was owned by one of the deadliest privateers from Dyraith."

He was lying. She could see it in the subtle shake of his head. Still, he didn't move the knife from Ceylon's throat.

"I'm not giving you the painting." This was a waste of time. They both knew Malachi wouldn't—couldn't—harm her. It was late, and Ceylon had better places to be.

"Ah, see. That's what the knife is for. Now, I'm not asking, I'm just going to take it." He opened the tube and reached inside only to find it empty of any Louvel.

Ceylon laughed as confusion marred his face. "You think I wouldn't secure it as soon as I left? You've taught me many times not to trust you, Malachi."

He lowered the knife from her throat.

Ceylon rolled her neck, fingers just brushing where the knife had been.

Malachi laughed, a low, amused thing, and Ceylon's fists clenched. What did he have to laugh about?

"I have to admit, you are quite fun to toy with."

She frowned.

"You believe all my actions tonight were an accident? I let you do all the hard work, and you practically told me where the painting was going to be. A colleague is picking it up." Malachi spun the knife in his hand absently.

The world tilted; the painting was hers. She knew exactly where it was. She'd won this round. Hadn't she?

"Don't be cross, you were just outplayed." He lifted a hand as if to pat her reassuringly on the shoulder. Ceylon snapped her teeth at him, and he withdrew his hand.

"How do I even know you have it? How do I know you're not just playing me so you can search the alleys once I'm gone?" she growled.

"I believe it was the...third, no, fourth brick from the left behind the Owl and Fox. Clever trick, leaving it where the guards frequent. A truly poetic touch."

She tightened her grip on the dagger, her spare hand curling into a fist. "What's stopping me from pummeling you into oblivion right now?"

"That's in poor taste. Besides, it won't get your painting back." He crossed his arms over his chest smugly.

Ceylon let her fist fly. It connected with Malachi's nose with a satisfying crunch. It was definitely broken.

"I guess my taste has always been poor since I chose to hang around you."

Malachi made a wounded noise. She shook out the ache in her own hand as she stalked away. There would be some bruising in the morning, but it had been worth it to sock that idiot just once. She had been waiting a long time to do so. Now, she questioned why she hadn't done it sooner.

As Ceylon stepped out onto the main road, a good distance from Lord Granvilles' estate, the bridge to the Underworld loomed before her. She considered the next encounter she was about to have, and she had to force her feet to keep moving. The home base of the Scourge, her father's guild, was an hour's walk away.

She had an hour to come up with an explanation if the Lord of the Underworld would even hear it.

Two

Malachi

Malachi watched Ceylon walk away, his chest tightening with every step she took.

He gingerly touched his nose to see if it was broken. The delicate contact brought searing pain; there was no denying the damage. Still, he wasn't affronted. Ceylon was a handful, but he had provoked the incident. There was no need for him to taunt her so. He could have just taken the painting and left, but it was just too easy to tease her.

Malachi examined the blood on his clothes. It probably wouldn't come out—another fantastic outfit forfeited. Silk of such quality was fickle. He tilted his head back to slow the bleeding and tasted the metallic essence in the back of his throat.

"Are you alright?" Domenyk asked, peeling out from the shadows, canvas in hand.

Dom, Malachi's second, placed a hand on Malachi's shoulder, inspecting the broken nose. His flaming red hair glimmered like fire in the alley-light.

"Fit as a fiddle," Malachi said with a nasal tone. Domenyk's hands clenched as he stomped in the direction Ceylon disappeared, ready to fight for Malachi's honor. Loyal to a fault. "There's no need to let it get to you. It was entirely my fault."

Dom paused, sighed, and turned back. He held up the roll of canvas. "You know, for a guy who just bested the Daughter of the Underworld *again*, you're rather subdued."

Malachi grinned and then winced at the shooting pain.

"You need to let her go, Mal," he continued. "She's nothing more than an annoyance, not to mention a member of the most dangerous family in Yvelle. We could have hundreds of jobs without ever encountering her."

Domenyk was a necessary and valued member of the Forsaken. He was logical and honest. But his attempts at curbing Malachi's impulsive nature weren't always the most welcome reminders.

"In a different life, she would have been one of us. She needs to see the truth about the Lord of the Underworld. Maybe one day she'll realize he's not the great leader she makes him out to be," Malachi said.

He had always been fascinated by Ceylon's tenacity and drive. When he was younger and learning his way around the streets, Ceylon was pickpocketing the king's sentries so precisely they didn't even notice.

But Malachi had seen.

Her auburn hair had been tied back high on her head, swishing behind her as she walked away. She didn't need to run because no one knew to follow her. It was in that moment Malachi resolved to be just as good.

It wasn't until later that he realized who she was. Rumors spread about the thief of the Underworld. Some even mentioned dark magic. Malachi hadn't believed it for a second; Ceylon was too talented to require supernatural assistance.

But even King Owynn's sentries couldn't stop the gossip from twisting around town. Fear, the final remnant of the Battle of the Burning Sea, was still palpable in many parts of Yvelle, though King Owynn and his armies had managed to eradicate the dark mages years ago. Victory came at a great cost. The sentries around Yvelle were now a sad display compared to the might the king once held. It set his citizens on edge for what might occur should the dark mages ever rise again.

Malachi had taken one look at Ceylon, though, and wondered how someone with so much finesse and grace could possibly be considered evil. He'd seen her skill develop, and he knew there was no magic involved. Just sheer determination. Everyone knew she was Bronn's daughter, even though there were no records, no ties—the apple doesn't fall far from the tree. Yet, even if her origins were questionable, that meant little in the Underworld.

Malachi had begun to follow her around, to learn from her. But then she saw him watching.

She'd marched over from a bread stand, a bite of stolen goods in her mouth. "Who'r'you?"

"I'm nobody," he'd whispered back, awed she was even speaking to him.

"You've been following me. What do y'want?"

Malachi was stunned; how had she seen him? He had been very careful not to be noticed, to remain in the shadows.

"Just observing."

Ceylon smirked, but then her face shadowed. "Observing what?" She thrust the stolen breadstick at his chest. "You're not gunna tell the sentries, are you? 'Cause my father is very powerful, and if you tell, you'll only bring trouble on yourself."

Malachi's mouth fell open. He raised his hands in surrender. He was mesmerized. Her spirited green eyes, her threatening words. He'd been outmatched, but he found it hard to be annoyed.

"I won't speak a word of it, I promise." He shook his head.

Ceylon removed the breadstick from his chest, crumbs dropping to the ground. "Good. Guess I'll see ya'round, Nobody."

She'd sauntered off into the crowd. It only took a second for Malachi to lose her among the surge of bodies.

After that, he followed her more closely, to learn of her jobs before they happened. He came up with reasons to see her, to speak with her. As he grew in his abilities, it became his goal to prove himself and to have her take him seriously.

Sometimes that meant getting in her way.

Domenyk's feet shifted on the stone road, and Malachi returned his attention to his still-dripping nose. No way to fix that here. He ripped off a corner of his tunic, gently holding the cloth in front of his nose.

"Let's go," he said. Dom gave him one last exasperated look before following Malachi down the alley. "And keep that painting away from me, no point in destroying a perfectly good canvas with blood."

Dom made a snorting sound Malachi elected to ignore.

As they crossed the bridge over the Suri Kulu and into the Underworld, the well-kept structures and cobblestones of New Town crumbled into dilapidated dwellings and darkened doorsteps. The Underworld shouldn't have felt like home—he'd been born in New Town, and the Underworld was the bottom of the barrel; a place for the ruthless, the hopeless, and the abandoned—but he'd found more family among the outcasts than he ever had with his blood.

Malachi felt his shoulders loosen with every step, his chin drifting higher, and he couldn't help the delight that bloomed across his face—even if it did hurt his nose.

"Keep your head down, Mal. You never know who might be on these streets," Dom grumbled, reaching to pull Malachi into the dark.

"You know, you could really be more flexible. Enjoy the fresh air. Look at the stars," Malachi said as he danced out of the way of a couple of drunks.

"And you could be more cautious." Dom let the couple run into him, giving them a disapproving stare. They flinched back, muttering slurred apologies, and ducked into an adjoining street. "I guess neither of us will ever be entirely pleased."

Malachi snickered. Indeed, they would not.

They rounded one final corner that led to the abbey. Malachi had gone to great lengths to ensure no one would enter here unless they were a member of the Forsaken. He'd spent a fortune on the charm that hid the abbey's true nature from prying eyes. To those without a token, it was haunted, rotting, a place to fear. No one set foot within a block.

It kept them safe.

Still, Malachi glanced up and down the empty streets before ducking through the side door.

There weren't many people awake in the abbey at this time of night. Malachi gave Dom a few instructions concerning the Louvel and the completion of the sale.

Dom grumbled, then threw over his shoulder, "The roof in the east wing is still leaking. I'm not mopping all day if it rains again."

The words sent a warmth through him, comfort—his own dysfunctional family.

Alone, Malachi took in the stone walls, the wooden doors; it had been his home for years, and the one place he felt truly at ease. It was a simple building, not like the king's citadel in New Town or the grand townhouses in Wellborn. It was a place of refuge. He would give his life to defend it, if it ever came to that.

He ambled through the wide, stone halls of the abbey, sconces lighting the way, and paused in the courtyard garden. The scent of fresh herbs and blossoms enveloped him. Out here, he could take in the stars. It was one of his favorite things to do, admire the night sky. He didn't feel quite so insignificant when there was so much wonder to be explored.

Before the chill set in, he returned inside. His chambers were at the far end of the dormitory hall. Only two torches were lit here as the rest of the Forsaken were likely asleep. It wasn't often he slept in his own room, regularly choosing one of the empty dorms, but the private quarters were a gift.

Bookcases filled with his rare books ran along the walls, lit by the large hearth resting to the side. It cast a warm glow around the room. He often came here when he wanted to read by the fire during the cold winter months. His guild knew that and so they kept it aflame whether he came home for the night or not.

Deep blue linens covered his bed, imported from distant kingdoms he had a hard time pronouncing. Or at least, that's what he'd been told.

Malachi stood at the end of the bed, staring at the gold embellishments sewn into the edge of the linens, remembering an injured man gripping that very fabric like it could save him.

He must be destroyed, Malachi. You know what needs to be done, the man whispered.

The door slammed open, and the memory faded into smoke. Malachi leaned casually against the bedpost.

"Please, do come in," he greeted the resident healer and cook.

"Hush and set your butt on that chair." Ayleth pointed by the fire. Her back was hunched, and she didn't so much walk as shuffle.

He wandered over, sprawling into a velvet chair by the fire.

"...Domenyk *demanding* it couldn't wait until morning," she muttered.

"My apologies, Ayleth. It appears my mouth has run away with me again."

Ayleth plopped herself in front of Malachi with her bag of gauze. She glared up at him.

"It's not your mouth that's the problem." She grabbed his chin, yanking him toward her with surprising strength. She tilted his head this way and that, staring at his nose. "Broken."

Malachi leaned away as she reached into her bag. "Could have told you that myself."

"Well then, I guess you won't be needing my assistance?"

Malachi stiffened, smiling awkwardly. "I didn't say that."

She stared at him. In one swift movement, she grabbed his chin again and snapped his nose back in place. Malachi howled, tenderly pressing a hand to the bridge of his nose. Ayleth shoved some gauze at him as she stood.

"Don't get blood on the carpets. I won't be cleaning them because of your stupidity." She set a small vial of cream on her vacated chair. "Use that and your pretty face will be back to normal in a few days."

Ayleth trudged out of the room.

Malachi gave a tired grin and slumped back into the chair. Ayleth had hard edges, but he knew she, too, would defend the Forsaken with her life. If only for the sake of her late son.

His reflection in the golden mirror above the hearth caught his attention. Bruises had begun to form under his eyes, deep purple things. His nose was straight again, but dried blood still crackled under his nostrils and down his chin.

He glanced at the vial. What right did he have to heal himself? Tonight's escape came at a cost. He'd seen Bronn's wrath from a distance one too many times, and he didn't wish it on anyone, but he had to get through to Ceylon somehow. Still, he deserved to feel at least a little of that pain. The thought of Ceylon at Scourge Manor sent a chill raking through his body. He turned toward the dying fire. She was tough—she would survive this. Malachi only hoped that survival would be enough.

THREE

Ceylon

The walk home felt especially long. Ceylon ran through a list of excuses. There were those who had angered the Lord more than she might have—maybe she could propose revenge. She could always offer Malachi's head on a platter. Those promises seemed to please her father.

But the closer she got to her home, the more she realized she would have to tell the truth, some version of it at the least. She had let Malachi distract her. She had been cocky and wasn't watching her back or her hiding place. He had used her confidence against her, and Ceylon had fallen for it. The fault was entirely her own.

The manor stood on the corner of two generally busy streets in the Underworld, the grimy sibling to New Town, which lay across the river. At this time of night, the crossroad was deserted—not only because of the hour but because everyone knew whose house this was.

While the Lord of the Underworld was known to be ruthless, he never acted without purpose. He wasn't one to strike someone down simply for walking by his property.

No, his wrath was reserved for those who had truly messed up.

Like her.

Ceylon shivered against the punishments that flitted through her mind—things she'd experienced before for less.

The mahogany doors stood before her, towering over her at twice her height, a reminder of how small one was in the realm of their Lord. But no one could call her a coward. She pushed them open, wincing as they creaked. There was no way of entering the manor quietly.

When she was younger, she used to climb through the windows so she could sneak around undetected. That ended the day she'd dropped into a very important meeting involving a duke and some rather compromising information. After patching things up with the client, her father yelled at her about the impropriety of sneaking into business meetings. Ceylon knew part of him was proud of her for being able to make it into the room at all. Or, at least, she assumed he was proud.

The Lord of the Underworld was hardly a beacon of compassion, but he did have his moments. He never smiled, but sometimes her performance during her training would provoke a single nod. Afterwards, Ceylon would discover that the kitchen staff had been told to leave out a custard pie just for her. It was those days she knew she did well, even if he never said it to her personally.

Most of the house would be asleep now. Maybe her failure could wait until morning. If she was lucky, the scout her father sent hadn't noticed Malachi.

She tiptoed up the grand staircase, the runner stark against the dark wood, muffling her steps as she made her way to her room.

"...the whole shipment?" her father's voice was cool, laced with anger.

She slowed, relieved not to be on the other end of that conversation.

"Yes, My Lord. The Forsaken managed to intercept the shipment before—"

"I don't care *how* they did it. I care that my own people couldn't handle the task of keeping out a few children!" the Lord of the Underworld yelled. A shuffle. "Find it. We can't move to phase two without all the shipments—that includes Yru."

Ceylon flinched. Her room was on the top floor, she'd have to walk past the office to get there, but maybe if he was distracted enough...She took one more silent step before the boom of her father's voice reverberated through the foyer, calling her, and her stomach turned to stone.

Ceylon continued up the stairs as someone she didn't recognize scurried down, a man with wide eyes and early wrinkles. She logged the man's face away to consider later. Inside the office, she found her father sitting in his imposing chair behind the desk, as usual. A knife the length of Ceylon's forearm notched marks in the tabletop, unusual. She tried not to let the tremor she felt show.

Her father's light brown hair brushed his shoulders, a groomed beard trimmed short framing his stern face. The man was as sturdy as Ceylon was nimble, as immovable as Ceylon was flexible. If she was being honest, there was very little physical resemblance between them. But she'd been raised by this man. Her character was shaped and molded after his very own. She never missed the chance to prove her relation.

To his right stood Brutus. He was wide as a door, dark as the night, and broody, but he was truthfully a kind soul. Unless her father had a job for him, Ceylon had learned to stay out of his way. Leaning on the desk to her father's left was Alfie.

Of course, he was the scout for this take. His gaunt frame hunched over the tabletop like a vulture circling carrion. He had a habit of tattling on the crew. While he wasn't good for much, he had a skill of getting into tight places. And blowing things up. Ceylon was tempted to slap the smirk off his face, but that wouldn't help her case.

The Lord of the Underworld didn't look at her as she entered. Ceylon stood across from him; in this room, the distance felt like miles.

"You lost the Louvel." It wasn't a question.

Her fingers worried at a loose thread. "Lost is a harsh word—"

The Lord slammed his free hand on the table. "You either have the painting, or you don't. Do not test my patience with technicalities, girl."

Ceylon knew better than to say anything. Alfie was practically beaming at her reprimand. She may have framed him a few too many times. At least the next time, it would be well deserved.

"We had been following that trail for weeks—one of the few Louvels still in circulation. Wasted because you were played by a child of the *Forsaken*."

Ceylon cringed. Malachi was her age, and she was *not* a child. But she kept very still; her father maintained an air of composure, but his pinched lips told a different story. She could feel his anger radiating across the room. Brutus grimaced for her.

At least someone cared for her wellbeing.

Malachi would have already sold the painting, but she might still be able to salvage the situation. "I can get it back. I'll leave right now."

He shook his head. "The damage is done; the painting is inconsequential now. You've cost us a good deal of money and our reputation. It will not be easy to recover."

"Tell me what to do and I'll do it. You know I'm good for it, father."

The Lord of the Underworld winced at the word. Ceylon never knew why, but he hated it when she called him anything familial. He was Bronn. That was his name, and so it was forced to be her title for him, externally at least. She couldn't bring herself to call him lord. Internally, she thought of him as father, which was why she would occasionally slip. Now couldn't have been a worse time.

"Perhaps I should lock you in a cell for a few days. Maybe that would cure you of your confident delusions." He rubbed his temples. "Your arrogance will be the death of you."

Ceylon's breath hitched, a shot of fear piercing through her heart. She had spent time in the cells before. Practically every member of the Scourge had. The days of no sunlight, endless isolation, and starvation assaulted her mind. Her stomach growled in response. No, she did not wish to be left in a cell.

"My Lord, I think you've scared her enough," Brutus said quietly. He did not touch Bronn. Smart man.

"Fine." Bronn lowered his hand, flipping the knife and finally looking at Ceylon. "The painting was a disappointment, I admit. We're on the cusp of amalgamating the final guilds, and I don't need anyone questioning my position. But it is only part of the reason we're meeting tonight."

Ceylon clenched her jaw to keep it from dropping open, subtly wiping her palms on her stealth suit. That was it? He wasn't going to punish her?

Alfie stared at Bronn incredulously. "Sire, ain't she got to pay for losin' the Louvel?"

Bronn was on Alfie in a blink, knife behind one ear, the other hand clutching Alfie's shirt. "Do you need two ears to scout?"

Alfie's eyes darted between Brutus and Bronn. "Y-yes, My Lord?"

"Question me again, and you'll have to make do with one." Bronn snarled, holding Alfie for a moment longer before shoving him away. "Get out of my sight before I change my mind."

Had Ceylon not been in danger of a similar fate, she would have laughed as Alfie sped past. As it was, she could barely keep her breathing even, and she was thankful for the space in the room.

Bronn settled back into his chair, dignified, the knife point resting on the table. "There is a job being planned. Limited knowledge, need-to-know only." His eyes pierced through Ceylon, holding her to the spot.

Her hands began to tingle. They always did when she was told of large takes like these. They were her bread and butter. Well, except when Malachi just *had* to butt in.

"What do you need me to do?" Ceylon asked, convincing herself the turn in her gut was excitement.

"Prove yourself," Bronn said. "If this job is going to be successful, which I anticipate it will, I'll need my best team on it. Your failures over the past year have made me question if you're the right fit for this particular crew."

Ceylon's heart dropped into her stomach. He was sidelining her?

"I promise you, Bronn, I'm fully capable of any job you require of me."

"I will decide that for myself." He cocked his head to the side. The knife spun absently in his hand as he looked Ceylon over from head to toe. The corners of his mouth pulled downward. "If I deem you unfit for the crew, Gideon will be named my successor."

Ceylon's mouth did drop open then. Gideon was strong, fast, handsome. Everything Bronn could possibly wish for in a second. But he was not blood. He was not her, and she would not allow that boastful cretin to take her rightful title.

"Tell me how I can prove myself." Ceylon held her breath.

"A different job. One I give you complete freedom to execute on your own terms."

She bit her cheek to hide her smile. She was rarely given such a gift.

Bronn traced a finger over the table like they were discussing the weather and not her one chance to be named heir.

"The Forsaken have become a problem I can no longer ignore. I want you to steal their leader's heart."

Ceylon was sure she'd misheard. "Like, literally? You want me to bring you his heart?"

Brutus coughed, hiding his mouth. Bronn just rolled his eyes.

"Stupid child. I want you to make him fall in love with you."

He must have been joking. No one had seen the leader of the Forsaken. He was rumored to be the youngest boss of an Yvelle guild ever. But how was Ceylon supposed to find him? The only real connection she had was Malachi, and she'd been exhausting that outlet for years with no results.

And it couldn't *be* Malachi. He was annoying, sure, but he was hardly a leader. He was a lackey, someone who did the grunt work and got in her way. He was nowhere close to her level.

The real leader could be eighty for all they knew. And better yet, how was she supposed to make him fall in love with her? She wasn't sure if she even knew what love was. This wasn't a real job. Not one she had been tasked with before.

"The Forsaken have been a thorn in my side for years. If they won't kneel, they will be destroyed. I don't just want them gone, I want them annihilated." He set the knife down, his fingers folding together, knuckles whitening. "Get close to them, get them to trust you. Once they do, take them for everything their useless lives are worth."

Ah. There it was. This was a test for Ceylon, but it was also a way for Bronn to get the Forsaken to fall in line. They had been searching for the proper leverage for months. Maybe they had just been looking in the wrong places.

"I'll do it." The words tasted bitter in her mouth. Never had she been reduced to her feminine wiles before. Her stomach churned. But her father needed her. If she didn't see this job through, her entire future was in jeopardy. She would not bow to Gideon for the rest of her life.

"You have one week." The Lord of the Underworld stood and then paused. His head tilted to the side, and he gave an almost imperceptible nod. Ceylon's heart soared as Bronn left the office. He believed in her; she could do this.

Brutus hesitated in the doorway. "He loves you, you know." He looked like he wanted to say more, but he strolled out of the room, closing the side doors behind him.

Ceylon clapped her hands together. One week was barely enough time to plan an easy heist, let alone one with so many variables and a subjective outcome. She may not know much about love, but even she could tell a week didn't feel like nearly enough.

Her mind reeled at the possibilities. Never having been in a relationship—she was much too busy for that—she didn't even know where to start.

Once, when she was about twelve, she thought she felt something for Gideon. Turned out it was just loathing.

Lost to her thoughts, Ceylon drifted through the halls to her room. It was one of the smallest in the manor, but it was on the top floor and the only one with a window seat that overlooked the city. She felt calm when she could see how small her world really was.

Her plan to sit on that window seat and think was quickly thwarted when she found Gideon already occupying the space. Ceylon sighed heavily.

"Get out. I'm in no mood to deal with high-born pretty boys right now." She didn't know what time it was, but she was certain it was well past midnight.

"Aren't we feisty tonight? Is it the fact you lost a Louvel in a simple break-in?" The look he threw her way said he was perfectly happy she'd failed.

Ceylon pulled out one of her daggers and threw it at his head. He dodged it, barely. The dagger stuck into the wood frame behind him, humming as it vibrated.

"The usual charm, I see." He stood from the window seat, smoothing down the front of his tunic. "I sure hope those aren't the tactics you plan to use on the Forsaken."

Ceylon snarled at him. He always seemed to know everything that went on in this house.

"I thought I told you to leave."

"Oh, you did. I elected to ignore it. After all, you're not the successor yet. I have no reason to follow any of your orders."

"Well, you won't be saying that for long." Ceylon fluffed her pillow though she had no plan to use it. She just needed to look busy until Gideon finally decided to leave.

Gideon brushed a small speck of dirt from the shoulder of his long leather coat. She didn't know why he wore it. Maybe he thought it made him look more regal. It looked ridiculous and was probably going to get him killed one day when it caught on something.

Perhaps, in that case, he should wear it more often.

"Does the great Daughter of the Underworld have a plan already?" He raised his eyebrows. "I hate to break it to you, but finding employment in the closest brothel probably won't work. You don't even know what the master looks like."

Ceylon's teeth ground together, but her mind began to turn.

Gideon's footsteps drew close behind her.

"Maybe I could show you a few things," he whispered in her ear. His hands landed on her hips, and nausea rolled through her.

Ceylon lashed out, hitting him below the belt with her elbow. When he staggered, she grabbed his throat, shoving his back against the wall. Her free hand snagged the dagger from the window frame and pressed it against his throat.

"Do you need two hands to be a thief? Or do you think you can keep them to yourself?" she hissed in his face as blood roared in her ears. She willed stillness to her hand, hoping he couldn't feel it shake.

Gideon's breaths came in ragged spurts. He managed a grin. "Scared, lovey?"

Ceylon slammed his head back against the wall. He let out a cry of pain.

"Just know the only reason I'm not currently slicing your throat is because my father would be disappointed if you couldn't use that silver tongue of yours." Her eyes roamed his face—his handsomeness was his most prized possession. She slashed downward, starting just above the left eyebrow and ending at his elegant cheekbone. Not deep enough to be a danger but enough to leave a scar. Gideon shrieked. It resonated somewhere deep within her, bolstering her. This was her father's second choice?

"Every time you look in the mirror and see that scar," she said, "I want you to remember to keep your hands to yourself."

Ceylon threw him into the hall as he clutched his face, blood slipping through his fingers. But she didn't watch for long because the annoying twat had given her an idea.

She couldn't make any kind of reliable plan without knowing who the master of the Forsaken was. And there was only one tavern in the Underworld the Forsaken were known to frequent. Granted, it was also the only establishment that hired mercenaries to keep the Scourge out. Just stepping foot inside could have her thrown into a deep hole she might not come out of, but at this point, if she had any hope of becoming the successor, it was a risk she needed to take.

Ceylon only had a week to find the master and make him fall in love—if it even *was* a him. Not that it mattered either way. At the least, she needed to find their hideout tonight.

Ceylon checked her suit, restocking her weapons, grabbed a cloak, and slithered out of her window back into the darkness.

FOUR

Ceylon

Ceylon weaved her way through the Underworld. The night chased at her heels, whispering silence. She was swift but didn't draw attention. The tavern was on the southwest side of the Underworld, and it was not a short journey.

A body caught in her vision; the way it swung from the lamppost made her shiver. There were no marks identifiable from this distance, but it was the signature execution style for someone accused of working for the Scourge in secret. Her guild. Ceylon didn't recognize the body, so there was no way to be sure. Honestly, Ceylon found commoners much more frightening than anyone she worked with. Fear could wreak havoc on an otherwise peaceful community. It made people unpredictable.

The Battle of the Burning Sea caused a rift between those who could afford to live and those who could not. The guilds formed out of necessity, providing goods for those that New Town and Wellborn would not sell to. Until her father began uniting them, the guilds had been at odds.

Many refused to see the good Bronn was doing for the Underworld. They called him fanatic, cruel. And yet it was because of him they could find food or have a place where the king's sentries did not roam. It added at least a small amount of security to their lives.

With only the Iron Clan and the Forsaken outstanding, the Underworld was well on its way to unification.

Shuffling feet and whispers sounded down the lane. Ceylon tucked further into her cloak until the two men lumbered past, muttering over a few coins as they checked their shoulders. She shook her head. Amateurs.

Ceylon counted their steps until they were out of earshot. She continued on her way.

Anger wove through her as she contemplated having to attempt this stupid plan. But with the amount of time her father had given her, she didn't have a better one.

Ceylon would just have to hope one of the Forsaken was at the tavern tonight, and they wouldn't take too long getting home. She didn't know their faces—not many did—but they all carried the mark of the guild with them. A small disc with the image of a rose losing its petals, similar to a coin, with a hole in the center so it could be tied to a leather cord. It was generally hidden somewhere on their person.

Half an hour later, the old tavern loomed before Ceylon, its tired exterior sagging from years of overuse. Torchlight poured from its windows, even at this hour. Chatter and cheering echoed down the street; an acrid stench drifted from an open window, something that seemed to accompany all the taverns in Yvelle. But unique to this tavern were the two mercenaries who guarded the door.

She pulled her cloak tighter, her hood concealing her face. This was her one chance to make it in with the Forsaken, as she would be quickly recognized by security in a place that prohibited the Scourge.

Ceylon approached the front entrance. Her fingers curled into a fist, preparing for some well-placed blows, but at that moment, the door flew open, and someone stumbled out. They were still holding a mug of ale, sloshing it all over the street and the two mercenaries. Ceylon narrowly missed being doused herself.

The mercs shouted, raising hands. They pushed the person out into the street, turning their backs to the door. For a moment, Ceylon just watched, stunned at her luck that they didn't even notice her. But with a quick prayer to Magum Makaio, she snuck through the open door.

There were three exits she could see: a back door behind the counter, a hall leading off to the right, and the front door she had just used. A handful of grime-smeared windows lined the walls. Fire roared in the hearth to her left, making the already warm tavern stifling. The scent of sweat and booze wafted through the air, clinging to her, and Ceylon feared the effort that would be needed to remove the stink.

The attention of the room, including the barkeep, was fixed on some kind of gambling. Ceylon observed the room as she took a seat at one of the tables far enough from the door, and with a perfect view of the betting.

Most of the other tables were empty as people crowded around the game where two very large men sat across from each other. Mugs littered their table. Some were empty, others were not. They lifted mug after mug, guzzling its contents before slamming the empty glasses down. Ceylon could tell right away the man on the left was going to win—the one with the flaming red hair.

He was cheating.

He managed to lose most of the ale on his clothing without the crowd noticing. The other man was rocking in his seat; he still had two mugs to go. For a moment, Ceylon debated challenging the winning man. She could drink him under the table in a fair fight. But she had a job to do.

A quick glance at the patrons revealed crude alliances. She recognized the tattoos of the Iron Clan—the guild known for smuggling people in and out of Yvelle. A few scantily clad patrons were draped over other unsavory-looking characters in dark corners. Some faces she remembered seeing on the street, pilfering what rubits they could. She was surprised they had the coin to afford anything. On the other hand, there was more than one guest from Wellborn attempting to hide their wealth in worn fabrics, but it would take years to remove that air of self-righteousness.

From Ceylon's cursory investigation, she couldn't identify any Forsaken. No, she needed to get a marker out in the open. She shifted in her seat, intending to head for the crowd.

"...that old man from New Town was arrested last week," the guest at the next table murmured to his companion.

Ceylon froze, ears piqued to Yvelle's gossip. Secret conversations were more valuable than many realized as even rumors were often based in truths.

"That crazy one who's always babbling about the dark mages from the South Continent?" the friend asked. "'Bout time those ramblings of doom were shut up. Dark mages. Honestly."

"Not so, my sister saw a healing mage just yesterday—one of the ones in Wellborn that came from the mountains to the north, from Yamah. Those nomads know what they're doing. High-borns can't look that pretty without some help," the first said with a growl.

"Yamans don't practice dark magic, just the innate stuff," the friend replied.

The first glanced around—Ceylon hunched farther over her table—and leaned closer to his friend. "But Netta, from next door, told me her cousin came to visit. In a different body. She said the Necromancer brought him back."

The friend scoffed. "The Necromancer is a myth; she's no realer than my fortune. And Netta's been batty since her cousin died. She'd see him in a pig if it made her feel better."

"Maybe, but you didn't see her, Landry. Her eyes were clear for the first time in months. I'm telling you, something's happening to this kingdom. Ever since the eldest prince disappeared—"

"Come on. Yvelle is as safe as it's ever been. The dark mages are gone, there never was an 'eldest prince'. The former king and queen died of a sickness. Don't start with all your controversy. Netta's just crazy. All that's left are some charms and potion-makers. And a good king to boot." He lifted his glass, spilling ale over the table. "Those pirates from Ranniko, on the other hand, can't seem to keep them out of the king's coffers."

Ceylon shivered. She'd heard whispers of the Necromancer in Yvelle for years. Some said she was the most powerful dark mage in history, others that she was no more than a tall tale. Yet people still made their way to the forest at the eastern edge of the Underworld after the passing of a loved one, with the hope she would bring them back.

The missing prince, though...that was a phrase she hadn't heard much. The Scourge had their hands in a lot of pots, but even there, whispers of the royal history seemed a mystery.

Ceylon rolled her shoulders and cracked her neck; she'd heard enough. The commotion of the gambling tables reached its peak as the man on the left placed his mug down a moment before the contender fell out of his seat.

There were boos and the sound of coins being exchanged. Ceylon placed herself in the middle of the crowd. No one would know where the shout had come from, and she didn't need them to know. She just needed to check their pockets.

"I've been robbed!" she bellowed.

Cursing echoed around the tavern as every patron stopped their conversations and frantically patted themselves down. Ceylon scanned the crowd for the token.

She wasn't disappointed.

The man who had won the round of drinking carefully pulled out a Forsaken marker. Anyone else wouldn't have noticed, but Ceylon had been waiting for it.

The crowd quickly dispersed, everyone worrying about losing their hard-earned winnings. Ceylon allowed herself to be carried with the current as she kept her eye on the red-haired winner.

He glanced up a warily as he tucked the winnings into a pouch. Red Hair's eyes skipped over her as he stood from the table.

She had her mark, and almost her freedom from the crowd, but then she noticed the mercs checking everyone who walked out. Checking for the fake robber Ceylon herself had fabricated.

At the last second, Ceylon stepped out of the current and into a waiting chair. It wasn't ideal; her back was to the man, but with less people also came less noise. And it gave her a moment to figure out how to follow the man and get past the mercs.

The man strolled over to the barkeep. They had a short conversation she couldn't make out, but then he strode for the door.

Ceylon hunched, the breeze of his pace rustling her hood as he passed. Just like that, her time was up. Ceylon told herself there was nothing to worry about. It's not like *she'd* stolen anything, yet. The mercs would search her and let her pass like everyone else.

She waited for a handful of breaths and then stepped through the door.

The mountain of a guard turned. Ceylon's eyes narrowed, calculating the distance she would need to pass him and avoid that meaty grasp if they didn't let her go.

"Hey, we didn't let you in," the merc said, hand extending.

"You must have forgotten." Ceylon stepped forward, but the merc slapped a hand on her shoulder, wrenching her back.

There wasn't enough space. And worse, Red Hair was about to disappear around a corner.

Her hood slipped and light cut across her face, her hair. The merc's eyes widened with recognition. Now, the second one also turned toward the commotion.

Ceylon groaned. She didn't have time for this.

"You're the Daughter of the Underworld!" the second merc shouted.

Ceylon gave a slight bow, making room before she surged upward. She pinned the first merc's hand to her shoulder, grabbing his elbow and forcing it upward with a satisfying snap. He screamed, buckling.

The second leaped for her. Ceylon dodged, slamming an elbow into his back as he stumbled forward. He grunted and his knees crashed into the dirt.

But this one was faster, and he was back on his feet momentarily.

"Just stay down," Ceylon muttered.

There was some distance between them now. Enough that she could make a break for it, but it would be close.

She pushed off. The merc just missed her arm, fist closing on her cloak instead.

The cloak tightened around her throat. Ceylon scrambled at the closure, coughing and sputtering. The merc dragged her backward, and the fabric strangled her.

Finally, Ceylon's fingers unsnapped the clasp. The cloak flung from her shoulders, sending both her and the merc to the ground.

With a gasp, Ceylon shot to her feet and took off down the street. She didn't look back. Her feet only slowed once she soared around the corner.

Ceylon heaved down breaths as she searched the shadows for Red Hair. There, just turning left down another road. She tried not to rush to catch up, taking an even pace and walking with intention. She doubted she'd find another chance if she gave herself away before seeing the hideout.

Ceylon turned the corner as Red Hair walked back her way. He startled but just stepped aside and carried on. Ceylon did the same. A clever switchback. Whoever this Forsaken was, he knew how to lose a tail. She could afford one pass unnoticed, but not two. Ceylon peered after Red Hair. When he was a comfortable distance away, she followed, keeping to the darkest shadows. It was fun, at first, dipping through alleys and tucking into doorways. But after what felt like the fourth hour, Ceylon began to get bored. There were only so many times she could pretend to be a wall.

Finally, Red Hair approached an old abbey only a few blocks from the tavern he'd just visited. They were at a side door, not the grand doors at the front, but it was still a sight to behold. Old and forgotten, the grey stones stretched three stories into the sky, tinted with the sadness of inattention. And yet there was still a grandeur to the structure.

The small wood door was tucked into a dark alcove. It was shielded from the lamplight—a perfect hiding place—and located in a rarely-used alley.

A strange sensation snaked through Ceylon from across the way where she observed. A sense of foreboding before a storm or the dread of waking from a nightmare. Ceylon wasn't one to shy away from danger, but something about the feeling made her want to run.

She'd heard the rumors of the abbey: haunted, infested with rats, its roots to the dark mages. They'd all seemed far-fetched, but standing before it now, she wasn't quite so sure.

Red Hair disappeared inside. She waited for a guard or the hitch of a lock, but no sound followed him. With a frown and a glance down the alley, she made her way to the door.

The feeling worsened the closer she got. Ceylon's chest tightened, her breath hitched. As her hand brushed the door, a spike of panic surged through her. But then it quieted, as if a wall had been placed between that feeling and her.

Ceylon removed her hand from the door to inspect her palm. Nothing abnormal. She touched the door again, but that feeling didn't return. It was a distant memory. She tilted her head, attempting to figure out the puzzle before her.

But she didn't have time to figure it out now.

Ceylon gripped the handle and pulled. To her surprise, it clicked open. They didn't even lock the door.

The latch clicked softly behind her. Inside, the hall was just as antiquated. Grey-stoned and lit by wall sconces. A few more corridors branched off, leading to places unknown.

To the right, a half-wall opened into a garden courtyard. It was ethereal in the moonlight. She didn't have the time to examine the botanicals, though she wished she did.

Laughter echoed farther to the right. She turned, following the sound, and wished she still had that cloak to hide better. But she was the Daughter of the Underworld; Ceylon didn't rely on cloaks.

She swept quietly across the stone hall. About thirty paces away was a double door in the same dark wood as the side door, soft light emanating from the inch it stood open. No one stood guard. In fact, aside from the laughter, she didn't hear anyone at all.

Strange. Scourge Manor had guards on every level, at every door. The lack of presence unnerved Ceylon. She couldn't decide if they were stupid, brazen, or both.

Through the opening, she could just make out parts of the inner sanctuary. Like the rest of the abbey, it was old and crumbling, but wooden timbers marked the ceiling far above. Pews were arranged in a circle. Members of the Forsaken were turned in toward each other but facing the front of the sanctuary. The dais was just out of sight.

Ceylon stepped back and searched for another way in. The hall ended a short distance to her right, but there was one more door. After pressing her ear to it and determining there was no one inside, she pushed it open.

A spiral staircase twirled upwards. She took the stairs two at a time, feet light, unsure where it might lead. But after only a handful of bounds, she found herself in a loft. There wasn't much in it: a few empty mattresses and a locked chest. The wood ceiling bowed to a point above her. Directly in front was a railing overlooking the meeting. On the other side of the sanctuary, vibrant stained-glass windows of all colors peered back at her, massive and beautiful.

Ceylon wasn't here to admire the architecture.

She sank into a crouch as she approached the railing. The Forsaken sat in a circle. And sure enough, they all looked toward a raised dais with a hand-carved chair—throne-like in nature. But pacing at the end of the dais was Malachi, hair slicked, eyes bruised.

Her teeth ground, but she tuned into the conversation.

"...tell me what you found," Malachi said, pointing to a boy in the first row with a smile.

The boy, blonde-haired and slight, stood. "The Marquis left thirty rubit in his carriage this morning. I was sure to help myself to the lot as he didn't seem in need. This is the third time this month he's done something of the nature."

The Forsaken laughed, hooted, clapped hands with one another. Malachi pointed to someone else who shared a similar story—interesting they looked to him for direction—and so on. A game. Each person managed to take more, whether it be money, information, or time. Some of the things they mentioned even Ceylon didn't know about—turns out that the Duchess of Southward was scared of ravens.

Ceylon's jaw clenched. She should have known Malachi was close to the leader of the Forsaken, given his intel and haughtiness. But it was that very insolence that had her believing he had no chance of leadership whatsoever. He wasn't calculated, scheming, he was just...Malachi. She couldn't help the spike of irritation that shot through her.

She was about to leave to collect more information when the crowd quieted. A small girl with a shock of white-blonde hair stood. "What did you get, Master?"

Ceylon's blood ran cold. The girl stared at Malachi. *Directly* at him. There was no question who she was speaking to.

"Well, Anya, I may have come into possession of the last genuine Louvel," Malachi crowed.

Ceylon stepped back, bumping her heel against that locked chest. It made a soft thud, barely louder than a whisper, but a sound nonetheless. Malachi's smile flickered. It could have been the lamplight. Ceylon's heart pounded in her ears as she waited for any response. Slowly, Malachi sat in the chair, tapping a hand twice on the armrest.

"Of course, that's nothing compared to what some of you found. It seems I've lost this round to Purdy!"

More cheers rang out. Ceylon sighed and straightened to leave. But as she stood, her face met a broad chest. Her eyes caught Red Hair. Ceylon only managed a gasp before a hand was over her mouth and a bag over her head.

FIVE

Malachi

"This is bad," Dom said as he paced Malachi's office. "How did she find the abbey? How did she even *get in*?"

Malachi sighed, rubbing his eyebrows. "I don't know."

"What are we going to do?" Dom continued.

He peppered the Master of the Forsaken with questions as Malachi's heart grew heavier and heavier. He'd always wished for Ceylon to see the abbey one day, but not like this—not now. She'd put everything in jeopardy just by knowing.

"Dom!" Malachi yelled.

His second startled, coming to a halt on the worn carpet. Malachi rarely raised his voice in such a way.

"Your pacing is driving me mad."

Dom clenched his jaw and set himself in the empty chair facing the desk. "Then what do you suggest? We can't let her go."

"I know," Malachi breathed.

He wandered to the window, high enough to see out over the Underworld and almost to the Suri Kulu. It was a peaceful view. Tonight, however, he barely saw anything through the glass.

Malachi grabbed the bottle of whisky from the sideboard and took a swig, holding it out to Dom. His friend took more than a healthy drink.

"Look, I know what she is to you, but we can't give her the opportunity to go spreading your name to the Scourge," Dom said.

Malachi nodded.

"I know we're not really into the whole violence thing, but if she's breathing, she's dangerous."

Malachi's eyes shot to Dom as adrenaline curled in his gut. "We're not killing her."

Dom raised his hands. "I'm just saying, there's probably more than one person waiting out there with a freshly sharpened knife."

"It's out of the question, Dom." Malachi sank into his own chair behind the desk. Was he being soft? Would things be better if Ceylon was gone? The pressure in his chest told him it wasn't just sentimentality holding him back. "If we kill her, we become just like every other guild: bloodthirsty, merciless, only interested in making money. I'm not going to tarnish Wildar's legacy like that."

Dom raised his eyebrows but shrugged and leaned back in the chair.

"Then what do you plan to do with her?"

Malachi's fingers tapped absently. He shook his head. "I think we need her."

Dom snorted. "Okay, now you've truly lost it. What could we possibly need from the Daughter of the Underworld?"

Malachi leaned forward, elbows on the desk. "Information. Wildar saw what Bronn was doing; he wouldn't have tasked us with stopping the Scourge if he wasn't sure who we were up against. Who better to help us than Bronn's own daughter? She's got to know more about their inner workings than anyone we've come across."

Dom leaned into the desk, mirroring Malachi. "It's too much of a risk. She'll destroy us before we get anywhere."

But the wheels were already spinning. They couldn't let her leave now that she knew who Malachi was, or they would risk the lives of the entire guild. They were already the largest mark in Yvelle because of what they knew, the jobs they interrupted, the clientele they stole from, the reputations they destroyed.

If Malachi was gone, the Forsaken would never be safe.

They needed to keep Ceylon. Two birds with one stone: the Forsaken kept their anonymity, and they would fulfill Wildar's dying wish.

Dom continued, "You've seen her in action. She's a force of nature."

"Then we better have the right guards."

SIX

Ceylon

Ceylon was really beginning to tire of Magum Makaio. They'd placed her in an old prayer room. The stained glass lit the small room in reds and golds and blues. A faded façade of the ancient mage, whom some believed to be the first to wield magic thousands of years ago, holding out his hand to his love, Lady Laenyr.

When they first threw her into the room, she paced, then she pounded on the door, and finally, she sat in front of the stained-glass window contemplating, longing for a true ray of sunlight.

The mage was taunting her from beyond the grave.

What is love, truly?

There are mages on both continents of Artyra—the North and South—who believe in the simple story of their love and sacrifice. That it was Lady Laenyr's sickness that drove Makaio to search all of Artyra for a cure until he came across magic far north in the foothills of Taefarus. White magic, borne from nature, was rare but more powerful than any other kind, which gave him the ability to share magic with the rest of Artyra. But it was all too far-fetched for Ceylon. Especially since the old mage kept all the secrets of love to himself.

She much preferred the story that it was a wayward traveler, stumbling across a lost palace brimming with knowledge in the darkened mountains of Sobravar, who unlocked the true potential of magic. A thief, some might say.

Ceylon huffed. Malachi, the master, leader of the Forsaken.

On one hand, she was grateful. The master could have been someone incapable of being wooed, whether by age or preference. On the other hand, it was *Malachi* who had crushed her good standing with her father, threatened her reputation in the Underworld, and was a supreme pain in the ass.

At least she knew him. Maybe she could use that to her advantage. Her skin crawled. If she pulled this off, it would be her greatest heist to date.

As the sun rose higher, Ceylon sat before Magum Makaio and she plotted. What she'd seen of love was in darkened doorways, hushed whispers. It was tough but subtle. For that, she would have to get Malachi alone, which would be all but impossible unless they let her stay in the abbey. Which meant proving to the Forsaken she could be trusted—at least on some level.

Ceylon flopped onto her back with a groan, arms sprawling by her sides. The cool floor seeped through her stealth suit and grounded her.

She would convince them to let her stay because if she didn't, she would never be the successor. And Ceylon refused to relinquish her birthright.

Through the small, barred window in the door, Ceylon noted her guard shift. He was sturdy but untrained. She would have no trouble beating him one-on-one. But that wouldn't solidify any trust.

She pushed herself to stand and approached the door.

"Hey," she said.

The guard shuffled but didn't turn her way.

"Hey, call for Malachi," she said.

"We don't summon the master," he replied over his shoulder, which hitched toward his ear.

Ceylon rolled her eyes. "I have information he might find useful. I'm just trying to help."

The guard turned to face her then. His lips pulled into a frown, eyes pinched. "Then let me have it, and I'll be sure to pass it along."

Ceylon tried not to laugh, and the guard set his jaw.

"Sorry, it's just...you're new to this, aren't you?" she said.

He didn't respond.

"I'm not trying anything. Only that my information is all I have to bargain with right now. You're the ones who locked me in this cell. Why would I give up my only chance at freedom?" she asked.

The guard's frown wavered. "We don't get many prisoners."

"Right, well, as someone who has experience in *secure accommodations*, let me give you some pointers: Get someone to bring Malachi, I'll give him my information, and then he can decide what to do with me." Ceylon nodded, taking a small step back from the door.

He straightened. "How do I know your information is good? How do I know you're not just trying to get him close so you can kill him?"

Ceylon shrugged. "Like I said, you're the ones who locked me up. So long as he's outside the door, there's nothing I can do to him."

The guard glanced to his left down the hall with nervous eyes. Ceylon kept her most innocent face on. *Just go get the master, you dimwit.*

He opened his mouth once more, but it was not the guard's voice that traveled down the hall.

"Planning your great escape, Ceylon?" Malachi said.

Ceylon steeled herself as she plastered on a pleasant expression, thinking her happiest thoughts. Malachi's dark head popped around the corner. He fiddled with a tie on his silk dressing robe. A *dressing robe.* How pompous.

The red-haired one stood just behind, aggravated as he shooed the guard away.

"Why would I want to leave such a beautiful place?" Ceylon asked. "Magum Makaio and I were just getting to know each other."

Malachi looked past her to the well-lit stained glass. "I didn't think you believed in the Magum."

"You'd be surprised by the things you don't know about me." Ceylon stepped closer to the door, peering through her lashes.

Malachi's grin never wavered. He leaned in as he whispered, "You'd be surprised how much I know already."

Ceylon's lips pressed tight as she tried not to grimace.

"So, what do you plan to do with me? Throw me from the tallest tower? Feed me to the wolves?" She pretended to inspect her nails as she waited.

"If that's your preference, I could arrange it. But I have a different proposition for you."

Seven

Malachi

"You want to make a deal with the Daughter of the Underworld?" Ceylon asked with a look that said Malachi must be dumber than she thought.

Dom took a step forward, reaching for the dagger in his belt, but Malachi waved him off.

"I would think one would show more respect for the Master of the Forsaken." Malachi stared her down. He watched Ceylon flounder, his pride soaring now that he was in control for once. His heart beat evenly as he looked at the girl, for she *was* only a girl.

A girl who clearly wanted to throttle him as she tried to keep her composure.

"You made me wait all night for a *proposition*?" she cried.

"I'll have you know I take sleep very seriously. Your arrival last night caused quite a stir." He brushed a speck of invisible dust from his shoulder. He didn't mention he hadn't been getting much sleep before she had shown up.

"How does no one know who you are? The Lord of the Underworld has been trying to learn your identity for years," Ceylon asked.

Malachi had managed to evade even the best of the Scourge's spies. It wasn't all that difficult when they stood out even amongst the rabble.

Bronn chose his people carefully, but they were well-known faces among his own people.

"Flood the Underworld with enough rumors, and it becomes difficult to tell the truth from the lies," Malachi said with a wave.

Ceylon's brows raised, and her head twitched in the slightest of nods, but then it was gone. Her tells were so small that only a trained eye could spot them.

He tamped down the thrill that passed through him. This was his chance.

The Forsaken were a protective bunch; they had fought and grown together. Many of them were here because of Bronn's way of keeping order: dead parents, unpaid debts, lost homes. That kind of pain was not easily forgotten.

Was he making the right decision?

"Fine, you're a genius. What's the deal?" Ceylon crossed her arms, leaning on her back leg like she didn't have a care in the world.

"Straight to the point, aren't we? Not much for poeticism." He leaned against the doorframe. "I believe you just said you had information for me."

Ceylon's foot slid against the stone, her eyes flicking away and back. For a moment, he wasn't sure she was going to say anything, which was to be expected. Just another ruse to get to him.

But then Ceylon huffed and said, "There's a weakness in the Scourge—one of the members has been leaking information to the highest bidder. He's been collecting for months, things I'm not sure Bronn is even aware of." She glanced past Malachi to Dom. "I didn't know about it until recently."

Malachi stared at her, examining her soft eyes. But he knew by the set of her jaw she was lying. What he didn't know was whether she was lying to save her own skin or to break down his defenses.

"I think you're lying," he replied.

Ceylon's eyes widened subtly. But then her fingers tightened around her arm. "There's a possibility I could be convinced to give you something more if you let me out." She paused. "Or I could just double that shiner you're still sporting."

Malachi let out a deep, hearty laugh.

"You're persistent, I'll give you that. The thing is that you know who I am now. That puts a lot of people at risk." He scanned her face. "A lot of *innocent* people. I can't let you out to run back to Daddy."

Ceylon rolled her eyes. "If you hadn't taken my Louvel I wouldn't be here. At least part of this situation falls on you, *Master*."

Malachi tilted his head back. "But letting you and the Louvel go would have been a shame. We were having so much fun."

Malachi smiled, the kind of smile that came easy to him. One that won over peddlers and nobles alike. But Ceylon's lips only pulled downward in what might be considered a frown.

"You said you had a proposition."

Malachi took in Ceylon's custom suit, her bored demeanor. But her index finger tapped against her arm—she was nervous. She'd infiltrated the guild for a reason, one that held great weight for her, and maybe he could use that to his advantage. He had been hoping for an opportunity like this for years.

"I can't let you leave, but I also admit I don't want you dead. It leaves me in a bit of a predicament, doesn't it?" Malachi said.

Dom coughed beside him, shaking his head lightly. Malachi winked, but he wasn't so foolish as to trust her.

Ceylon snarled, her hands clenching, but nodded. "Sounds like a *you* problem."

"As it turns out, though, keeping you around might prove to be more useful." Malachi stepped right up to the door, looking deep into her mesmerizing green eyes.

"I've witnessed your heist skills enough to know that I could ask you to steal the crown off King Owynn's head, and you'd find a way. So, I'll let you out, and you'll be free to wander the abbey, granted you do what I ask without question. All supervised, of course. Can't have you running away with the candlesticks." He winked at her again.

Ceylon's eyes flicked between himself and Dom. Malachi couldn't tell if she was looking for a secret or keeping one of her own.

"That's it? I just have to stay here and do what you want?" she asked.

Malachi nodded.

"For how long?"

"Well, seeing as I don't trust you, I would suspect you'll be here for quite a while."

Ceylon's eyes narrowed, calculating. But then she glanced at the door.

"And what *do* you want, master?" she breathed.

"I guess you'll have to wait and see."

Ceylon chuckled with an acquiescent nod. "Doesn't seem like I have much of a choice. But if you're offering me food, I guess it's not the worst deal ever."

"Excellent!" Malachi said, stepping aside to let Dom unlock the door.

His second gave him a wary look as he passed, which Malachi ignored. There was risk wherever Ceylon was involved; they might as well use her while they could.

The door clicked open, and Ceylon took a suspicious step out. But Malachi stepped in her path, arm reaching to the opposite frame.

"I should ask how you got in. I don't like holes in my ship." Malachi peered down at her.

Ceylon looked between the Forsaken like he'd asked a trick question. "The door was unlocked."

Malachi's hand slipped. He glanced back at Dom, who was staring at him just as incredulously. The door *was* unlocked because the charms around the abbey were strong enough to divert even the fiercest intruders. The fact Ceylon hadn't even mentioned their effect—or having a token—was...unusual.

Clearing his throat, Malachi dropped his hand.

Ceylon stepped into the hall. She looked left and right, then straightened and turned toward a dead end. It was only three steps later she halted, shoulders tensing like she didn't want to admit to a mistake.

Malachi forced down a laugh. "Lost your way, dear Ceylon?"

She pursed her lips. He motioned toward the dining hall.

This was going to be interesting.

EIGHT

Ceylon

They didn't kick her out. It made sense; she knew who the master was, and that put the Forsaken at risk. Little did they know how well that played into her own plan.

Still, Ceylon had a feeling there was something underneath the façade of protecting the Forsaken, and it made her the slightest bit wary. Why couldn't he just leave her alone? What could he possibly want from her?

Malachi hadn't been kidding about being supervised, either. The little guard followed Ceylon everywhere. She went to the privy, she counted the tiles in the sanctuary, she even sat in the loft for a few hours and the whole time, her guard was with her. Poor girl must be bored out of her mind.

Her name was Anya—the one from the first meeting with the shock of white-blonde hair. A shy little thing but very stubborn. Couldn't have been taller than four and a half feet, and she was quite skinny. She looked about eleven, though the girl assured Ceylon she would be fourteen in a week. Must be good at getting in and out of places unseen. No one looked twice at a child.

Anya had mentioned—in between her bouts of silence—that she was an innate mage. Ceylon had worked with mages before; it wasn't hard to find a backwater magician offering questionable spells and concoctions in the Underworld of Yvelle. While the dark mages might be gone, the innates simply went into hiding, their memory tarnished by the destruction their cohort left in their wake.

The rare few that weren't shunned by society had become healers. The ones on the fringes would sell tonics and serums to aid in recovery, but their magic only went so far. Many left for kingdoms that valued their gifts. Places like Sobravar—the land of the dark mages on the Southern Continent—or Yamah—the northern mountains where the nomads roamed. There, rumors of free mages with a variety of magics were easy to come by. There, mages were even revered.

But Yvelle was different. No level of power could stop you from being feared or controlled.

Ceylon logged away the knowledge. Anya could prove to be useful.

Eventually, Ceylon asked Anya to take her on a tour. She needed a plan, even if it wasn't as solid as she might like. With only a week, every advantage helped. And knowing the ins and outs of Forsaken Hollow would give her more opportunities to get Malachi alone.

If they ever crossed paths again.

He hadn't stopped by since letting her out of the cage. Her fingers itched at the waiting. If she didn't have enough time with Malachi, she would lose her chance of becoming the next Lord of the Underworld.

Anya was more than happy to oblige. She showed Ceylon through—almost—the entire building, including the bell tower and crypts. But her favorite part was the courtyard she'd spied when she'd first entered the abbey. It was completely closed off from the street, but far above was open sky. There were plots of sage and chamomile and some more nefarious-looking plants she made a mental note to inspect later.

A few trees graced the space, bordering stone benches and a dried-up fountain.

Anya raced for the lowest branch, easily swinging herself up and climbing to the top.

"When did you come here?" Ceylon asked from the ground. She craned her neck to see Anya through the branches.

"When I was ten. I tried to help a sick squirrel, and someone saw me. My mum said I wasn't supposed to use my gift, but I couldn't let the squirrel die." Her gaze grew distant. "Whoever spilled about me told the wrong person. The Scourge showed up to take me away, said they needed a necromancer. Mum tried to protect me, but she wasn't a fighter."

Ceylon stiffened. She knew the Scourge were brutal, but those that died at the Scourge's hand deserved it. Anya was young; she must not have known what her mother was really doing. Still, Ceylon couldn't quell the familiarity—that little piece of herself that knew what it was like to grow up without a mother—and she tried to stomp out that bit of weakness, that connection. She wasn't here to make friends.

She focused on the part she knew would be useful. "Necromancy?" Ceylon asked.

Every child in Yvelle had been told stories about the Necromancer. Ceylon had never been able to shake the feeling that they were rooted in truth.

"That's what they thought I was doing. I couldn't even bring back a worm if I tried. My gifts are in the mind, not the body." Anya spoke casually.

"Malachi knows about your gift?" Ceylon asked, rubbing a leaf between two fingers as if the answer didn't really matter.

"Yeah. He even lets me practice, altering memories and such." She hopped down from the tree, landing beside Ceylon.

"You can do that?"

She gave a shrug as if it were nothing. "Sometimes. It doesn't always work, but if I focus really hard, I can do it." The joy in her face cast the shadows from Ceylon's mind, blonde hair blowing in the breeze, and once again, Ceylon had to stop herself from being sucked into her charm.

"Show me," Ceylon said, holding out her hand.

Anya looked at it. She tilted her head. "Most people don't ask to be fooled."

"I'm not most people." Ceylon wiggled her fingers.

The girl shrugged. Her hand folded around Ceylon's, light and gentle. Her touch was warm and welcoming. Never had she been held with such tenderness before. Bronn would never get close to her, not unless he was showing her a new way to take someone down. His touches were rough, brutal, effective. Anya's touch made her want to pull away, suddenly uncomfortable with the care.

"What do you want me to do?" Anya asked.

Ceylon paused, shaking off her discomposure. "Can you make Dom look like a goat?"

Anya grinned, closed her eyes, and took a deep breath.

Ceylon watched the fair girl intently—so fair she could have been from Zymah, the ice kingdom to the south, but they rarely breached the Frysta Abyss.

Anya's face relaxed, her limbs loose. But the longer time drew on, a frown deepened, her grip tightened. After a moment of silence and waiting, she opened her eyes.

"It's not working. It feels like there's something blocking me," Anya stated, releasing Ceylon's hand.

"Does that happen often?" Ceylon asked. A chill snaked up her spine.

Anya shook her head. She gnawed at her lip absently.

Ceylon's eyes narrowed, but she let the thought drift from her. Anya had said it didn't always work; the girl just wasn't practiced enough.

"Have you ever used it on Malachi?"

Anya shook her head vigorously. "I would never use my gift on the master."

Right. Good to know.

Ceylon glanced up into the sky, surprised to find it was beginning to glow orange. They had managed to wander the whole day, and Ceylon had never even chanced past Malachi.

At least this girl could help her. The more information she had, the easier it would be to win over Malachi. "Do you know what he—"

"Anya," a smooth voice sang from the shadows.

A girl about Ceylon's age sashayed into the courtyard. Ceylon tried not to stare as the stunning woman approached. It was as though the sun radiated from her; her dark, glossy hair shone in the dying sunlight, dusky skin absorbing the warmth. Her eyes sparkled, and on the breeze, Ceylon caught a trace of cinnamon and wild oranges.

This girl looked straight through her like she was nothing, a phantom. Ceylon took one step back, then cursed herself for being so weak.

"You shouldn't divulge such information to the enemy," she stated, coming to a stop a foot away. Her hip popped out to the side, arms crossed.

"Don't be silly, Willow. Just because she's from the Scourge doesn't mean *she's* evil. Ceylon's too kind for that," Anya replied. Ceylon looked at Anya, feeling both grateful for the defense and guilty for having to deceive the child.

"What have I told you?" the girl, Willow, asked.

"Everyone is an enemy until they prove otherwise," Anya cited, rolling her eyes.

"Precisely," Willow said. Her stare remained on Ceylon. Her eyes were hypnotic pits of darkness; Ceylon couldn't look away, and yet it felt like they were piercing her very soul. "Go inside, Anya."

"But Malachi said—"

"I will deal with the master. Go inside."

Anya sighed and slumped away. Willow circled Ceylon, taking her in from her black boots to her flowing auburn locks.

"Make no mistake, Daughter of the Underworld. We are well fortified here." Willow stopped in front of Ceylon, leaning in to whisper in her ear. "If you hurt the master, I will kill you."

Ceylon held her ground. Her stomach flipped, and she hated that Willow put her on edge. The girl was clearly trying to start something. Ceylon mirrored Willow's assessment, coming to rest on her fearsome eyes, and cocked her head to the side.

"You could try."

Willow took one step forward, reaching for the dagger at her hip, and stopped abruptly. She took a deep breath, chest rising and falling. Then a false sense of hospitality wisped across her face.

"Maybe another day. Please." Willow motioned for Ceylon to head back inside.

Ceylon gave the girl a final look. Her fingers twitched for a knife she didn't have, and her skin prickled. Ceylon made a mental note to keep one eye open around her.

Willow led Ceylon to her quarters through wide stone halls, Anya already sitting on a bed. The room was quite sparse. They probably hadn't changed much since the abbey was used for its intended purpose. A tiny window was set in the stone wall across from the door. It cast an orange glow through the room. There was one sconce on the wall, two small beds, and a side table. The rest of the room was empty.

"Enjoy your stay, madam," Willow sang, striding past and setting herself gracefully on the bed to the left. Ceylon stared at her. Willow ignored the look, closing her eyes and leaning her head against the bare wall.

Ceylon walked over to the second bed—the one Anya sat on—testing the mattress. It was hard, nothing like back at the manor. There it was soft, and she had the lushest silk bedding. She sighed. No need to be thinking of such luxuries, it would only make her more miserable. She needed to be at her best if she was going to get this job done—if she was going to woo Malachi, of all people. Nausea roiled in her gut.

Anya giggled.

"What are you laughing at?" Ceylon chucked the pillow off the bed at Anya. It hit her in the face. Anya erupted into laughter.

A laugh burst from Ceylon, and she clamped a hand over her mouth. She wasn't used to there being much genuine joy around, just the pleasure of the latest take. She was the only child that had grown up in the Scourge—everyone else had joined as Bronn recruited them for their skills. Her laugh died away and she cleared her throat, unsure what to make of this child in a guild growing up...happy.

Ceylon had been trained and lectured and disciplined as far back as she could remember. There were dear moments that it felt like they were truly family—moments when Bronn would sit and eat dinner at the same table or show her how to repel down a fifty-foot shaft to steal a single hairpin. But training came first. She didn't get this good without knowing where to focus her attention.

Fingernails bit into her palms. Ceylon glanced down at the tiny impressions. She wiped her hands on her stealth suit as if it could wipe away the trace.

"This is for you, too." Anya tossed a shift at Ceylon unceremoniously.

Ceylon sank onto the cot beside Anya. There was barely enough room for one person on the bed, let alone two. She glanced at the waifish girl, sighing at the arrangement.

"I feel like the loft would be more comfortable..." Ceylon whispered to Anya, shift crumpling in her hands.

"The loft is for special guests, and right now, you are neither special nor a guest," Willow stated. Ceylon made a face at her closed eyes that set Anya giggling again. "Try anything tonight and it will be the last thing you do."

NINE

Malachi

Malachi skimmed over the most recent reports on his desk. His office—a well-kept secret—was behind a hidden door in the east wing. Only a few Forsaken even knew where it was, Dom being one of them. The cold bit into his skin through his light cotton shirt, and the dying sun cast harsh shadows over the room, making it look even broodier than normal.

"This is a terrible idea," Dom stated. He, once again, paced the length of the worn purple carpet.

"Horrible," Malachi agreed. "But those are the best kind."

Malachi smiled grimly, imagining the girls meeting for the first time. Willow was a tempest, and Ceylon was a hurricane. Both had a certain propensity for destruction.

Dom came to rest across from him, pressing his hands into the top of the ratty old guest chair. "You shouldn't have given the order."

"They would have met eventually. Willow is loyal; she'll do as she's told. Besides, they need the time to work things out amongst themselves, establish their own hierarchy."

Malachi placed a stack of reports in with the others—ledgers of their storerooms, recent movements from rival gangs, any word on Bronn's purchases and when they might be best intercepted.

Dom's face fell, just for a moment. "Malachi, you know I'm not usually one to stand firm against you, but this is cruel. You know how Willow feels about you. You know what Bronn put her through. How could you force her to guard the Daughter of the Underworld of all people?"

Malachi's gut clenched, and he glanced to the whisky on the sideboard. Dom wasn't wrong; forcing Willow to watch Ceylon *was* cruel. Willow was his closest friend after Dom. But that's all she was, a close friend. Sooner or later, she would have to realize he would never feel the same way she did.

Malachi's mouth was suddenly too dry. "Willow knows her place."

Dom snatched Malachi's hand from the papers, his fingers digging in painfully. "That girl is giving up her heart for you, and you're letting her."

Malachi stared at his friend's hand. Dom had come to the Forsaken lost, sat in a corner, knees to his chest, silent. Malachi had made it his job to make the newcomers feel welcome. He'd sat beside the red-headed boy and told the tale of the intrepid jester until the smallest upward curve tugged at his lips.

Dom had a frighteningly quick temper, but there were only a handful of times it had been directed against Malachi. He looked into his friend's eyes, fire shining in them.

"This is the only way she'll get it back," Malachi whispered, gently peeling Dom's fingers back. "She won't talk about it with me."

"You know how I feel about you and Ceylon—"

"So you don't need to remind me." Malachi's chest ached, but—as he had told Dom—this was the only way he could help Willow move on.

Malachi could never love her the way she wanted. "Now, what were we saying about that horrible idea?"

Malachi pushed out of his chair, making for the bottle of whisky.

Dom grumbled, "You shouldn't let her stay."

"What else are we to do with her? We need her. She's our best lead to take down her father. We earn her trust; we gain her knowledge. I just need to play along with her little games long enough." Malachi didn't mention how those words left a bitter taste. "Besides, I want her to see what life is like without Bronn. I want her to see what I've built."

The thought of Ceylon seeing, truly seeing, what he'd done at Forsaken Hollow created a lightness in his chest.

"There are some who would say you're mad." Dom plopped himself into the guest chair with a withering stare.

"Most likely," Malachi replied. "But those people are fools."

Malachi poured two glasses, handing one to his second. Orange flared around the office as the sun set over Laoryf Bae.

He took a long sip from his tumbler. The whisky burned on its way down.

Putting the girls together...Dom was right; it was a recipe for disaster, and more than one person was likely to get burned.

Dom downed his drink in one go. Malachi knew he cheated at the taverns, but that was only to ensure he would win. There were very few people Dom couldn't out-drink.

"Wildar never would have allowed her to stay."

Malachi's grip tightened on his glass. "You're wrong. He would have gone and brought her in himself."

The sun slipped below the horizon, a burst of red before the sky was coated in darkness. Malachi downed the rest of his drink.

"She's just one girl," Dom said as he examined the master.

Malachi's heart flipped at his words.

"Wrong again, Dom."

The secret passage to his office spiraled down a level in tight stairs; a few windows, cut into the thick stone sprayed moonlight across Malachi's path. He hesitated as he stepped into the hall, his chamber door looming across from him. But the silence that greeted him was ubiquitous and gave him nothing to focus on but his thoughts. He frowned as he pressed forward, quietly tucking into his room.

Dom was right on some accounts. Having Ceylon stay was a risky move. She could find a way out, give them all up. Malachi had no doubt Bronn could find someone to null the charms protecting the abbey, and the Forsaken were no match for the Scourge in combat. But at the same time, it was no riskier than any of the other jobs they did. He knew every inch of this abbey, and there was nothing material he wouldn't mind losing. But losing his family—the Forsaken—was another matter.

Even in dim firelight, he knew his way around this room. He stepped around the chair, avoiding that squeaky spot in the floorboards, and leaned in front of the fireplace, staring into the flames like they might tell him how to handle the situation.

"Hey stranger," Ceylon sang.

Malachi had a firm grip on the hearth, so he didn't leap a foot in the air. With a deep breath, he schooled his features into amusement and spun around.

Ceylon lay on his bed, her fingers painting invisible lines across his silk bedding. Hair cascaded over her arms and shoulders; he'd never seen it so undone.

He swallowed, cleared his throat. "I thought I had two guards on you."

Ceylon glided off the bed, walking toward him with bare feet. If he was cold in his cotton shirt, she must be freezing in that shift.

"You really think they could stop me?" she asked.

Her face was twisted in a look resembling alluring, but it was wrong. There was something in the tightness of her mouth, the stiffness of her shoulders, that told him she was uncomfortable, but she was trying very hard not to be.

Malachi closed his eyes, tilted his head back.

"I thought they would give you at least a bit of a challenge," he said.

Ceylon stepped closer until they were only inches apart. He could feel her warmth, even sandwiched between the fireplace and her body. She smelled of...earthy musk, a freshness permeating around her.

She reached for his chest, leaning in, and Malachi froze. His eyes popped open as her fingertips brushed the fabric of his shirt. He was barely breathing.

And then his mind caught up. Ceylon didn't do anything without a goal. He pushed past her, ripped the throw off his bed, and wrapped it tightly around her shoulders.

Ceylon stiffened but pulled the blanket tight around her. Something like relief washed over her features, mixing with a touch of...genuine disappointment.

"These abbey walls are not what they used to be. Drafts and all. Wouldn't want you to catch a cold." Malachi shrugged, tucking his hands into his pockets.

"Who knew the master was so thoughtful." Ceylon smirked. She dropped into the chair closest to the fire, drawing the blanket tighter.

"I have my moments." Malachi smiled, and it was genuine.

He wished they could stay here. The world was so quiet.

"So," Malachi sat down across from her, "are you visiting all the men this evening? Or am I special?"

Ceylon scoffed, her nose scrunching. "Please, don't flatter yourself."

"But you are here. In my room. In a shift." Malachi couldn't help the smirk pulling his lips upward.

Her cheeks warmed to a lovely shade of pink before she said, "I was disappointed with the room you gave me. The Daughter of the Underworld does not share a cot with a child. Your bed was the only one that seemed fitting."

He searched her face for the lie, but this time he found no tells. Either she was telling the truth, or she had convinced herself she was. He didn't know how to feel about that.

"Well, I'll have to see about getting you something more appropriate."

Ceylon narrowed her eyes. "Liar. You're not even going to try."

Malachi shrugged. "I have to keep things fair. Besides, you're on probation; you don't deserve a better bed. And after that clever maneuver in New Town a few years back, I don't trust you."

A warm memory, but a lifetime stood between then and now.

The warmth in her expression didn't meet her eyes. "I'd be worried if you did."

Malachi glanced over her face. There was a heaviness, a detachment. Maybe it was part of the reason he felt so compelled to follow her all these years. The weight in his chest returned, and as if in answer, his nose gave a painful tweak. He stood, grabbing the water pitcher and pouring a glass.

He held it out to her. "I think you could use this."

"Trying to poison me?" She took a careful sniff.

Malachi's lip quirked. "It's just water."

She raised an eyebrow but ultimately rolled her eyes and took a sip.

Malachi dropped back into the chair. "So, what did you do to Anya and Willow? Drug them? Tie them up?"

"Actually, they fell asleep, and I had to pee. That's what you get for sending a child to guard me."

Malachi hid his grin. "Possibly."

He leaned back in the chair, steepling his fingers.

"I must admit, I do kind of enjoy playing with you," he said.

"Of course you do. You could never just let me go." Ceylon frowned.

"Well, *you* were the one who broke into my home with unknown intentions." He gave her a smile that made most want to run. But Ceylon only sat up straighter, leaning forward. "How could I let someone like that go?"

TEN

Ceylon

Ceylon held her hands in her lap to keep from throttling him. Her bare foot tapped a steady rhythm on the stone.

Her best efforts at seduction had seen a blanket thrown over her head. And though it foiled her plans, she had to admit she was grateful for the extra time. No matter. There would be other moments. Malachi seemed preoccupied enough with her, so she hadn't completely failed. However, he said he liked to toy with her. Maybe she was just reading into his attention.

"Well, I guess if I'm not entitled to your chambers, I should be off to bed," Ceylon rose, allowing the blanket to slip from her shoulders.

She didn't miss Malachi tracing her form as he rose from his seat. Her blood pounded in her ears.

"Leaving so soon?"

He blocked her path to the door. Ceylon tried to keep her eyes steady on him, even as they wanted to drift to the exit, wanted to escape the job her father had given her. But if he was going to play her like that, she wouldn't back down from the challenge.

Ceylon took another step toward him. She intended to get close, lean in, only he stepped back, and his absence nearly sent her stumbling.

"Why don't we make things interesting?" Malachi lifted his chin.

Malachi's version of interesting generally ended with her losing something important. And she had a lot to lose right now—her whole future, to be exact.

"Interesting how?" Ceylon asked, strolling to the bookshelf and picking up a tome.

"Seeing as you're in my care for the foreseeable future, I figured I might as well keep you busy."

Malachi closed the distance between them, nearer than most people got without her knife at their throat. But being close to Malachi was what she came here for tonight. So she forced down her instincts to step away, determined not to lose.

"I'm listening." She crossed her arms, aware that their faces were inches apart. A simple step would have them breathing the same air.

He took that step, and they were nose to nose. She pressed the book to her stomach as their chests brushed. His light green eyes shone in the firelight. She'd never noticed the tiny flecks of yellow strewn throughout his irises.

"I want you to pay attention," Malachi breathed.

"To what?"

"To the Forsaken. To the Hollow. To every word and breath and laugh uttered inside these walls." Malachi stared her down with an intensity she had rarely seen.

For a moment, Ceylon couldn't find words. "Why?"

"Because there is a world you refuse to see."

"Maybe I'm not the only one." The bookshelves pressed into Ceylon's back painfully, and yet she barely felt it.

"Perhaps." The twinkle in Malachi's eyes dimmed a fraction. "I need you to make me a promise, Ceylon."

She blinked. "You would trust me at my word?"

Ceylon didn't know if that made him a fool or a mastermind.

"I have no other choice." Malachi closed his eyes. "I need you to promise you won't tell Bronn who I am."

Ceylon stiffened, her head shook. "You know I can't do that."

When Malachi opened his eyes again, they were filled with pain. "The Forsaken are a family. If you give me up, they have nowhere to go. I'm prepared to face whatever wrath comes my way for the things I've done, but my guild doesn't deserve it. If there's even the smallest sliver of humanity left in you, you'll keep my name to yourself."

She wanted to believe he was kidding. Because if he was serious, he was weaker than she thought. Not willing to own his reputation, the fact that the safety of an entire guild rested on his name being kept secret. Those were things that should have been thought through. Those were things he had to know would come to light eventually. And Ceylon wasn't quite sure why that was so disappointing.

But another feeling tugged at her gut. A heaviness that sat, making her stomach turn and her mouth bitter. For whatever reason, she found herself nodding. Although she was certain it was only to gain his trust.

The relief that shot across his face was fleeting, replaced by his usual smolder.

Malachi took another step forward, forcing her even closer to the bookshelf.

He quirked his head. "Now, where were we?"

"I think you were about to kiss me." Ceylon smirked. She didn't want to give the impression he had her rattled.

It was subtle, but Ceylon didn't miss the choked sound Malachi made.

"I think you need to learn to read people better."

"I'm reading you just fine," Ceylon bluffed.

Just to be sure, she watched him, noticing the slight tremor in his hand, the hitch in his breath, the wideness of his eyes. Now she had *him* flustered, and she leaned into it, placing a hand on his chest.

Malachi was a statue.

"The master of the Forsaken is such a *legend*. Do you think your perfect little family can actually accept someone like me?"

His expression grew dark. She blinked at the transformation; this wasn't the boy she knew. He closed the space once more. His arms caged her as he leaned on the shelf.

"If you think this is a perfect family, you really are blind." He was low, direct.

Ceylon wished she could take back the taunt.

"Ceylon, the Forsaken have suffered at the hand of the Scourge for years. Many of them are here because of your father. There is nothing I can say that would make them forget a lifetime of pain."

Blood drained to her feet. What did she have to be sorry for? Bronn was focused on the greater good rather than the plight of the few.

"Then why keep me at all?" she breathed, not backing down, her arms dropping to her sides.

Malachi straightened. His usual swagger snapped back in place but with a hint of something she couldn't quite place. Like this was exactly what he wanted.

He flicked a stray hair from his eyes. "Because I still have use for you yet."

Ceylon stared at him, at whatever secret lay just behind his eyes. Malachi was the only thing between her and leading the Scourge. Just seven days, and she would be named successor. Based on their interaction this evening, it seemed she was well on her way.

But she couldn't stop a strange tendril of unease from snaking through her.

Ceylon pushed off the shelf. "Well, then I guess it's a good thing you're not the worst company."

Malachi's fingers tightened around the tome she handed him. "I guess so. Goodnight, Ceylon."

Ceylon stared at him for a moment longer. "Goodnight, *Master*."

His shoulders hitched. With a nod, he turned and dove under his sheets.

Ceylon's lips pursed at the dismissal. When it was clear he would say no more, she marched to the hall, slamming the door behind her. The sound echoed off the walls. Something clattered to the floor in Malachi's room. She hoped it shattered.

Ceylon wouldn't let him rattle the Daughter of the Underworld.

Ceylon tossed and turned, mind racing.

Anya was passed out on the bed when she finally made it back to the room, same with Willow. Or at least, they looked like they were asleep. Ceylon hadn't tried to be quiet or graceful when she shoved Anya over and laid beside her.

Hours—or maybe minutes—later, Willow woke Ceylon with a pillow to the face as the sun peeked in through the window. She informed Ceylon of a mandatory guild meeting, then simply stepped out and waited in the hall.

Anya, on the other hand, was very chatty. The girl didn't stop talking as Ceylon brushed out her hair, tied the green dress someone had provided, and laced her leather boots.

In the dining hall, Willow never looked away as Ceylon took her time with the porridge she had been offered. It wasn't the Scourge's five-course meal, but it was better than nothing. Regardless, Willow ate her porridge like a lady, using a napkin and a spoon.

Ceylon had been taught etiquette—it was necessary to blend in with the nobles of Wellborn when she wore the mask of Lady Ceylon of Townsend—but she only used it when she needed to. Watching Willow made her feel like a street rat. Ceylon shoveled the dish back with a sneer.

Willow scoffed and glowered over her own meal. Ceylon knew a thing or two about grudges, but she honestly had no idea what she had done to the girl.

After breakfast, she let Anya drag her through the abbey. They passed a couple of members of the Forsaken on the way. Each one greeted Anya and Willow pleasantly and looked at Ceylon like she didn't belong. In the Scourge, no one greeted anyone.

Ceylon had a good chance to examine the crew at this meeting. There couldn't have been more than thirty members in total; the Forsaken were much smaller than the Scourge. But that could also be due to the amalgamation her father had instigated. Yet, despite their small numbers, the Forsaken had managed to create a name for themselves that even her father couldn't destroy.

Knowing Malachi was their master, Ceylon was beginning to understand how they had survived for so long. And she couldn't help but feel just the slightest bit impressed.

It took twenty minutes for all the Forsaken to assemble. Only after everyone was seated did Malachi take his place on the dais, the rustle of his coats heard even in the back of the room.

"Good morning, Forsaken." There was a mumbled greeting that surged through those gathered. Even Ceylon managed some kind of acknowledgment. "There has been a development; I wanted you all gathered here to make you aware."

A murmur from the crowd, eyes flicked her way accusingly. Ceylon tensed. All Malachi had to do was imply she had acted violently—even though she hadn't—and the Forsaken would likely take her out on his behalf. She knew better than to trust his word.

Malachi glowed as though this was the best day of his life. "Ceylon, would you join me?"

All eyes turned on her now. She gritted her teeth, sighing through her nose.

Slowly, she stood from her seat. Anya beamed at her from the bench while Willow glared. Her footsteps echoed through the hall.

Malachi offered a hand. She was a little offended by the gesture. The platform couldn't have been higher than a foot off the ground; there was no need for assistance. Still, she accepted it so as not to offend the crowd, and as her fingers slipped into his, a slight warmth shot through her—like stepping into a ray of sunlight after miles of shadow. She stole her hand back, fingers tingling as she stabilized. But she couldn't determine the feeling.

Malachi placed a hand on Ceylon's shoulder as she turned to face the Forsaken. She distracted herself by scanning each one of their faces, judging their height, build, and possible proficiencies. But the glares shot her way made it clear they didn't trust her.

Rightly so.

"Ceylon will be staying at Forsaken Hollow for the foreseeable future." Shouts erupted. Malachi waited, and slowly the dissent quieted.

Ceylon could feel the hostility in the air; it would light at the smallest spark.

She caught Willow's eye, and the fury made Ceylon's lungs constrict. She searched for anything else to look at, settling on the stained glass at the far end of the room—one of the only things untainted since her arrival—with a calming breath.

"Forsaken," Malachi said. Their anger simmered. "I understand how you feel, and it's justified. Bronn has brought nothing but pain, and welcoming his daughter would be like accepting the things he's done. But that isn't the case. We know what it means to choose our family.

"The former master brought us all here. He chose us. And when Wildar passed, he also passed on his mission to me, to *us*. Who would we be if we didn't carry on the former master's last wishes?" He cast a meaningful gaze over the crowd. Some nodded, others glared, but the atmosphere lightened a touch. It left Ceylon wondering what that final wish might be and what it had to do with her.

Ceylon looked closely at Malachi's face, calm and controlled. A part of her thought he genuinely cared whether or not she stayed. But there would be very little reason, aside from information, that a rival boss would welcome a member of the Scourge into their fold so freely.

"Now, Forsaken, I ask for your assistance. I'm invoking the rights of Master; I've agreed to this arrangement of my own free will, and I expect you to treat her as you would any other new member—to the best of your ability." He winked at the crowd. "Trust in me. This is our home. I will not fail you."

As Ceylon viewed the crowd again, the looks she received now were indecisive. They weren't hateful, but neither were they endearing. A blank slate.

The Scourge would never have been so accommodating.

Malachi asked the Forsaken to line up, each one facing the east wall, so they could be properly introduced. They moved quickly and efficiently. As Ceylon scanned them, walking down the line, she noticed none were older than twenty-five, except for one sour-looking woman who could have been ancient. Most looked to be closer to Anya's age.

Malachi gave a short rundown of each member and their talents. Ceylon listened, nodding when it seemed appropriate, memorizing everyone's faces.

Dom looked pained at having to welcome her; he kept glancing at Malachi like a puppy betrayed by its owner. Anya was a ball of energy, her excitement radiating from her slight frame. Willow fumed.

The Scourge had never known how big the Forsaken were. And, despite the inconveniences they caused the Scourge—stealing from high-profile clients, ruining takes—numbers were numbers, and Bronn wanted as many as he could get.

Now Ceylon, the future leader of the Scourge, knew everyone.

Malachi took a step forward, addressing the crowd.

"Let's show the Daughter of the Underworld what true hospitality looks like." He turned to Ceylon. "I trust your stay will be enlightening."

He grabbed her hand, placing a gentle kiss on her knuckles.

It will be, Ceylon thought.

ELEVEN

Malachi

The Forsaken dispersed, leaving a trail of uncertainty in their wake. Ceylon stayed rooted to her spot beside him, likely unsure of where to go. He had work to do, as he was sure Ceylon did, but neither could be obvious about it.

Willow marched up to him. He could practically see the steam rising from her ears. He winced internally and raised his hands in surrender.

She grabbed a fistful of his shirt, pulling him closer. Willow was tall, almost as tall as Malachi, and their eyes met as she leaned in.

"One day. That's what you told me."

He placed his hand over hers. "I said *at least* one."

Willow shoved him backwards. He stumbled.

"How could you even let her stay, knowing who she is? Do I mean so little to you that you would make me *watch* her? Make me live *with* her?" Willow's face dropped, and her hands fell slack at her sides.

Malachi didn't know what to say. The truth was he needed Willow, just not in the way she wanted him to need her. Willow was his anchor, his lighthouse, the one constant in a sea of uncertainty. No matter what happened, she would always be there.

"Don't be like that, Low. This isn't personal."

Dom attempted to still Willow. She didn't move her gaze from Malachi, just flicked Dom's hand away.

"With you, everything is personal. I'll support you because I trust you, but don't you *ever* ask me to do something like this again." She turned to Ceylon, and Malachi took an unintentional step forward. "Just remember your place, girl. You don't belong here; you never will. And if you step out of line, I will make it my life's mission to ensure you suffer."

Willow turned on her heel. Dom shook his head as he followed their friend.

Ceylon let out a low whistle. She rocked back and forth and said, "What a family meeting."

"Just don't. You don't know these people," Malachi replied and sank into his seat on the dais. He dropped his face into his hand. The lack of sleep was catching up with him, making him emotional and unstable. He couldn't afford that kind of weakness, not now.

Ceylon shuffled toward him. He lifted his face. Her expression was softer than he expected, apologetic but more on the edge of indifference. Still, it was something he wasn't used to seeing from her.

"For what it's worth, it's not your fault." The Daughter of the Underworld stood on the dais staring at the master, hesitating. His heart fluttered at her words—her encouragement. For a moment, she looked like she might say something else as she lingered, but then a redness tinted her cheeks, and she turned and left the sanctuary.

Malachi thought about following her. From what he knew of Bronn's plans to take over the Underworld, he didn't have much time, and he needed to figure out why she was here.

But he also needed to think.

He stayed in his chair for a long while. He hadn't been expecting her to agree, to stay, to show up. Maybe he *was* making a mistake—letting his feelings for Ceylon cloud his judgement, even though he tried to push them away. But the truth was, Wildar's last request was that the Scourge be destroyed. They had been strategizing for years, searching for anything to exploit. Anything that would give them an edge. Their best option just happened to amble in on her own.

His stomach gave a nauseous twist. He was using everyone he knew to make this work, everyone important to him.

They would forgive him. When the deed was done, and Bronn had been knocked from his reign, they would see his reasoning. At least, he hoped.

All he needed was one shot.

Malachi sighed. There was work to be done, he couldn't spend the whole day wallowing. He stood from his chair, smoothed back his hair, and readied himself for work.

He found Ceylon wandering the halls of the third floor. She looked out a window, the sunlight glittering in her warm hair. It pooled around her shoulders, curling softly at her waist.

"Are you going to stand there and stare at me all day?" she asked, her gaze remaining on the world outside. His footsteps had been silent; he stayed in the shadows. Her ability to sense people amazed him.

Malachi shook his head. *No distractions.*

He walked toward her. "I have your first job," he stated.

Ceylon looked at him through her lashes. "Excuse me?"

"You agreed to do whatever I asked." He came to a stop a foot from her, staying just outside the rays of sun that poured through the glass. Malachi didn't want to disturb her portrait.

She turned from the window, squaring herself.

Her eyes were like the color of foliage in late spring. He reached a hand up, brushing away a strand of hair from her forehead. She quirked an eyebrow at him.

Malachi stiffened, dropping his hand. "You're coming to the docks with me."

He turned and made his way back to the stairs, forcing her to follow.

"The docks? What do you have there?" She tried to contain the excitement in her voice, but he caught the speed, the inflections.

"Business to take care of. I've heard news of a shipment I'm rather eager to intercept. I'd like to remind Yvelle that the Forsaken are independent for a reason."

Ceylon snorted. "You can't take me for that. No one would believe for a second I was cooperating with the Forsaken."

"Luckily, I may have a spare obstrepat charm lying around." Malachi smiled over his shoulder. "Domenyk!"

Where had Dom run off to?

"So why am I coming? I could just as easily stay here."

"You, dear Ceylon, are the distraction." Malachi paused in the middle of the sanctuary. "I feel much better when I'm the one keeping an eye on you. You have a tendency to sneak through guards."

Dom lumbered through the archway. His temper had calmed some, but he still sported a scowl as he approached.

"You called?" Dom grumbled.

"Yes, gather the team. We're heading to the docks."

Dom glanced at Ceylon, his eyes wandering over her green dress. His nose twitched with distaste. "And her?"

"She's not exactly a prisoner, Dom. It's in her best interest to assist us while she's here."

He gave her one final, scalding look. "Fine, we'll meet you at the door."

"You're all lovely, really. Very accommodating. I feel so very welcome." Ceylon crossed her arms.

Malachi gave her a slight frown.

"I'm nothing if not honest," she retorted.

"If I thought for a second that I would find honesty woven through even a single hair on your head, I wouldn't be taking you with me." Malachi grinned at her.

She returned the look.

Malachi counted heads as the crew converged by the door. Ceylon rubbed at the obstrepat charm around her neck. Dom and Willow strapped on weapons. Leo, whose thin frame made him perfect for sneaking, and Venus, an expert with explosives, were reading the notes they'd received yesterday. This wasn't the first job like this the Forsaken had taken on, but it never got any easier. In fact, the guard around Yvelle had increased recently.

Willow glanced up as their steps sounded down the hall. She took one look at Ceylon and said, "You can't be serious. Did you tell her—"

"Ceylon is here to help. She won't be a problem," Malachi interrupted.

He gave Willow a meaningful look. Willow narrowed her eyes, judging Ceylon, and turned away. Ceylon hid it well, but he could tell she was intrigued by their interaction. And that was a dangerous thing.

"I will permit you one dagger," he said. He reached into his own stash to find the least threatening one. It was small, not even the full length of his palm, but he knew Ceylon could still make it deadly.

She tucked it into her shoe. "Do I at least get to change before we go?"

"Consider it gift enough you even get to come," Dom growled. He tugged on the straps at his shoulders as he turned to face her. "Willow won't hesitate to kill you if you try anything. I hope you know that."

Ceylon just waved a hand. "Yes, yes, she was kind enough to inform me when I arrived. Really, death threats are a regular occurrence for me. I thought the Forsaken would be more inventive."

"Enough," Malachi said as he strapped on his own weapons. "She's coming, and that means we're going to have to work together. Stop bickering."

The group formed a circle just in front of the door.

"Now, once more for the newcomer," Malachi began. "The shipment is moored on a private dock toward the end of the pier. That dock will have at least five guards. Ceylon, you're with Dom. You are to distract the guards at the dock and do *nothing more*. Do you understand?"

Ceylon raised her hands, palms out. "You think I would try to ruin your plan?"

Malachi gave her a sharp look.

"Fine, I'll do what I'm told, *master*."

"Good." Malachi looked at the rest of the crew. "You know what to do."

The Forsaken grumbled but didn't press their opposition. The group turned to leave the abbey, filing out one by one.

"Wait, that's it? What's the rest of the plan?" Ceylon asked, lingering.

Malachi glanced back at her. "That's need-to-know."

He held out a hand and ushered her into the alley. She paused in the doorway, studying him. The moment seemed to last a lifetime, but then she was outside, trudging after the Forsaken.

Malachi felt the tug of energy as they slipped through back alleys, that *zing* that accompanied him before a challenging job. Sometimes, he thought he did these things just for the thrill of it. But he also had people to protect—that was his first priority, no matter how much he loved being a pebble in everyone's shoe. So he threw on a hood, and they made their way to the docks.

Malachi trusted Ceylon to follow closely down the narrow alleys with the rest of the crew sandwiched at her back. He didn't bother taking a roundabout way. He knew no blindfold would stop her from finding her way back to the abbey.

Leading her to Forsaken Hollow was a mistake. Even unintentionally. She was ruthless, self-interested, and far too clever for her own good. The guard needed to be tight; they were risking the entire guild having her there.

And yet, he was glad Ceylon had come, whatever the reason. There was something in her. After watching her these years, he knew a piece of her hadn't been tainted by Bronn, that there was still a heart beating under her stony façade. And, as much as he tried to deny it, he liked having her around. He could already see the small ways she was relaxing, the way her eyes softened when she thought no one was looking. Clearly, she still wanted something, but there was curiosity too. Malachi just hoped it would be enough to convince her to stay.

"So, why did I find you at Forsaken Hollow?" Malachi prodded as they followed the twists and turns of centuries-old houses.

"That's need-to-know," she replied with a mocking glance. "But maybe it was my intention all along."

Malachi studied her; Ceylon's face remained blank. A heavy weight settled in his gut. The longer he went without answers, the more dangerous it was for her to stay. He probably knew her better than Bronn himself, but the list of possible reasons for her arrival was longer than he was tall. Still, keeping her in sight was better than letting her free or killing her.

"Well, here we are," Malachi said, pointing to a door on their left.

It was a rickety thing leaning on its hinges. Years of use and wear had thinned the wood. He pushed it open and took the stairs two at a time, the sunlight warming his skin as he made it to the roof. The scent of salt and brine wafted in off Laoryf Bae. Malachi smiled as the Forsaken poured in behind him.

"Here we go," he whispered to the wind.

Twelve

Ceylon

Laoryf Bae sparkled blue in the afternoon sunlight, tucked into the west corner of Yvelle. Ships of all kinds harbored there, docking and unloading. She noticed sails from their neighbors to the east, Dyraith, as well as the islands of Ekean, and even two from Orthyr and Yru, kingdoms of the South Continent.

The docks themselves were packed, merchants bustling shoulder to shoulder. Ceylon had been there a few times—Bronn had shipments like everyone else did, goods from the South Continent that were hard to acquire like weapons and foods and magical items—but she'd never seen it from the rooftops. Up here, it was obvious why Yvelle was the trade capital of the Northern Continent.

"That's the one we want." Malachi pointed to a ship with no colors flying on the southern end of the docks.

It wasn't a large vessel, appearing instead to be built for speed and discretion. Whoever's ship it was, they didn't want to be noticed, which made perfect sense as to why Malachi would target it.

He looked everyone in the eye. "We meet back at the Hollow when it's done. If you're not back in two hours, we come looking."

The crew nodded. Ceylon glanced at Leo and Venus, but she said nothing as she followed Dom down the stairs and out toward the water.

Ceylon kept her hood low as they jostled through the crowd. Here, the classes mixed like paint on canvas, crowded and vibrant, with voices blending in the air. Dom rested a hand on her shoulder, directing her through the traffic. No one paid them a second glance.

She hadn't had a chance to see how the obstrepat charm had changed her. Although she was never able to see the transformation like others could. She just felt the tingling rip through her and knew it was working.

As they neared the ship, a clear divide separated the private docks from the boardwalk. Five guards blocked the entry to the dock, where the unmarked ship was the only vessel moored.

She knew she was just a distraction, but should they need to be more aggressive, Ceylon couldn't exactly take the guards out one by one in the middle of a crowd. She may be good, but five missing guards would be noticeable in a heartbeat.

Dom raised a hand like he was going to greet the men, but Ceylon didn't trust any plan that wasn't her own. So, thinking on the fly, she threw her arm through Dom's and said, "Smile and laugh. Just follow my lead."

Dom growled—they were too close to the guards for him to object.

The man in charge stepped forward. "Halt," he said.

Ceylon added a lilt to her voice as she said, "Oh, I'm sorry. My fiancé and I were just so hoping to get a private tour." She leaned in. "We're *obsessed* with foreign ships."

She turned to Dom and giggled. The tightening of his hand on her arm told her everything she needed to know of how he felt as he laughed with her.

"This dock is off-limits to the public. I'm going to have to ask you to move along." The man in charge looked past them, dismissing them out of hand.

Ceylon stepped forward, Dom's fingers biting into her arm, signaling her not to do anything rash. Like she would be so foolish.

Her hood tipped back. Out of the corner of her eye, she saw Dom's face drop. He tried to pull her back, but she was already in motion. Ceylon glanced up at the guard. "Couldn't you please—"

The guard looked back down, his eyes widening.

"My apologies, Miss. I didn't realize it was you. Please." The man stepped aside, motioning her and Dom forward.

Ceylon hid her frown and squealed as she passed, unsure what else to do. She wasn't sure what the obstrepat charm made these men see, but she was grateful either way.

"Thank you so much. We'll just be a moment."

She searched the docks for Malachi as they boarded. He was staring daggers from the boardwalk, mouth pinched into a thin line; Willow shook her head just behind him. But with every step Ceylon took, they seemed to realize she wasn't leaving. Malachi gave an intentional look to Dom, and they disappeared into the crowd.

Dom released a breath as their feet met the deck but immediately pulled her hood back into position. "Keep your face covered. You look like you," he muttered.

Ceylon was about to scoff when she glanced down. Was she seeing what everyone else was seeing? Her hand brushed over the braid, but she kept her hood in place.

The deck wasn't busy, but there were a few deckhands hauling crates up from the lower levels. Three masts with square-rigged sails surged from the sleek, wooden surface. All were spotless and well-maintained even after crossing the Sea of Cator. However, for a ship meant for speed, it was sitting rather low in the water.

The main guard for the dock hollered something over the rails, granting Ceylon and Dom the freedom to move about however they wished. They caught a few glances, but no one bothered them as they perused the crates.

Dom nodded to the stairs beckoning to the lower deck. Ceylon led the way.

It was darker below, but sunlight still peeked through from the stairs and some open ports. Hammocks were slung between the beams wherever there was space. Ceylon and Dom went lower still to where all the crates were stored.

The workers kept unloading, so Ceylon and Dom casually picked an unoccupied corner to review the contents of a crate themselves.

Dom whipped out a long knife, wedging it under the sealed wood and lifting off.

Ceylon frowned at the contents. There were many things she didn't recognize: vials of liquid, precious rocks and metals, but there were also weapons. Pistols from the pirates of Ranniko, white with gold filigree. Non-descript shotguns. Even what appeared to be some grimoires.

Ceylon picked up the pistol and examined it closely. "Dom, what is this? Whose ship are we on?"

Dom scowled as he looked at the contents. "It doesn't matter."

He glanced through the rest of the cargo hold. Another box was lifted to the upper level. Dom sighed, pointing to a barrel toward the back wall.

"Use that powder. You take this side and line the deck with it. I'll start from the other side, and we'll meet in the middle." Dom pressed an empty bag into her hands and walked away before Ceylon could object.

Ceylon's lip curled at the rudeness, but she just tucked the pistol into her satchel. She wasn't sure why she took it, but something told her she might need it later. At the very least, it was insurance should all this end badly.

She did as Dom commanded, making her way amidships. But she couldn't help peeking inside some already opened crates—more non-descript weapons with no distinct tracing or name. Whoever owned this ship was bringing a lot of unmarked firepower to Yvelle. They could make an army if all the crates were filled the same way. And if the grimoires were any indication, it might not be simply an army of men but of dark mages as well.

Ceylon glanced across the endless expanse of crates. How did Malachi know about the shipment when she didn't? There was something she wasn't seeing. Something that felt so obvious and yet just out of her reach.

A long, dark coat swished at the edge of her vision. Before she could react, a hand clamped over her mouth and pulled her backward.

Ceylon slipped the knife from her boot, her heart slowing at the thought of a fight. She hadn't had a good one in a while. She let the hand lead her to a room next to the cargo bay.

Ceylon attacked, slashing with her knife. The assailant dodged.

She advanced, keeping the knife high and slashing again.

Her assailant didn't have a weapon, coat billowing as he spun. He blocked her knife with his forearms, metal clinking at every move.

"Ceylon, stop," he growled.

She halted mid-swing.

"Gideon? What the hell?" Ceylon sheathed her knife and threw her hood back.

There he stood in his pompous glory. The cut over his eye was deep purple—he must be using a healing salve.

"You shouldn't be here," he said, eyes filled with fire and something that looked an awful lot like fear.

"Neither should you—" And then everything clicked into place. Her hand tightened around the hilt of her dagger. "This is Bronn's ship."

Gideon's mouth pressed to a thin line. He didn't respond.

Ceylon groaned. "That twat has me blowing up my *father's* ship."

"Who?" Gideon asked, stepping forward.

Ceylon raised her knife again. "The master. He didn't give me the details; I didn't know we'd be interfering with the Lord of the Under-world."

Gideon raised his eyebrows. "And who might the master be?"

The words caught in her throat. She could give Malachi up now. It might even change her father's mind about her own mission. But she wasn't the kind of thief who gave up on a job just because it was a challenge.

"Like I'd tell you, just so you can run back to Bronn and inform him yourself." Ceylon bared her teeth. "Tell my father I don't need a babysitter this time. You can run home."

"You'd help the Forsaken work against your father?" Gideon crowed. He surveyed her with something more than malice.

"I need them to trust me somehow." Ceylon crossed her arms, chang-ing the subject. "Why does Bronn need all these weapons anyway? What isn't he telling me, Gideon?"

Gideon's mouth transformed into a sneer, but it didn't meet his eyes. "If he isn't telling you, it's probably because he's second-guessing your position in the Scourge."

Of course, Gideon wouldn't tell her anything. She was wasting time.

"Sorry I can't stay and chat, but if I'm gone too long, they'll think I've run away." Ceylon turned to leave the room, planning to have a long chat with Malachi. But Gideon's hand wrapped around her arm, pulling her attention back to him.

"What's the plan, Ceylon?" His eyes were wild.

She frowned as she leaned back. "I know Bronn won't be happy, but we're blowing up the ship."

Gideon's hands loosened a fraction. He released a breath and gave the slightest of nods.

"Your turn. Tell me why Bronn needs all this. He already has the guilds. Now, he plans to weaponize them, too?"

He paused, staring into her eyes, searching. She was just about to ask what his problem was when he said, "I can't tell you."

Ceylon wrenched her arm free. "Why will no one tell me a *damn* thing!?"

Gideon just stared, eyes blank, that usual hint of mischief absent.

Ceylon turned again to leave. "If you're not going to help me, just run back to Daddy like you always do."

"Bronn will want to see you if he hears about this."

Ceylon scoffed, even as dread pooled in her gut. "I'm not some servant who can be summoned. I'll come if it suits me. Make sure you tell him that."

"Ceylon," he said, and she paused at the worried tone. "Be careful."

She ignored him, striding back into the cargo hold and replacing her hood.

She hated Gideon. She hated everything about him. Ceylon understood why Bronn would choose Gideon to supervise her; he would do anything to throw her off balance. Her job was to steal the master's heart, while Gideon's was to disorient her, to challenge her. Bronn would have nothing but the best, and she wouldn't let herself be goaded by the competition.

The darkness of the hold enveloped her as she dumped the contents of her satchel while she walked. Dom was easy to spot—even in the dark—his height and fiery hair peeking out above the crates. He was trying not to look frantic, but his eyes were wide, his head on a swivel.

Ceylon rounded the corner to meet him as the last of her powder ran out.

"Where have you been?" he demanded.

Ceylon rolled her eyes, motioning the way she came.

"Don't lie to me. I've been searching for you, there's no way I just overlooked you."

She grinned. "Maybe it's not that you overlooked me, but simply that I wanted to be overlooked."

He glared, scrutinizing her before his expression shifted to one of self-doubt. He shook his head, eyeing her. "Fine, let's get out of here."

Without another word, they returned to the main deck, running with their heads down. Once cleared, together they yelled, "Fire!"

In the chaos, they blended into the fleeing deckhands. Ceylon didn't look back as everyone cleared the ship. The shot rang out, drowned out in screams and shouts. And then the explosions began.

THIRTEEN

Ceylon

Dom repeatedly asked for Ceylon to slow down on their way back to the abbey. She'd been so quick that she'd arrived well before the others, leaving her to grind her teeth, pace inside the side door, and wait. Willow laughed and joked from the alley beyond. As soon as Malachi stepped through, she was shoving him back against the wall, dagger to his throat.

"You didn't tell me it was my father's ship," Ceylon snarled, nostrils flared, angrier at herself for not figuring it out.

A cool blade met her neck, pressing but not cutting. Dom, Leo, and Venus raised their own weapons, calling for Malachi.

"Drop your knife and step away from the master," Willow commanded.

Ceylon did no such thing.

Malachi shook his head minutely, but Willow also refused to relent. His hands were raised, empty, palms facing outward.

"Would you have come if you knew whose ship it was?" he asked.

"Of course not! I would never move against my father like that. You forced my hand." She pressed the knife closer, and Willow's bit into her skin in response.

"You need to see who he truly is, Ceylon. He already has the guilds. Why is he bringing in so many weapons? Why is he bringing in dark magic?" Malachi's eyes were pleading.

"He manages the Underworld. That is no small task." Ceylon wanted to rip the knife through his neck, and yet no matter how many times she envisioned it, she knew she couldn't. That weakness was a persistent thorn, the source of her anger.

Killing him only leads to her failure—a dead man can't fall in love, and a sensible man wouldn't love a woman with a knife at his throat.Howe ver much she disliked it, Ceylon needed Malachi. She needed his trust.

She swallowed deliberately, taking a measured breath.

"If you want my help, you tell me the truth."

Malachi nodded, glancing at the knife. Ceylon lowered it, and Willow snatched it from her hand.

Malachi pushed off the stone wall, keeping his hands raised. "This isn't the first shipment like this. Honestly, I'm surprised he's still using the docks. But I don't want those weapons in my city, and I sure as hell don't want another mage battle."

Ceylon studied his face. His eyes were a pure light green, no darkness hiding in them. And his mouth was loose, no tension. No lies. As much as she wanted to find fault, part of her had to agree. She trusted Bronn; she trusted in his plan for the Underworld, but that *was* a lot of firepower. Whatever he was planning was much bigger than she had anticipated.

A tendril of unease settled in her gut.

Malachi seemed to sense her shift. He motioned for the dining hall, uncertainty lingering. "Well then, shall we prepare for dinner?"

The Forsaken slowly filed out of the antechamber, Ceylon plastering on a semi-apologetic smile. She couldn't predict what was coming—with the Forsaken or with her own father. It set her more on edge than she would like to admit.

⁓

Anya was chatty and animated, asking for all the details on their afternoon excursion when they caught up after dinner. Willow glowered, but Ceylon ignored her. She largely ignored her meal, too, focusing instead on the room. It allowed her to confirm some vital intel—there were somewhere between thirty and forty Forsaken at the abbey.

Malachi said there was one last errand to run before the evening was up, but he insisted it was one he needed to do alone.

That suited Ceylon just fine.

She watched with a careful eye as he removed himself from the cafeteria, smiling and shaking hands with those he considered family. The family that he chose. Not the one that was forced on him. A sliver of jealousy rang through her. She shoved it aside. She would be the next Lord of the Underworld. She could have any family she wanted, including this one.

Ceylon chuckled at something Anya said as the rest of the table erupted in laughter. She hadn't heard the words, but it didn't matter.

Malachi's kindly façade slipped as he left the room, a weight on his shoulders. He seemed tense, and his smiles no longer met his eyes. Curiosity filled her like the wind in a sail.

She glanced around the table once more. Willow rested her head on her hand, staring at nothing. Anya kept the table entertained. Ceylon was on the end, close to the door, and no one was looking at her.

With everyone distracted, she dropped her fork to the floor, waiting a moment to gauge the reactions. No one even looked her way. She folded, slipping under the table, and waited once more. Nothing.

And so she crawled. The door was only a few paces away. The cook, burdened with a large iron pot, was returning to the kitchens; Ceylon slipped out from under the table, walking beside Ayleth until they were through the door.

"Really excellent meal tonight," Ceylon said.

Ayleth grunted, not even giving her a second glance before disappearing into the heat emanating from the kitchen. For a moment, Ceylon stood in the empty hall, surprised she managed to escape so easily. But she'd been fooled before into thinking she was alone; she wasn't about to fall for that again.

Ceylon scurried down the hall on silent feet, listening for signs of Malachi. She didn't catch any, but aside from the kitchen there was only one direction. His dark hair disappeared down a hall to her right—headed toward the side entrance.

Ceylon paused in the middle of the hall, pretending to drop something, and checked her surroundings discreetly. No one in the shadows. No one she could sense or see. Pressing her back to the wall, she peered around the corner. Malachi was at the door, throwing on a cloak. He didn't even look back before stepping onto the street. Ceylon pattered swiftly after him, slipping through the door before it closed. Malachi was already on the main street.

This wasn't her first time tailing someone. That was when she was six and Bronn had challenged her to find the home of one of the king's sentries. It was an easy enough job when no one looked at a child, let alone one who appeared to be nothing more than an urchin.

But this was different. Malachi wasn't a fool, and while he hadn't been cautious when leaving the abbey, he was now. He circled blocks, doubled back, tied a shoe with no laces. He was even more meticulous than Domenyk had been.

It made Ceylon dizzy—she ducked into doorways, continued past him with a staggered gait, or simply slumped against a wall like a drunkard. There were only so many times she could duck into the shadows out without raising suspicions. But if Malachi knew she was following him, he didn't show any sign of it.

Malachi finally slowed outside of an old graveyard at the south-west edge of the Underworld. A small church, rundown and falling to pieces. Just a single room with a roof, really, bordered by a short wooden fence collapsing in on itself. Even the headstones looked like they were tired from standing all those years.

One in the center, the one at which Malachi stopped, was cleaner, straighter, newer. Ceylon tucked herself in the door of the church to watch.

It wasn't anything special. He knelt in front of the headstone and sat, muttering some words, but she was too far away to make them out. She didn't want to risk being seen.

The city had an eerie feeling this far south. Citizens of Yvelle avoided the forest for various reasons, but here it was like the dead stood watch. A gentle fog guarded the tree line. No one else was around aside from the two of them. The moon lit the area with a soft glow.

She didn't know who might be buried here, but she would have chosen a nicer resting place. A place that seemed peaceful.

Her toes were numb by the time Malachi stood. She pressed closer to the door, hidden by the alcove, as he walked past. She watched to see which way he went before jogging over to the headstone.

Wildar

forever forsaken
forever loved

Nestled in the grass before the stone was a single black lily with a rubit.

It meant nothing to her; she didn't understand the gift. But she did recognize the name of the former master of the Forsaken, and she understood that loss.

Ceylon had never known her mother, Adelaide, who'd passed away during childbirth. Bronn wouldn't talk about it, leaving a hole in Ceylon's heart. She never let herself consider for too long. Love made her weak. She couldn't afford that.

With a shake of her head, she took off after Malachi. It didn't take long for her to catch up.

He was headed toward New Town, but not by a path she would take. Malachi dipped down darkened streets, zigzagging across desolate alleys. The effort to keep up was exhausting. Still, she followed.

As he approached the bridge over the Suri Kulu, he turned left, skirting the river until he reached a building with a single torch lighting the door. A sign illuminated by the firelight: Madame Dabney's Home for the Abandoned.

Like most buildings in the Underworld, the orphanage could use a good patch job. The door was old, with some cracks in it opening to the interior. A pane of glass on the upper floor was missing completely; someone had hung a sheet over it that flapped in the light breeze.

Malachi pulled a pouch from his cloak, leaving it on the doorstep. He didn't knock or linger, he just dropped it.

Malachi, leader of the Forsaken, visiting a home for abandoned children. Confusion froze her to the spot.

Malachi turned, eyes widening as he spotted Ceylon in the middle of the street, the only sign he was surprised to see her. She'd bask in the pride of having followed him undetected, if not for the sinking feeling of guilt in her stomach, like she was intruding on a scene she wasn't supposed to have seen.

"You're not meant to be here," he said.

Ceylon rubbed the back of her neck, shrugging. "I get that a lot."

His surprise turned to anger as he stalked over to her, grabbing her by the arm and practically dragging her back down the streets.

"Ow, let go!" she grunted, ripping her arm free.

"Can't you just stay put for ten minutes!" he yelled, the sound echoing off the empty streets.

"I'm sorry I'm not some loyal dog like Dom or Willow."

Malachi crumpled, sighed. He rubbed a hand over his face. "How long have you been following me?"

"Since you left."

Malachi's head shot up, that rage flickering once more, but it faltered.

"I suppose I should have expected as much." He motioned for them to continue walking. "Silly of me to think I'd get any privacy with you around."

It was then Ceylon realized how truly alone they were. The city was asleep. They weren't close enough to the taverns to meet anyone else.

Her options were limited in the middle of the street. Could she force him up against a wall? Would he let her? Her heart hammered in her chest, her palms starting to sweat.

Malachi glanced at her, brows drawn. "Are you okay?"

"Of course, yeah, I just—I missed—" She looked around for any excuse for her behavior but found only brick and stone and dirt. "There's a pebble in my shoe, and it's really uncomfortable."

Ceylon cringed internally. It was the worst save she could have made.

But Malachi laughed, a deep, hearty sound that echoed off the stone, filling the space with warmth.

"You are many things, Ceylon, including a terrible liar."

She bristled at the comment but found herself laughing too. Because it was a terrible lie, and they both knew it. She couldn't remember the last time she'd had a conversation with someone that wasn't about profits or takedowns or motivated by something other than friendship. The way Malachi looked at her now was like she was the only person in the world—and she wasn't even trying to hold his attention.

She liked being around Malachi. It was easy with him—it's why they'd been friends before, why they'd worked well together on jobs. If only his constant presence hadn't left her reputation with her father in tatters.

That lingering sentiment was a dangerous thing.

"While you're being transparent, now seems like a great time to ask you why you came to the abbey in the first place. If I were to guess you came to steal a very secret, very specific item few aside from those in the Forsaken know we're in possession of...?" he asked.

Ceylon cocked an eyebrow, thankful for the distraction. "If you want me to answer, you'll have to be more forthcoming than that."

"I may have relieved a noble or two of some prized jewels from a distant land." Malachi observed his nails.

She had to remind herself not to let her jaw fall open. "You stole the royal zymrat from Zymah? They said those gems fell into the Suri Kulu."

Malachi shrugged and popped into an alley.

"How'd you do it? The Zymavians never cross the Frysta Abyss. Their shipments have something like twenty-five mercenaries guarding them," she trailed off as she followed him.

"Anything is easy enough to grab if the subject is looking in the wrong direction." He waggled his eyebrows at her.

Ceylon shook her head, and the conversation stalled. They walked a few more blocks in silence. She should say something, do something. She should be using these moments alone with him to her advantage—no distractions. She sidled closer to the Master of the Forsaken.

"You never told me how *you* ended up at the abbey," Ceylon said.

A small smile played on Malachi's lips.

"A man named Wildar caught me trying to steal from him. I needed rubits for dinner. I was eleven, and I thought myself an adept pickpocket. But Wildar was better. He trained me himself, raised me. And I wasn't the first. When Wildar died, he named me his successor. In return, I promised to maintain the Forsaken for what they were, a family for those who had none." Malachi paused and looked at Ceylon. "A safe haven in a world of danger."

Wildar, forever forsaken, carved dutifully into the headstone. She'd never heard the name before arriving at the Hollow; it frustrated her how much Malachi had managed to keep secret. She'd thought she knew him, saw through him.

It made a poetic sense why they had never joined her father's ranks. The Forsaken were a family in their own right, having chosen one another when they had no one else. Malachi was their leader, the head of the household. Until he stepped down or died, they would follow no one else.

Ceylon admired that kind of loyalty.

Bronn led with coercion. Everyone followed him because you were punished if you stepped out of line. It was effective. It kept the Underworld in some kind of order. What Malachi had with the Forsaken was beautiful, but it was a dream.

Malachi's gaze fell upon her, and she debated—just for a moment—what it would mean not to follow her father's orders.

By the time she looked up again, they'd made it back to the abbey. Malachi said nothing as he held the side door open.

She paused for a moment as she stepped through, their faces only a breath away. Malachi was staring at her lips, and a thrill ripped through her. Without permission, her body leaned toward Malachi, closing the distance—

"There you are," Anya cried.

Ceylon jumped, backing into the wall faster than she'd ever moved.

"I knew I'd best you, snuck out right beneath your nose," Ceylon said, cocking a hip and crossing her arms.

Anya frowned. "Don't do it again."

The girl glanced around Ceylon to Malachi. Ceylon didn't turn, but the weight of the master's eyes pressed heavy on her back. Anya narrowed her gaze, and then grabbed Ceylon's hand and dragged her back toward the dining hall.

"Come on! They've challenged Dom to a drinking game. No one has ever beat him."

Because he cheats.

But Ceylon allowed herself to be guided, thinking a drink might be just the thing she needed.

FOURTEEN

Malachi

The cafeteria was raucous with jeering. The Forsaken huddled around a table as taunts were thrown back and forth between Dom and Alexei. The younger boy would never learn that Dom was unbeatable, but Malachi wasn't about to spoil their fun. He was still tight as a spring himself. As Ayleth brought in the ale, he debated having a glass, if only to loosen up.

But then Ceylon slid onto the bench across from Dom, shoving Alexei aside. Alexei gave her a look, but Ceylon didn't even glance his way, eyes locked on Dom. Dom stared back, challenge in his eyes.

This couldn't be good.

But then again, a drunk Ceylon might mean a loose-lipped one.

"So, are you going to cheat again, or is this a fair fight?" Ceylon asked, elbows on the table.

A chant started from somewhere in the crowd, low and inviting, building to a crescendo as the Forsaken watched, Malachi included.

A glimmer of mischief passed through Dom's eyes. "I didn't know the word 'fair' was in your vocabulary."

Ceylon tossed her hair back over her shoulder. "I happen to know a great many words, some that might even make you blush. But I can play nice when I want to."

Dom looked her up and down, eyebrow raised. But then he nodded, and Ayleth set the tray of mugs on the table next to them as the onlookers cheered.

"First to finish their drinks wins. Quit, vomit, or pass out, and you forfeit." Dom raised his first glass.

Ceylon matched him.

Leo stepped forward and raised his arm. "When I drop my hand, you begin."

Silence filled the room. Malachi pressed forward, throwing a casual arm around Alexei. He wasn't sure if he wanted Ceylon to win or to see her put in her place.

Leo's hand dropped, and both Ceylon and Dom shoved their mugs to their lips. The cafeteria filled with shouts and pounding fists. This wasn't the first time they'd hosted a drinking contest, but it was the first Malachi wasn't certain Dom would win.

Ceylon pounded her first glass on the table a fraction before Dom. The two kept their faces to the ceiling as they downed their second glass.

On the third glass, Dom slowed, his mug hitting the table just after Ceylon's.

Malachi pushed forward so his hands were pressed into the table. The Forsaken also pressed in, stomping a rhythmic beat that filled his head.

Dom lifted the fourth glass, paused with a deep blink, but shook his head and continued.

The energy in the room shifted. The Forsaken quieted with the realization Ceylon wasn't slowing.

By her sixth glass, Dom was nursing his fifth, his cheeks rosy red. A hiccup startled him, and he dropped the glass.

Ceylon slammed her final mug onto the table and pushed to her feet. "I knew it! You only win because you cheat."

But she was swaying too, words slurring. Ceylon leaned over the table, bracing her hands on the edge.

"I don't know what we were betting, but you owe me." She winked.

"You—" Dom moved to stand but instead tripped over the bench and landed on the floor.

The tension in the room evaporated as everyone burst out laughing, Ceylon included.

She was the sun, bright and life-giving. Malachi didn't know if he'd ever seen her so uninhibited before, so wholly herself. Why couldn't she see how well she fit in?

"More drinks!" Ceylon shouted.

Ayleth, still looking sour as ever, brought out another tray for the rest of the crowd. The cafeteria collapsed into casual banter and laughter. His family. His home. These were the people he would do anything to protect. Ceylon included.

Malachi made his way through the crowd, lightly touching her shoulder. Ceylon spun, hair twirling. Her smile faltered as she saw him but then a cheeky grin replaced it.

"Care to challenge me, too?" she mused.

But Malachi just nodded toward the hall. She followed.

"We just did this, master. Care to have another go?" she asked. The noise of the cafeteria dissolved behind them, and she raised a brow suggestively.

The moonlight in the hall cast a cool glow. The sconces on the walls didn't provide much in the way of light. Malachi's heart raced. Ceylon padded down the hall, stumbling; her arms out as she twirled in circles, staring at the ceiling. And for a moment, he debated not saying anything, just living in this one peaceful moment. But his stomach twisted, and he knew he had no choice.

"I used to believe I was going to be king." Malachi's words broke the silence like shattered glass.

Ceylon startled when he spoke, but then she laughed. A belly laugh that had him both smiling and growing irritated.

"Why would you think that?" she asked. "Kingship's hereditary."

Malachi sighed. "My mother. She brought me up to think that was my place."

"Where is she?" Ceylon asked, walking to an open window and closing her eyes against the cool breeze.

He couldn't stop the look of disgust that flashed across his face. "She spends most of her days chasing after whatever man can supply her with the most ale."

When Ceylon said nothing, he continued. "My mother was a fine woman," he whispered. "She used to be. We weren't wealthy, she worked as a maid. Her job meant she spent her time with nobles in Wellborn who insisted on basic knowledge. They taught her to read and write, and she bestowed that knowledge on me. She told me I was going to be king one day, and I needed to make sure I was prepared."

Malachi stepped beside Ceylon, leaning against the wall, watching her. "All that changed on my tenth birthday. She came home from work, already drunk. She took one look at me and told me I was worthless. Over the next year, I learned to take care of myself until eventually I realized there was no point in being with a mother who didn't care I existed. I was fending for myself already, I might as well find my own place, too."

Ceylon didn't look at Malachi. "Where was your father in all this?"

"I never knew him. Mother said one day he would come for us. I tried to believe that for a long time. The day I left I realized my father didn't matter. He was never coming back."

A crease formed in Ceylon's brow. "Why are you telling me this?" she whispered, resting her head against the cool window.

Malachi took a deep breath. "Because I want you to know me. And I need you to see that everyone here has some kind of tragic backstory we're trying to overcome, including you."

Ceylon's eyes shot open, fire inside them. "I don't have a tragic backstory."

"You think because you still have a blood relative, that means your life has been peachy? Bronn doesn't love you; he sees you as a tool," Malachi said.

He immediately wished he could take it back.

Ceylon stepped toward him, stumbling but firm. "If you're trying to gain my trust, you're not doing a great job."

Malachi's anger rose. He closed the distance between them instead of slamming his fist into the wall to mark his point. "Haven't you ever thought about your father's methods? He doesn't hesitate to kill anyone in his way. Most of the Forsaken are here because he murdered someone in their family. Because they were inconvenient."

"No." Ceylon held her ground, even though she was a head shorter. "He can be ruthless, but he keeps everyone in line. If anyone died, it was their own fault for not following the rules."

"Bronn made this personal when he left children without their families." A brief glimmer of doubt shot through her eyes, and Malachi pressed. "You believe that—with all your heart—he's just a leader? Even seeing what he's bringing into Yvelle, the army he's trying to build?" His voice dropped. "Even after seeing the way the Forsaken operate?"

Ceylon scoffed, throwing her arms in the air. "The Forsaken are unique. They've grown together. The real world doesn't work that way."

"But it could. Ceylon, your father needs to be stopped." Malachi fumed. "Are you so naive to believe he feels an ounce of love for you? Or for anyone other than himself?"

The two stood in the empty hall, inches apart, and yet a chasm stood between them. Bronn had blinded her; she couldn't even see the damage he was doing. His hope crumbled as Ceylon's face closed off. He wished she had punched him instead.

Ceylon straightened and took a step back. Not a retreat, but an end. "Whatever you may think of him, my father does have a heart. It might not look like the one you want him to have, but it's there. I know he loves me in his own way, and when the time comes, he'll give me what I'm owed." Her breath shuddered. "He doesn't act rashly. Every move is calculated. I'm here because I have to be, but I'm sure as hell not going to turn against him like that. I helped you once against my conscience. I won't do it again."

She spun, her feet catching. He reached out, grabbing her arm and righting her before he could even process the movement.

"Ceylon, please, take a minute. You're not being rational."

She shrugged him off. "Not being rational? You're asking me to go against the man who raised me. Tell me you wouldn't act the same way if I tried to convince you to take out your mother. They may not be the ideal parents, but they're the ones we have. At least I know mine still cares about me."

Malachi was sure, now, there must be a hole straight through his gut for how much it ached. Her lips pursed—a flicker of apology—but then she was marching down the hall.

"You might keep me in your castle, but you don't have my loyalty," she said over her shoulder.

And Malachi could do nothing but watch her leave.

FIFTEEN

Ceylon

Malachi hadn't been kidding when he told her she was going to be put to work. She'd spent the morning sweeping the third-floor corridors while coughing up dust, wiping sweat off the mats in the training room, yanking soot from a clogged chimney, and washing kitchen utensils until her fingers were pruned—and that was only half the list. It was menial and demeaning. She was surprised to learn that she was not to wash the floors.

The pounding in her head from all that drinking didn't help.

Just a few more days. Dread ripped through her. She may have spoiled her chances after last night—telling Malachi off like that. She should have held her tongue.

Malachi seemed interested, at least. Ceylon's mind hadn't stopped whirring all night, wondering what might have happened if Anya hadn't interrupted them in the corridor. She gave herself a light pinch as that fluttery feeling grew in her stomach—still unsure exactly what it meant.

But did interest count? What did it look like when someone was in love? She needed to get him alone again. Ceylon wouldn't botch this job. She wanted to make her father proud; she wanted the Scourge.

There was no choice.

They had finished lunch about an hour ago, and she still had a handful of tasks to complete before sundown. She'd get them done—they wouldn't mind if she found time for a task of her own that needed doing. Bronn would want to see her after the whole shipment fiasco, and she needed to ensure her guards wouldn't follow her.

Ceylon wandered the halls, a pitcher of water at her hip. It had taken all her cunning to convince that hag in the kitchen to let her take it—what with all the nonsense Ceylon might try to poison Malachi. Like she'd ever resort to something as lazy as poison.

Ceylon moved purposefully, appearing aimless to onlookers. A left at the treasure room and then Malachi's bedroom door loomed before her. She surreptitiously glanced in both directions down the hall. There was no one to be seen.

Gideon had always struggled with lock picks; Ceylon did not share his mediocrity. Malachi's door clicked open on her first try. She shut it behind her, locking it with a flick.

When Ceylon turned to survey the room, she gave a low whistle. There hadn't been time for her to truly appreciate it in the darkness two nights prior. The four-poster bed was covered in the finest deep-blue linens—imported from Lylow. A rug with bright weavings in swirling patterns lined the floor, and two antique wingback chairs sat in front of an imposing fireplace. It reminded her of her own room, although the architecture of this one was much grander, with exposed beams and intricate carvings. And the bed looked like it hadn't been slept in.

A sideboard lazed next to the door, with some miscellaneous items strewn about—alcohol, a silver brush, and a broken pocket watch frozen on three-seventeen. She set the pitcher on the sideboard, shifting a deep green bottle to make space. A quick swig told her it was whisky. It burned on the way down before the warmth filled her.

She sauntered around the room, opening drawers here and there, but she was more interested in the massive bookshelves that stood sentry beside the windows. Each tome was a relic, rare books she'd been seeking for many years—just to say she had them. Titles like *An Account of Ekean Customs* and, ever popular, *The Monster of the Frysta Abyss*.

She spied a copy of *The Blacksmith's Boy*, a favorite of hers growing up, the author weaving a tale of mystery and magic. She'd sit in the window seat of the Scourge Manor library, the sun warming her skin as she flipped through the pages in her spare time. Its rebellious overtones saw it outlawed by the previous king around the same time as he outlawed all mages only a few decades ago. Prince Owynn never amended those decrees when he ascended to the throne. Maybe, if his so-called brother had truly existed, things would have turned out differently.

She picked up the frail tome, feeling the soft leather in her hands. The smell of aged paper and ink filled her lungs as she thumbed through the pages. It was a well-loved copy. Some of the pages had been creased, the corners of the hardcover were soft and worn—the color fading from its original deep green. A peace settled; it appeared she wasn't the only one who liked the story.

Ceylon set the book back on the shelf, careful to replace it exactly as she had found it and flopped onto the bed. The sheets she remembered, so soft and smooth. There was more than enough room for her, Anya, and Willow, unlike the tiny cot they'd had to share.

The lock clicked. Ceylon shot up—she was less worried about being caught in Malachi's room again than she was of him ruining her evening plans.

Her frantic searching revealed no good places to hide. She considered the chimney of the fireplace but refused to dirty her nice new dress—a purple one to replace the dirtied green. Ceylon sighed. She would rather get caught than ruin the velvet with soot.

Under the bed it was. She had no delusions about getting off scot-free.

Footsteps entered the room. The door swung closed. Bolts were replaced. There was only one hopefully unobservant person.

A shirt dropped onto the floor. Oh. Ceylon had seen enough at the Scourge and wasn't uncomfortable with nudity. Still, she wasn't looking for a show.

The rustling stopped. She could see boots at the bookshelves she had recently vacated.

"You can come out now."

Malachi.

Ceylon cringed before crawling from her hiding place as gracefully as she could. There were very few ways to look less than shameful when caught trespassing.

She stood and smoothed down her skirts, the depleted obstrepat charm clinking around her neck. Malachi faced the window, wrapped in his dressing robe, an open book in his hand. The same book she had just been rifling through. Ceylon gawked. Not at him, but at the fact she was certain she had replaced the book exactly as she'd found it.

"You have good taste in literature. Is this what you came for?" He snapped the tome shut, placing it gingerly back onto the shelf.

"Possibly. You do have an impressive collection." She approached him. "How did you get so many rare titles?"

Ceylon kept her eyes locked on his. As long as his attention was on her...

Malachi shrugged. "I stole them."

Ceylon glared in exasperation.

"A few governors, a lady or two, the king..." He made his way across the room, plopping into a chair by the fireplace. He looked like he owned the place.

Because he does.

"So, you rob rich people?"

"We tend to acquire goods from those who can afford to lose some."

That wasn't news. The Forsaken had a gnarly reputation, but they were rarely spoken about for causing harm to the commoners. They were famous for making a raucous with the higher class. Setting things on fire, stealing, ransoms. There were never any mentions of killing, but that could have been an oversight.

Malachi inspected his nails. Ceylon was sure they were spotless. "Enough about me, what brings you to my chambers?"

"Maybe I really did come for the books." Ceylon lifted her chin.

Malachi raised his eyebrows. "The ones you left on the shelf? I thought the Daughter of the Underworld was a better thief than that."

This boy. Ceylon was certain she was going to murder him before she left.

Feeling entirely too exposed she decided to lean into her discomfort, attempting to distract him from her unmerited presence. Besides, they were alone again, which was what she had been hoping for. Ceylon stretched her arm like she'd seen the girls of the open-door district doing, placing it high against the bookshelf—the very one she'd been pressed against only a few nights ago. She lengthened her body, flicking her hair left and right.

Malachi blinked at her, his lips twitching. Very much like he was trying not to laugh. Ceylon grimaced internally.

"If you're trying to distract me, it might be working. Keep up those convulsions, and I might need to call for Ayleth," he said.

Ceylon bit her cheek to stop her retort and dropped the act.

"You're such a pain. Why do you bother me so much anyway?" she said through gritted teeth.

"Why else?" Malachi sat up straighter. "You make it so easy. You're just as much an open book as any of the volumes on my shelves."

There was no way he knew that much about her. Ceylon had spent years controlling her emotions, tuning her face to neutrality. Granted, she may let something slip every once in a while—people had the tendency to be rather irritating—but she was certain Malachi would never guess why she was truly here.

"An open book in a language you don't understand, I would think," Ceylon stated.

"I know you've always had an eye for flowers. That you never sleep with your back to the door, and you never lead with a left kick because your knee is weaker on that side. I know the corner of your mouth pinches when you're lying, and I know you've always wanted to see the world, but Bronn would never let you go. There are so many things I know about you, Ceylon." Malachi's stare pierced through her, his eyes dark pits. "So I guess we'll just have to wait and see. Whatever you originally came for, though, clearly has something to do with me."

Ceylon kept her face impassive, her breathing steady, even as her heart rate spiked. She crossed her arms. "And what would make you think that?"

Malachi just stared at her, that irritating smirk on his lips. The longer the silence held, the more her discomfort grew. After what felt like an eternity, she turned and headed for the door.

"Ceylon, be careful. I would hate to see you stabbed in the back by your own blood."

If she didn't know any better, Ceylon would have thought Malachi knew she was intending to see her father. He couldn't know that, and he clearly didn't know Bronn either. Her father could be ruthless, but he would never betray her.

Malachi is the one who should be careful.

Ceylon didn't respond as she let herself out.

Ceylon had quickly become accustomed to the daily schedule of the Forsaken. Dinner was strictly at seven o'clock, and she made sure she wasn't late tonight.

As she entered the room, the voices quieted to a whisper and curious stares shot her way. She couldn't overhear their conversations, but she had little doubt they were about her.

Willow stood off in a corner, a stern eye on the proceedings. Ceylon pressed her palms to her thighs so they wouldn't form a fist. She didn't *want* to be the bigger person, but she needed Willow out of the way this evening. She made her way over.

Willow didn't look at Ceylon as she approached, choosing to keep her eyes on her friends. It wasn't until Ceylon was blocking Willow's view that she peered down her nose and said, "What do you want?"

"Look, I don't know what I did to make you hate me so much, but we're going to be stuck with each other for at least a few more days. I'd like to make the most of it. Would you sit with me?" Ceylon asked, motioning to a table.

Willow inspected her, eyes raking over Ceylon's new dress, her outstretched hand, the dagger tucked into her bodice. She squinted.

"What are you doing?" she asked.

Ceylon sighed. "Let's not make this a big thing, okay? I'm just trying to get to know you."

Willow pushed off the wall, leaning in close to Ceylon's ear.

"Don't," she said, checking Ceylon's shoulder on the way by before settling herself at a table on the far side of the room. The boys smiled and greeted her, laughing over some inside joke. Willow's face lightened at the interaction, changing from the dark scowl Ceylon always received.

Ceylon huffed. Well, that hadn't gone how she had hoped. She would need Malachi to distract Willow, but she also had Anya and Dom to worry about if she was going to sneak out.

A hand circled her wrist, dragging her toward a different table. She looked down to see that shock of blonde hair. Anya. Together, they plopped down on a bench hugging the wall. Ceylon had a decent view of the entire dining hall from here.

Malachi waltzed into the room, roguishness emanating from his being.

"Let's eat!" he shouted, and the room cheered. Fists pounded on the tables as the haggard woman brought the meal out on trays, assisted by a few faces Ceylon had memorized: Gibs, the expert storyteller, and Corrine, who could get her hands on any uniform no matter how obscure.

It didn't smell like the food she was used to, although she was becoming accustomed to Ayleth's surprising palate. The chefs at the Scourge were professionals; they used to work at the citadel before Bronn convinced them to come work for him instead. You didn't refuse Bronn, not even for the king.

This food had the fragrance of a peasant dish, brimming with bread and root vegetables. From the trays that swept by her, she saw no meat, just a slop of some kind of ill-enticing food. But she had learned from previous meals it often belied something unexpected and rather tasteful.

A tray was placed in front of her, and Ceylon poked what might have been a radish around the bowl.

Across the table, Anya dug in, munching away.

She lifted her spoon to her mouth, flavors exploding. She tasted *cadremic* from Veritas and *ystrali* from Koqet. Ayleth combined spices in ways she had never experienced, and she had to say it was quite good. She shoveled in a second mouthful. Anya grinned from across the table. Ceylon stuck out her tongue, reaching over and snatching the girl's bowl away.

"Hey!" Anya shouted, stretching across the table to take it back. Ceylon held it as far out of reach—and sight—as she could.

"Well, if you're going to tease me about it, maybe I'll just eat yours, too."

The girl smiled; Ceylon felt the bowl lift from her hands. Dom sat beside her, handing the dish back to Anya.

"Stop causing problems," he greeted.

Ceylon gave him an incredulous look. "Me? Causing problems? It was the sprout who started it."

Dom just glared at her, taking a large bite of his own stew.

Ceylon leaned closer to Dom. "Head still aching after that beating you took last night?"

Dom's hand clenched on the spoon. He opened his mouth to speak as Malachi sat on the other side of her.

"Getting along, are we?" he asked.

She sighed. "Swimmingly, except for your general over there. She doesn't seem to like me at all."

Dom stiffened; Malachi winced. "Yes, well, Willow has always made her own way."

Ceylon could tell that with one glance. Her issue was with how incredibly difficult it made it to execute her plan. Ceylon needed Willow's trust in order to move freely.

"Why *does* she hate me?" Ceylon asked.

Malachi's eyes searched her face with a look she didn't understand. Sadness? Confusion? And then it was gone, his usual irritation back in place.

"Who is to say what goes on in the mind of a woman?" Malachi asked dramatically.

Ceylon rolled her eyes. "Fine, avoid the question. It doesn't matter anyway."

Except that it did.

"Don't take it too personally, Willow isn't open with many people," Malachi said.

A rowdy laugh sounded from the opposite side of the dining hall. Willow's table was holding their sides. Willow snorted, sending them all further into their giggles.

Ceylon tilted her head toward Malachi, raising her eyebrows in question.

"Yes, well, there aren't many people at that particular table."

If Malachi wasn't going to help, she'd just have to be more forward with Willow than she would like.

The sun was going down, casting the corridor in a reddish glow from the tiny windows in each dorm room. Ceylon leaned against a stone wall, watching the sun's descent in the empty hall. She had been waiting since just after dinner. She hated waiting, but that was all part of the game.

Willow rounded the corner. Her silky hair flowed behind elegantly, as though she belonged to a noble family, maybe from the deserts of Lynlow or Koqet, not the urchin street gang family that she knew. Her eyes caught on Ceylon's, and her frown deepened.

"Isn't Anya supposed to be watching you?" she snarled.

Ceylon shrugged. "Lost her. Said she had something to do for Malachi."

Willow cringed at his name.

"Fine, just don't bother me." Willow spun into her room and sat herself on the bed. Ceylon followed her inside, pausing in the doorway.

"Just hear me out. If we have to be together, I'd rather not be such an inconvenience to you. Just have one drink with me."

Willow glared up at her. "If it weren't for Mal, I wouldn't see you at all."

Ceylon sat herself on the bed across from her.

"I know there's some bad blood between our guilds, but that doesn't mean there needs to be any between us."

Willow's eyes burned with fire. She was up from her bed and across the room in a step. Ceylon's head whipped to the side, her cheek stinging with heat.

Ceylon took one deep breath, two. She needed Willow in the right spot, and a fist fight wouldn't do it. Ceylon clenched her teeth.

"Did you just slap me?"

"Your father is the reason I'm here. Bad blood doesn't begin to describe the rift he created. He killed my parents. He *ripped* me from my family. You want to know more about me? Then know this: If I ever get the chance to send my knife through that murderer's heart, I will not hesitate."

Ceylon seethed, the sheets on the cot crumpling in her palms. No one threatened her father like that and lived. But she needed Willow, for now, because she needed Malachi.

She set aside all her creative ideas for retribution. Maybe next week.

"My father is the reason your sad little party can exist. Where do you think the Forsaken would be if there were no Underworld?" she prodded.

"Happy! With their families!" Willow yelled. A silence swept over the room and, just for a moment, Ceylon felt a tweak in her chest. A small, irritating notion she quickly smoothed away.

Anya stepped into the room, looking between the two girls, slicing through the tension.

"Don't leave her this time," Willow muttered as she stalked from the room. Anya stared after Willow, her face saying she wanted to follow. She looked to Ceylon expectantly.

Ceylon shrugged.

"I don't know what you're trying to do but don't push her. She's had a really hard time," Anya said, surprisingly somber. Ceylon had never seen the girl upset. She studied Anya's face—the lines there were too deep, too tortured for someone so young. But that was life in the Underworld.

Anya padded over the bed, flopping onto her side. She gave a gratuitous yawn.

"Anyway, I don't know why I'm so tired today, but I am so don't go anywhere and let me sleep," she said. She snuggled under the blankets, forcing Ceylon aside.

She sat with the girl until she was certain Anya would not wake up, satisfied that at least a part of her plan was working as intended.

Sixteen

Malachi

Malachi slumped into his armchair, relieved to find himself alone. He didn't like it, but there was a certain level of formality that had to be present while Ceylon was around—he couldn't very well look like one of the crew. But as he stared at the bed, he couldn't keep the image of Wildar—bleeding, dying—out of his head. That familiar kernel of shame and anger settled in his gut.

Wildar had placed all of his trust in Malachi as he passed. With him died a history tied to the bedrock of the Forsaken—a former Scourge, discovering what Bronn had planned and planning his downfall in turn. All that weight, in the hands of a boy. Because as much as he tried to prove otherwise, Malachi felt very boyish most of the time. Like he was playing at being a leader.

Like Wildar made a mistake choosing him.

Malachi turned to the window, trying to settle the nausea threatening to rise.

He shifted in the velvet chair, legs sprawling over the arm rest. The cast of the moon coated his room in blood. Everyone knew the blood moon was a terrible omen. He hadn't paid it any mind until she arrived, a sense of foreboding her constant companion. Ceylon had always had a way of getting under his skin, but recently it felt different. There was a danger that hung around her, sitting just beyond her shoulder. If only he could draw her close, maybe he would be strong enough to protect her. At least she would be safe, even if he was planning on betraying her again.

Someone pounded on his door, and he jumped. He sighed, throwing on his dressing robe and rising to meet his guest.

As soon as the door opened, Willow shot inside. Unsure what to do, Malachi waited, a stone in his stomach weighing him down with each passing moment. It was like a storm raged in Willow's mind, her body. Her shoulders jerked in unsteady motions. Just as he was about to say something, she spun on him, tears escaping down her cheeks.

He was doing this to her, keeping her with Ceylon. He deserved this discomfort.

"Willow—"

"I go along with what you say, you know. I trust you, Malachi. But that barbarian is too much."

Malachi wanted to reach out; he wanted to say he loved her, that he could make her pain go away. He wanted to say anything that would stop her from hurting the way she was now, even if it wasn't true.

But he had no words that would make it better. He stood, and he watched as she cried.

His hands hung awkwardly at his side. "Low, I can't make you do anything you don't want to do. I won't. But no one here understands what it means to take on the darkness in order to bring in the light. Not like we understand it. And in a way, I'm grateful we can protect the others, but that also means you're the only one I can trust with this."

Pain rippled across her face, a stone cast into a tempest. But with a deep breath, she forced her shoulders back, her head up. Willow let her tears hang where they were.

"I'm going to kill Bronn," she stated. "For what he did to my family, for every life I took to survive, for every family he tore apart. Even then, it won't be enough."

Her eyes were cold and dark. He didn't doubt her. He had seen that look many times when they were younger. Willow hovering in the darkness, blood dripping down her arms. Her face hollow. Before she'd come to the Forsaken, she'd been owned by a dealer in the Underworld who cared more about keeping his enemies in line than ideals. It was not an easy debt to pay off, and Malachi found himself visiting the despicable man more and more with his own shares just to get her out of there faster.

Willow left herself behind when she killed. It was effective and terribly frightening. He had been the one to pull her out of it.

"We're not going back there," Malachi stated.

Willow just pressed her lips together.

"Take a seat, Low," he said. She hesitated but sat in the chair facing the fire, leaving the one facing the window open to him.

He lit a sconce, fighting back the darkness of the room, then poured two glasses of water from the pitcher. He handed one to Willow and sipped the other himself, sinking back into his chair.

"We'll get him," Malachi said. "We'll make him pay for every evil thing he's done, but Ceylon stays out of it."

Willow glared, and it cut him like she knew it would.

His voice dropped. "We don't choose our blood."

"Maybe not, but we choose our alliances. That girl knows every-thing he's done, Malachi. She's in line to take over the family busi-ness. Did she happen to mention that?" Willow snarled before she downed her glass of water. "She's just as bad as he is."

He knew that. It was the very reason he was trying so hard to show Ceylon the truth—that Bronn was a monster, not a hero. That he led with fear, not with justice. If they had any hope of taking down Bronn—of changing how the Scourge operated—she would be the one to make it happen.

"We can find another way. She's not the only one connected to him," Willow prodded. She yawned, leaning back in her seat. "Someone's been feeding us his movements."

"There is no other way. Not without murdering the entire clan, and I refuse to sink to their level."

Willow languidly waved a hand in the air, dismissing his charitable heart. "We could just kill *her*. Get back at Bronn by taking the one thing he might actually care about."

Malachi bristled. He knew Willow would finish them all if he let her. She was a ghost.

But he wouldn't let her become that person again.

"You know why we're not doing that," he said.

She gave him a sharp look and let her head sag against the back of the chair, leaving it be. He sat for a while, just watching her breathe. She was a different person when she slept—calm, innocent. He wished he could keep her that way forever.

Sleep weighed on him. He couldn't carry her back to her room now, but he didn't have to. He picked her up, placing her in his bed and drawing the duvet over her.

After prodding the small fire, Malachi grabbed the extra quilt and sat back in his chair. The warmth from the flames calmed his tired body. He pulled the quilt up to his chin and leaned back.

His eyes drifted closed.

Seventeen

Ceylon

Waiting, again.

Ceylon lay beside Anya, the girl snoring lightly in her drug-induced sleep. It had been at least an hour since Willow had stormed off, and she hadn't returned. Ceylon didn't think that she would before morning, but still, she waited.

She didn't feel good about swiping that bit of pixy grass from the garden. She wasn't even sure they knew they were growing it. Adding a portion to Anya's dinner, along with Dom's, and a strategic placement in Malachi's water pitcher meant her ever-watchful sentries would be out for the night.

An hour passed, no one moved. The abbey better resembled a grave-yard with the rest of the Forsaken dead to the world.

Ceylon changed back into her stealth suit. She loved the dress, but it didn't quite suit furtive escapades. She set it, folded, beside her bed as she snatched Anya's token to get back in unnoticed.

With one final look at the sleeping girl, Ceylon left the dorm behind.

The abbey was eerily quiet at this time of night. It felt cavernous and empty, a tomb without the energetic Forsaken occupying every nook.

Ceylon trailed the route she'd memorized through dark side tunnels. The door let out to the same empty alley; it wasn't even locked. Ceylon supposed it didn't need to be if anyone who came close succumbed to unearthly fear. The benefit of charms.

The night was still young. Ceylon avoided the roads with popular taverns, opting instead for the alleys she was fairly sure would be deserted.

A few turns in and her fingers began to tingle, the hairs on the back of her neck rising. They were well-trained—whoever followed from the shadows was silent on their feet. She was being tracked.

Ceylon tensed, twirling a knife into her hand. She shifted her gait, lowering her center of gravity, but kept her steps even to feign ignorance.

The body loomed closer.

She rounded a corner, stepping into the darkness and pressing her back against the stone of the building. The man followed a moment later.

Ceylon grabbed his collar, spinning him around. The stranger gripped her wrist, attempting to offset her balance. She let him throw her aside. Twisting with the momentum, she pulled his weight with her, both of them collapsing in a tangle of limbs.

Gideon's priggish features peered at her.

She frowned and kicked his side, the air rushing from his lungs.

"Seriously, you need to stop trying to sneak up on me," she said, sheathing her knife.

He clutched his side. She didn't offer to help him up.

"Worried you might kill me and miss my pretty face?" he asked.

"More like Bronn would be upset I murdered his dog."

Gideon laughed, pushing himself off the ground. He held his ribs gingerly. She *had* kicked him pretty hard.

"Harsh words from such a pretty mouth. No wonder you're his favorite."

Ceylon snarled. "What are you doing here anyway? I told you I don't need a babysitter."

"Bronn is protecting his investment. Can't have you running off with the Forsaken, that would be a mess." Gideon's tone left little misunderstanding of how Bronn would tidy up that problem.

A shiver snaked through her. "So he knows then, about the ship." It had been foolish of her to hope it would be overlooked.

Gideon's grin flickered. "Yeah, he knows."

Ceylon nodded. "You know what, let's not talk."

She marched away down the alley, hoping Gideon wouldn't follow. Meetings with Bronn were intimidating enough without a cretin like Gideon goading her. She was already on edge.

Despite her request, Gideon prattled on the whole way to the manor. She tried threatening him, then ignoring him, and eventually just let him talk. Ceylon wouldn't allow him to get in her head. She focused on her breathing.

After what felt like an age, she arrived at the manor, her home emerging from the light mist as imperious as ever. It had only been a couple of days, but it felt longer. She had learned so much about the Forsaken that would be of value to her father.

Ceylon took a tentative step onto the property. It appeared most of the Scourge were asleep. That surprised her. Her clan never went to bed early.

She pushed open the double doors. Brutus was standing in the entryway, but no one else—no guards. He didn't look surprised to see her.

"Where is everyone?" she asked.

He gave a small shrug. "Boss sent them out to the taverns. Apparently, he received some good news."

Good news? This was what happened when she wasn't here? The whole guild got to go out and party while she was stuck being match-made with an idiot? That hardly seemed a fair lot for the Daughter of the Underworld.

"I'm here to see Bronn."

Brutus nodded, but he stayed where he was. A loud scream came from the basement—where the cells were. Ceylon sniffed.

"Right, well, come and fetch me when he's through," she said and strutted for the stairs. "But if he's not done in an hour, I'm leaving."

Gideon followed on her heels, his long gait catching her easily.

"Beat it. I'm home, there's no reason for you to watch me here," she snapped.

"On the contrary. I think you're even more interesting here." A glimmer of curiosity and mischief flashed in his eyes as he glanced at the spent obstrepat charm she hadn't taken off.

Ceylon turned on him. She stood a step higher, which put them nose to nose.

"I thought I taught you a lesson the last time I was home." Ceylon's smile had a manic edge as she ran a gentle finger over the scar across his eye.

Gideon seized her by the collar, his expression dark.

"You think your position here is so secure. One wrong move puts me on top and makes you nothing. I look forward to watching you beg me to stay," Gideon hissed.

The usual fire of conviction was missing from his eyes. She laughed lightly.

"Oh, but Gideon, I never beg for anything. I just take it." She wrenched his wrist backward. He managed not to cry out, but his knees buckled as she thrust him aside. Tutting lightly, she continued up the stairs; he didn't follow her this time.

Ceylon took her time on the steps, gliding her hand over the railing as she ascended. Forsaken Hollow was beautiful in a historic sort of way, but Scourge Manor was magnificent. Each piece of the house was meticulously built and maintained. Every railing was carved by hand, the ceilings painted gold, and the chandeliers *were* gold—she had acquired those personally from Count Destrian's enormous parade of carts he had intended to gift to King Owynn. Damsel in distress didn't take much effort. The challenging part was walking away with an entire cart in plain view without raising suspicions. But that was the fun of it, the risk. Ceylon only accepted a job if she knew she could come through.

This one was no different.

The doors to Bronn's chambers loomed before her. As Brutus had mentioned, no one was there. She took out her lock picks and made quick work of the door. Stepping inside, the world grew quiet.

Bronn had designed his quarters himself. It was probably the most elaborate room in the whole manor, and she imagined, though never having gone herself, that the citadel would look similar. The finest linens in the brightest colors lay on the four-poster bed; a massive fireplace with intricate carvings occupied the south side of the room, painted in brilliant shades of red and blue. Articulate tables were strewn throughout for things like writing, reading, and oil lamps.

Ceylon scanned the room. Bronn was a careful man, intentional about his privacy, and he rarely left a clue as to where he had been. She looked anyway, searching the floors for irregular dust patterns or a possible footprint. Nothing.

The locket she was looking for moved frequently. As far as she could tell, it was his most treasured possession. When she was younger, she had caught him gazing into the portrait and muttering under his breath. Ceylon had found it, after weeks of searching, hidden on top of the bedpost. The next time she looked, it was in a different location. Every time he picked it up, he changed where it was hidden.

Now, combing through the darkened room, she thought back to all the places it had been. He never picked the same spot twice, and there were only so many effective hiding spots.

Ceylon wandered to the windows, checking the ends of the curtain rods. Empty. The curtains themselves had no hidden pockets. The stones framing the windows were all solid—they didn't wiggle.

She contemplated the fireplace. There was one spot she had found a few years back. If she stuck her arm under the mantel and reached up, there was a little nook, only about the size of a teacup. It normally held a key for a lock she had never found. But today, as she reached in, there was the locket.

Soot covered the silver. She brushed it away to reveal the carving in the metal—it reminded her of the vagabonds who occasionally came through the market, peddling wares from the Cliffs of Dosevan, which separated the Northern and Southern Continents. The silver hadn't been made in Yvelle.

The hinge was well worn—it had been opened many times. As the locket clicked open, the pictures tucked inside warmed her with familiarity. Bronn didn't like to talk about her mother, Adelaide. Her portrait stared back with kind green eyes and auburn hair.

The picture on the left had always been damaged beyond recognition. It looked like it had been burned, but she had never figured out how one image suffered while the other was pristine. All she could make out was a short tuft of black hair.

She didn't know anything about her mother, so she had always wanted to believe that she'd been kind and soft-hearted, contrary to Bronn's own demeanor. But maybe losing her had made him that way.

"I won't let you down, Mother. I'll be his successor, like you would have wanted," Ceylon whispered.

She clicked the locket closed, leaning down to the charcoals and replacing the soot she had removed before carefully placing it back in the nook exactly as she had found it. Bronn was perceptive and would notice the slightest difference. Dusting her hands of the ash, she stood and felt a weight roll off her shoulders.

With a final glance back at the room, she closed the door behind her.

Bronn's office hadn't changed, a great, imposing thing that looked out over the street before the manor. It was an excellent vantage point with a terrible view. She had told him as much a few times to which he'd responded, "Not everything is about beauty."

She'd understood. He still should've picked a room on a higher floor.

Ceylon brushed her hands over the shelves, noticing not a speck of dust. Their cleaner, Winifred, was meticulous. She was also mute, which was part of the reason Bronn liked her so much. She looked on their proceedings with an uninterested gaze.

There were few times Ceylon was in the office alone. When Bronn wasn't in the cells or sleeping—which he rarely did nowadays—he was here mulling over his "kingdom". The Underworld was hardly a kingdom, but she'd learned not to disagree a long time ago.

Slumping into Bronn's chair behind the massive desk, she stacked her feet upon its gilded surface, the chair creaking as she leaned back. Papers were stacked neatly to the right and left; a quill and ink stood at attention in the corner, and she briefly debated signing a few papers herself. A single letter sat open in the middle, its abandoned but intact seal betraying its sender.

Ceylon leaned closer to inspect it, but she was not mistaken. The crimson wax was stamped with the mark of the citadel—the initials O.V. overlapping and surrounded by a laurel. She frowned. Bronn actively avoided the king. He would never have left a letter of such importance just lying there.

She reached for it, but faltered when she heard a mix of footsteps. She relaxed her hand and sank back into the chair.

Bronn was a stately man, yet he had learned how to make his footsteps soft as a child's, unless he wanted you to hear him. Brutus, on the other hand, was never nimble, his strengths lying elsewhere. Finally, she could make out Gideon and his eager gait.

The doors swung wide, and in the dim light, she caught the smallest speck of blood on Bronn's immaculate white shirt. Their washer would not be pleased about that, not that they would ever mention it to his lordship.

The Lord of the Underworld's muscular form took up most of the doorway, his mood flooding the rest of the room. His drawn brows and tight lips alerted her to the fact that he was severely unhappy. Good, so was she.

"Out," he growled to Ceylon, eyeing where she sat.

She didn't move. He scowled but settled for standing in front of his desk.

"You wanted to see me?" she asked.

"You blew up my ship."

Ceylon tensed. "As I told Gideon—"

"Quiet," Bronn interrupted. "I never sent Gideon, and I don't care for your lies. Not now."

Ceylon shut her mouth and glanced at Gideon. He kept his shoulders loose, gaze uninterested, but his fingers clenched too tightly for her to overlook. If Bronn hadn't sent him to the shipment, what was he doing there?

"Tell me what happened," Bronn demanded.

Ceylon turned her attention back to the Lord and straightened. "I made a call. I need their trust."

Bronn crossed his arms. "So you chose to work against me? You couldn't find a single way to thwart them while not destroying an *entire ship*?"

"There was no time." Ceylon kept her voice even. She would not be shamed for keeping her plan on track.

"Maybe I was a fool for believing you could come through. It's a good thing it wasn't my only ship." Bronn shook his head. "Tell me about the master."

Her throat tightened, the name catching. She didn't want to think about why. Before she could second-guess, Ceylon spat, "It's Malachi."

And her stomach churned.

Bronn made a sound somewhere between a scoff and a growl. "Hard to believe the little kitten that sulks after you has been such a thorn in my side. Although, he is clever, hiding in plain sight. He should already be in love with you," Bronn stated. "What of his...talents?"

"His greatest asset is his mind. He's clever. He grew up in the Underworld, and he knows the ins and outs."

Bronn scowled. "Of course he does." He unsheathed a knife with a grip like he could wipe the Forsaken out in one swing.

Ceylon nodded, the lump in her throat expanding. She didn't know what it meant, but her confidence slipped at the thought of all the Forsaken she was betraying just by being here. It shouldn't matter. They were a job, not an end.

And yet her next words croaked out. "There is another option."

The Lord of the Underworld set the full weight of his gaze upon her.

"I've memorized every member and their faces. We know where their hideout is. Now, I also know how to get in, and for the first time, we know who their leader is." She looked out at the room. Bronn's face was impassive. She didn't feel anything from him. Brutus looked like he could be in pain, and Gideon seethed.

"Why not plan a takeover like we have with all the other guilds? Apply some brute force and the Forsaken are yours. They're the only ones left next to the Iron Clan," she said. Still, Bronn's cool exterior persisted.

Ceylon's eyes tracked his minute movements, muscles tense.

"Did you bring the master with you?" he asked.

"No," Ceylon said. Feeling her confidence shrink even more.

"Has the fool fallen in love with you already?"

"No, but I—"

"Then why do you oppose me?" Bronn yelled.

If the manor had been full, she was sure the entire clan would have heard that question. His eyes pierced Ceylon's soul, and her ears began to ring. Gideon laughed behind her, setting her more on edge.

"Because the whole point of getting that imbecile to fall in love with me is to get you the Forsaken, and a takeover is the easier way to do it."

Bronn's features didn't soften at her words. He turned to the window, looking out over the streets, his streets. The king may reign, but Bronn was the one in charge. Fear is more potent than lineage.

"Did I ask you to bring me the Forsaken?"

"No..."

He faced her, his eyes bright with anger.

"Then why did you think I would be pleased? I sent you to do a job, one job, and you come back to tell me you've out-thought me? That you're smarter than I am? This was a test, Ceylon, a test to see if you could do as you were told. So far, you're failing."

Bronn turned back to the window. "Do you know how I became Lord of the Underworld?" She shook her head. This was a story he rarely told. "I gained my title because of my authority. I told people what to do and showed them what would happen if they disobeyed. After a while, they stopped disobeying." He ran a lazy hand over a paper on his desk. "Besides, I can't plan two takeovers at once. The Iron Clan are more vulnerable than they think."

Her stomach heaved like she'd been punched in the gut. It was worse than an insult. It was foolish to think she could make her father proud by bringing him something better than what he asked for; instead, she'd just made everything worse.

"If you want him to love me so badly, why not just marry me off?" she yelled.

Bronn's eyes cooled. "Do your job, Ceylon. From what Gideon tells me, the fool is at least interested already. You must be doing something right."

Her heart stuttered at the compliment, the approval. He still believed in her, she just needed to follow through.

"But your outburst means your timeline has just shortened. If Malachi doesn't love you in two days' time," he paused as his lip curled, "don't even bother coming back."

Bronn left the room, Brutus giving an apologetic look as he followed. Gideon started to say something, but Ceylon's swift toss of a knife had him exiting silently.

Ceylon was left sitting in Bronn's chair alone. Her heart raced, her throat tight. She would not cry. There was no need because she would get the job done. She would make sure Malachi was in love with her.

And she would be gone before the end of the week. She would not remain trapped with the enemy.

The reality of the situation sunk in. Her whole future rested on Malachi. She punched Bronn's desk, knuckles cracking with the force. How could her father reduce her so much? Why wouldn't he listen to her?

Brutus slipped back into the room. Ceylon's face heated seeing him again, but she didn't tell him to leave. At least Alfie wasn't hovering today.

"Up we come," he said, helping her stand from the chair. His words were soft, kind.

Ceylon felt numb.

"You're a smart girl. I have no doubt you'll get this job done, and Bronn will name you successor, no question. He still believes in you."

Ceylon met Brutus's eyes. They were full of hope. How could someone who had seen so much wickedness in the world still hold out for something better? Especially an enforcer of the Lord of the Underworld. He was required to do unspeakable things every day, and yet he was capable of such compassion. Maybe it was because they deserved their fates.

Brutus was the closest thing she had to a brother. She could choose to believe his words.

She paused at the door, glancing over her shoulder. For the life of her, Ceylon couldn't understand why a man who had very little love in his life was so insistent she succeeded at it now. But it was not her place to question the Lord of the Underworld.

Ceylon turned and left.

EIGHTEEN

Malachi

Malachi's neck hurt. He'd slept in the chair—as he usually did these days—but he had *actually* slept. Most nights consisted of him tossing and turning and trying to get comfortable.

There was a bitter taste in his mouth. He looked around the room to find Willow, still sound asleep, in his bed. He sighed. It had probably been a while since she'd had a good night's sleep, too.

His eyes landed on the pitcher of water, and an uneasy feeling bloomed in his chest. With silent steps he made his way over and inspected it. Nothing, no scent. He held it up to the light—it appeared as water, it tasted like water, but it was more than just a coincidence both he and Willow were knocked out for an entire night.

Ceylon.

Malachi threw on a new shirt and combed his hair back with his fingers. He didn't want to confront Ceylon. He hoped to find her asleep.

He strode into the hall, making sure not to let the hinges of the door squeak, and nearly collided with her.

She didn't say anything, but her mouth curved sensually. He tried not to let his confusion show. Eyes wide and innocent, she seemed her regular self, but he could see it. There. The corners of her eyes pinched tight. The slight puffiness under her eyes and the way her skin seemed to glow a little less. Something had upset her. She had been up all night. The laces on her dress were disheveled—as though she hadn't been paying much attention when she put it on. She was trembling, but the hall was comfortable.

"Fancy meeting you here," she said, stepping closer. Her hand raised to find the hair falling in front of his face.

Malachi gripped her wrists so she couldn't escape.

"What is it?" he asked.

Her smile faltered but stayed plastered in place. That was the girl he knew. The one with a thousand faces and the ability to hide them all.

"I just couldn't help but wander...straight into your arms, it seems," she whispered in his ear. "Don't tell me you haven't thought of me, master."

Malachi raised a brow before he shoved her away, the bitterness on his tongue reminding him what she'd done. "Why do you do that?"

Ceylon's cheeks flushed a slight pink. She hid it well, but she was flustered. He couldn't say he blamed her. His own heart felt like it was going to beat out of his chest. The girl he loved was throwing herself at him, but the drug in his water told him it was an act.

"Do what?" she asked as she closed the distance between them once more.

Malachi held up a hand. "That. Stop."

And she did. She halted in the middle of the hall and stared at him. He wasn't sure if she wanted him or if she wanted to throttle him.

"You know, I had an *excellent* sleep last night. Best one I've had in years," he said. Ceylon stayed very still, but her face remained calm, blank.

"Well, I'm glad you seem so rested." Her eyes searched his face.

"Yes, it's not often I find myself waking to the sunlight these days. I think Willow would agree, although she hasn't stirred as of yet."

Her eyes followed him as he circled her, her shoulders locked forward. She wasn't known as the Daughter of the Underworld for nothing. If he didn't know her as well as he did, she would have given nothing away.

"Oh? Does Willow also have trouble sleeping?" Ceylon asked.

Malachi chuckled as Ceylon continued, "The sunrise is quite lovely this morning."

"And how long have you been watching it?" Malachi came to stand in front of her again.

Her gaze flicked from his eyes to his mouth and back. She wanted to retreat, he could feel it, and yet she stayed rooted to her place. As if she couldn't walk away either.

From this distance, he could see the dark circles under her eyes. Her hair hung limp, framing her face, but her green eyes were as bright as ever. Her lips were stained a lovely deep purple. He had never noticed how bewitching her cupid's bow was before.

Malachi sighed. "Do you ever tell the truth?"

"It's not in my favor to do so. You should know that better than anyone."

He pinched the bridge of his nose. "...one thing. Just tell me one thing about yourself that's not a lie or a front or a job."

Ceylon swallowed. She searched his face, and her demeanor changed, shoulders dropping, eyes loosening.

She took a breath and shook her head. "You don't want to know me."

Malachi tipped her chin up. "Try me."

They stood like that for a while, in the quiet, his hand under her chin. Finally, she gave the slightest of nods. "I can walk Yvelle blindfolded—"

"I know that. I've seen you—"

It was Ceylon's turn to hold up a hand. "I can walk the streets blindfolded because Bronn trained me that way. One day, when I was ten, he took me to the outskirts of the Underworld in the middle of the night, threw a blindfold over my eyes, and told me to find my way back to the manor before sunrise or I'd spend days in the cells. On my first attempt, I ran face-first into a wall. That's how I got this."

She pointed to the scar over her left brow. Malachi tried to hold back his frown, hand dropping from her chin. It shouldn't have surprised him—that Bronn would leave a girl alone in the Underworld—but it didn't make him any less angry.

"On my way back, I heard people following me. I thought they might be slavers; turns out it was Gideon and his goons. Bronn told them to make it more difficult for me, and so they brought bows and arrows to trip me up before I made it back. That's when I got this."

Ceylon gingerly tugged at the neck of her dress, pulling it down over her right shoulder. A nasty scar marred her flesh, running almost the entire length of her collarbone.

"Your own guild did this?" Malachi asked, horror pooling in his gut.

"Bronn told them to make it a challenge. And Gideon's always leaped at my father's words. He shot me clean through the shoulder; didn't even give me a chance to breathe before I heard the bow straining again." Ceylon brushed a finger over the scar, her eyes distant.

Malachi wasn't sure how to respond. He knew she could be lying. She could have gotten those scars doing any number of things. But from what he'd observed of Bronn's training, it sounded right. He didn't know Gideon, but Malachi was sure if he ever saw the Scourge, he'd strangle him for what he did.

Malachi reached for Ceylon like he could wipe away the scar. Wanting to pull her closer just to keep her safe.

Ceylon's breath caught as his cool fingertips met her skin, but she didn't move.

The door to his bedchamber clicked open behind them.

Willow gave a small gasp. It was a quiet thing, barely audible over the sound of his heart beating in his ears. He turned to face her.

Her hair was in tangles, eyes glistening with the threat of tears. He closed his eyes, cursing himself for doing this here. When he opened them again, Willow's face was empty.

"Low," he started.

She pulled the door closed behind her and made for the stairs, moving as though it was the most casual gesture in the world if it weren't for the tension in her shoulders.

Malachi glanced uncomfortably between the stairs and Ceylon.

"Seems like you've got something going on there," she breathed.

He searched her face, seeing all the answers he wished he could have just out of reach.

"We're not done," he said as he bounded after Willow. Ceylon's eyes burned holes in his back as he left.

The morning chill clung to the walls of the attic. Willow sat, her knees tucked to her chest, looking out the small window. The abbey wasn't very tall, but it granted a view of the Underworld for a few blocks.

Crooks and criminals alike scurried along the empty streets. They wore dark colors, made harried exchanges; a couple looked like they might start a fight.

"You shouldn't have followed me," she mumbled. "I'm not a fool."

Malachi sat beside her, staring out the dirt-crusted window.

"I never thought you were."

"Then why are you here?" Her voice became more of a growl, a jagged edge that cut down to the hurt, broken Willow he once knew.

"I'm here because you're my friend, and I care about you," he said. He didn't make the mistake of touching her.

Willow grinned, more of a grimace in truth.

"I never asked you for anything, Mal. I know how you feel about her, and I know how you feel about me. What I don't know is why you're letting her cloud your judgment." Willow's shoulders slouched, pulling her into a tight ball. She rested her chin on her knees.

When he had first come to the abbey, he'd found her just like that on a night he couldn't sleep. Wildar had warned him—she didn't speak to anyone and spent most of her days up here. She would disappear for hours and randomly wander back in, mute, alone, empty. A specter.

Malachi knew that depth of despair, of wanting to disappear when no one wanted you around.

Wildar had drawn him out of that state, and he refused to let the effort go to waste, so he'd passed along the favor to her.

It took months. He would come up and just sit with her, not saying anything as they watched the people on the streets. Eventually, he started commenting on their lives, making up crazy stories about who they were and why they were important.

One day, she cracked a smile. It was subtle, but it was the first gap in her armor she had allowed. And so, he pressed onward.

In the years since, they had created a unique bond, markedly different from any at the abbey. They had each other's backs. He knew how she liked her knives sharpened, and she knew how he could never sleep in the massive bed that used to belong to Wildar. Their relationship had been comfortable.

Here, in the glistening cool of morning, he could see the change in her. The comfort had transformed into something else. Ceylon, her skills and the challenge she presented, the way she took whatever she wanted without an apology, had changed something in him. Willow saw that. They used to have each other's backs. It would be so easy to fall into that trust again. But Malachi knew he could never think of Willow the way he did of Ceylon.

It went unspoken. Both Willow and Malachi refused to let these feelings change the way they saw each other but try as they might, they already had.

Malachi sighed. "You're right. She clouds my judgement."

Willow stayed silent. A cool breeze whistled through the cracks in the window frame, rustling her hair and raising goosebumps on his arms.

Why had Wildar chosen him to lead them? Had he known anyone else would've caved under the weight of caring for so many lost souls?

"We shouldn't pretend anymore," she whispered. The words weighed on him, a small crease forming between his eyes.

"What do you mean?" he asked.

"I can't walk on the edge, Malachi. I can't keep hoping that one day you might change your mind and see me as more than just a soldier. It's fine, but I can't be your friend—not when she's here."

His heart stuttered. She never called him by his full name.

She wasn't leaving, but it felt like it.

"You know you're not just a soldier. Stop talking like that." But isn't that what he had wanted? For Willow to move on?

Malachi hadn't imagined this would be the way things went. He had hoped she would find someone else, that their friendship wouldn't change. He had kept her close, maybe too close, in the hopes he would always have her right where she was.

He'd been selfish.

"It's okay. I've known where I stand for a long time. I was just avoiding having to take the first step, just in case..." she trailed off. Willow didn't look at him. She stretched out her legs before getting to her feet. Her height in the attic forced her to slouch as she stood. When had she grown so much?

Malachi jumped to stand with her, not wanting her to leave.

"Low, don't be like that," Malachi said, lightly gripping her sleeve. As if that could keep her within reach, as if that touch could hold everything together.

Willow's brows pulled together. "You're really going to make me say it?" When Malachi didn't respond her voice lowered, "You love her, Malachi. And no matter what I do, you'll never look at me the same way. Bronn killed my whole family, and yet you still choose her over me."

Malachi sucked in a breath, gut clenching. His fingers loosened on her blouse.

"Don't go, please," he whispered. "I'm sorry."

Her eyes swirled with pain and sadness masked by steel. "I'll do almost anything for you, master, but I will not keep hurting myself to ease your conscience."

She pried away his fingers and stepped around him to the exit. He watched her go. Willow held her chin high and shoulders back as she descended the stairs. It was a façade he had seen her wear plenty of times before but never because of him.

His chest ached. This was his fault.

Willow was right. He had been holding her too close, relying on her too much. There were few he could trust, and he had taken her loyalty for granted. She deserved to find her own path.

And yet, he wished she would stay as she was. Just for a little longer.

Ceylon had complicated his life in ways he hadn't foreseen. What did he expect? That an enemy would wander into their home, and everything would stay exactly as it had been? Malachi shook his head. *Ridiculous.*

But if he was going to take down Bronn, she was the way to do it. Even if it meant sacrificing his own life, his own happiness, he would enact Wildar's last wish.

It was time to get down to business.

Nineteen

Ceylon

Ceylon's hands tingled at the near miss. Willow's interruption had saved her a great deal of embarrassment, but Malachi knew she had drugged the water. He would have figured it out eventually, but Ceylon still didn't want to have the conversation.

She couldn't help but relive the moments outside his room in her mind. Malachi was quite the specimen up close. One might even say he was handsome. Of course, that said nothing of his ego. But his lips looked surprisingly soft for someone with a silver tongue. If Willow hadn't interrupted, she would have been one step closer. She'd know what his lips felt like—

She shivered. What was she thinking about? Ceylon was here to make *him* fall for *her*, not the other way around. She wasn't some infatuated schoolgirl. She could ill afford to be so off-balance.

Focus. It had been an insightful encounter. Malachi seemed more preoccupied with her, which worked in her favor, although he seemed most interested in her when she wasn't actually trying. Infuriating, really—how could she measure that? How would she know when to make her move?

Ceylon groaned.

Her anger and embarrassment after meeting with Bronn had cost her the night's rest. She had paced, then schemed, and then finally changed and headed for Malachi's bedchamber. She'd forgotten about Willow, as though it weren't her plan for the girl to be there all night.

Instead, she'd stood hovering outside his door for hours. The corridor had been drafty and dark, but she'd stood in the shadows going over and over what she might do to draw his attention.

And when he'd rushed through the door, she had panicked.

Panicked! Her! Ceylon, Daughter of the Underworld, stood in the hall like a criminal waiting for the noose. She'd been weak. She wanted to hit something. She had never been made to look like such a fool as she had in the past few hours.

Ceylon trailed back through the halls to the training room. Right now, she needed a fight to clear her mind. The sunshine streaming in through the windows did nothing to improve her mood.

Wide mats and cushioning covered the floors, and rows of dull weapons lined the walls. She knew the whole room from top to bottom thanks to the robust cleaning routine she'd been set to. She arrived to find Dom sparring with Leo.

As she watched, she noted Dom tended to leave large gaps in his guard. He needed to tighten up, or he would lose.

Yet, he was not losing.

Leo was taller, thinner, and less solidly built than Dom, but he was quite perceptive. He had clearly noted the same thing Ceylon had, swinging rapidly at the holes in Dom's guard. And right when he did, Dom would dodge and strike.

She nodded. He wasn't very graceful, but he was smarter than she gave him credit for.

Ceylon strode into the room, and their eyes found her.

"Fight me," she said.

The boys paused. Dom slowly released his opponent, and they stepped away from each other.

"I know how you fight, and I'd rather not," Dom stated, his chest rising and falling with the exertion.

She rolled her eyes. "Too scared?"

Domenyk's opponent laughed, nudging his friend. "Yeah, Dom, too scared?"

"There is a difference between being smart and being scared. I fight fair; you fight dirty—which you exhibited once again thanks to my *excellent* sleep last night. I won't injure myself for your amusement." Dom walked over to the wall, picking up a cloth to wipe the sweat from his brow.

Ceylon raised her eyebrows. "You call that fair? You left your guard wide open, knowing full well where he would attack. It was inspired, but not what I would call fair."

"A fair fight is one in which you are both capable of winning. Leo knows how I fight, he could have strategized against it, but he got sloppy and tired and walked right into it."

His opponent frowned, grumbling under his breath about how he wasn't tired, he just let Dom win. She opened her mouth to say something else when Malachi walked in, the look on his face keeping her silent.

His features were even, but something was off. She noted the small crease between his eyes, the tension in his shoulders. Whatever conversation he'd had with Willow hadn't gone the way he wanted.

"I'll fight you," he said as he passed her.

He pulled off his shirt, throwing it into the corner of the room leaving his chest bare aside from an amulet. He tucked it into his pocket, keeping it on his person. She hadn't seen it before, but if he wasn't willing to leave it with his shirt it must have some importance. It may be worth something.

Malachi limbered up, twisted and rolling his shoulders.

She should say no. He wasn't in a good frame of mind for a match. But, then again, neither was she.

Ceylon rolled her own neck and shoulders. She removed the weapons she had tucked away on her person and placed them gently beside Malachi's shirt. She wished she had stopped to change into her stealth suit, but she hiked up her skirts, gathering them around her legs and knotted them around her waist.

"Still time to back out, pretty boy," she said as she took her stance in front of him.

"No talking," he replied and lunged forward.

A feint. He bounced from foot to foot.

Malachi was fast, nimbler than she'd like to admit.

Ceylon's blood pumped through her veins, her fingers tingling. She kept her hands loose in front of her face.

They circled each other.

"Going to stand over there all day?" he asked.

She smiled sweetly. "Why don't you come over and find out?"

He frowned but leaped anyway. She spun to the side, hair trailing behind her. Ceylon slapped her hand lightly over his.

Malachi growled and spun to face her.

"Stop playing and fight me!" he shouted.

The pain reflected in his eyes made her hesitate. But no. No mercy, that was the Scourge way.

Ceylon let him come. His anger made him sloppy. Her skirts softened the blow as she slid through his legs. Leaping to her feet, she threw her arm over Malachi's neck and tightened. His hair smelled like strawberries. Why was she thinking about his hair?

He grabbed her hand, spinning her around and pinning her arm to her back. Ceylon let out a small grunt, the only sign she would give of her discomfort.

"What were you doing last night?" Malachi's voice was a whisper, but she didn't miss the ire. She spun out of his lock and kneed him in the gut.

Both took a step back, out of reach, hands up.

"Don't get it twisted, *Mal*, you're the one who forced me to stay against my will," she taunted.

His gaze soured at the nickname.

Malachi lunged. He grabbed a fistful of the only thing he could reach, her hair, and tugged. Ceylon fell on her back, the air rushing from her lungs. She gave herself only a desperate breath to feel the pain. She punched him in the groin and he dropped. Using the momentum, she hurled her body weight over him. It took three attempts of Ceylon smashing Malachi's wrist against the floor for him to release her hair.

Too slow. She felt the world tilt as his weight shifted from below her to on top. It didn't stay that way. Ceylon used the motion against him, letting them roll apart.

Both sprung to their feet.

Dom and his opponent clapped from the sidelines.

"Feeling okay, master? You look winded," she panted, her lungs still clawing for air.

"I'm just fine. Don't get too confident, or you might just trip yourself up."

Ceylon dove in, feinting for a low attack and slapping him across the face instead.

He cupped his cheek, pulling his hand away like he might be bleeding.

"Did you just slap me?" he asked.

She shrugged.

Malachi stepped forward and threw one well-aimed punch to Ceylon's ribs. She let it hit, trapping his arm and pulling it over her shoulder. Malachi flew through the air, landing with a heavy *thud*.

He didn't get up.

She walked over and crouched beside him. "Was that challenging enough for you?"

Malachi's eyes shot open. He punched her in the face, her nose crunching beneath his fist. Ceylon slipped to her knees, crying out in shock. Pain she was familiar with, but rarely was she surprised. Wildness flared inside her—she couldn't believe he'd actually done that.

Blood dripped from her nose. Malachi groaned from the floor.

"Why did you drug us?" he breathed.

Guilt sliced through Ceylon. She pressed a hand to the mat beneath her, hoping it would ground her.

Leo and Dom flanked Ceylon as Malachi pulled himself up to kneeling. He braced his hands on his knees, the deep purple of the bruises under his eyes unmissable in the warm light.

Ceylon's eyes flicked between the men. She could still take them if she wanted to. But she could see from their faces they wanted information. And she might get some of her own by waiting.

She focused on the blood spilling over her lips. She spat on the mats.

"You're harboring the Daughter of the Underworld against the wishes of your guild," she replied. "You didn't think I was just going to sit around, did you? A demure house guest? A questionable choice and your friends here know it."

Malachi leveled her with a stare. "At least my leadership is not in question. Or did Daddy just hand you your position?"

A low blow. Ceylon snarled as she said, "When I lead the Scourge, we'll be stronger than any guild. My name will make history."

Malachi's eyes clouded. "You have no idea how to lead a guild."

Ceylon's chest tightened, throat closing. Her fingers curled into the mat. She knew how to lead a guild: with strength, power, and strategy. Not on well wishes and hope like Malachi.

But doubt swirled in her. Malachi *was* right. Bronn had sent her on this job and was losing hope in her; Bronn no longer looked to her as the only successor. And on top of it all, Malachi had a guild that had evaded the Scourge for years.

Ceylon forced the thoughts away, somewhere deep and dark. She was strong enough. She knew what she was doing.

Her fingers relaxed.

"What are you going to do? Torture me?" Ceylon let her head fall back, trying to stop the bleeding. "I've been taught to withstand every trick in the book."

"Taught? Or simply tortured by your own father?" Malachi whispered. "Why do you stay with him?"

She could feel the fire in her eyes. "I don't know if you've noticed, but I'm not exactly a good person, either. I do what I want when I want. I'd steal from the king if it suited me."

"But you know what Bronn is, what he's done, and still, you'd die for his approval."

Was that shame that made her gut turn? Her jaw set.

"You know what I am, and yet you didn't kill me. You even let me stay. How different are we, really?" Ceylon stared at him. "The world is not kind to those who can't help themselves, Malachi. You and I know that better than anyone."

Malachi's gaze pierced her. It wasn't the look of the boy thief who followed her around and ruined her reputation. This was the look of the Master of the Forsaken.

"You can't toe the line anymore, Ceylon. Bronn is making a move, a big one, and I can't risk the safety of the Forsaken for hope—that ship has sailed. You can help us, or you can leave."

"Malachi," Dom cautioned. He shuffled forward.

Malachi held up a hand, silencing him.

"You'd let me just walk away, knowing everything I do?" It had to be a trick.

"You'll do what you want regardless, consequences be damned. It's not like I can keep you here. And I will not resort to killing my enemies."

There was something in his eyes, something vulnerable she hadn't seen before. She had to ask. "Help you with what?"

Her eyes flicked between the Forsaken for any unspoken hints.

"The Scourge is a disease to the Underworld, and it needs to be dealt with. If Bronn keeps going as he has been, he'll have enough of an army to take over all of Yvelle—the whole kingdom under his control. No more innocents deserve to die because of him. He needs to be taken out."

Ceylon searched his face for the tells of a joke, but it remained cold.

"I'm sorry. You're asking me to help you end the Scourge?" She laughed. Pain shot through her broken nose, but she ignored it. "I'm not about to jeopardize my future like that. Besides, you'll never get close to touching Bronn. He's much too cautious."

"That's why you're going to help us. You know him better than anyone. Taking Bronn out would leave the Scourge in chaos. You could change the ways things are, Ceylon, you could make them better," Malachi said. "You could make them a family."

"You said I didn't know how to lead a guild, and now you're saying I have all that power. Which is it, Malachi?"

He huffed. "If all you use is fear, you don't know how to lead a guild. But I've already seen the way the Forsaken are changing you. Join us."

Ceylon studied him, looking for the lie, but she couldn't find a tell.

"What if better isn't what I want?" Her heart gave a precarious *thump*.

Malachi gave her a long, scathing look. "You've seen the Forsaken and where they come from. You're telling me there isn't a small part of you that feels guilty about what your father has done that brought them all here?"

The Forsaken may be young, but they know how the world works. Bronn's position means they have a place in the Underworld where they can fight for themselves. She wouldn't apologize for the empire she had helped create.

But she didn't say any of that. Ceylon could see, there, in the corner of Malachi's eye, a glimmer of hope. That she was a better person than she was. She could use that.

"And if I did feel that guilt?" she whispered, the pressure on her ribs lightening.

Malachi flicked his eyes toward Dom. "Then *help* us," he pleaded.

She gave him a hard look. "What's in it for me?"

"Who said anything about this being about you?" His mouth quirked up at the corners.

"I want to protect my investments. Wouldn't want to create a better world and all that for nothing, would I?"

Malachi sighed. "You would have the opportunity to lead the Scourge into a new age, one that benefited all the inhabitants of the Underworld, not just themselves. You could be as famous as your father, if not more so. What would it feel like to have people bow at your feet as you walked the streets because of how you helped them? Not because they feared you?"

The weight in Ceylon's chest was replaced with a sense of warmth.

Maybe things could be different, but they would never be that different. She could still become the successor of the Scourge and create her own legacy. Suddenly, her path seemed clearer. Bronn saw things the only way he knew how: through fear and violence and ultimate power. Ceylon wanted that power, but she wanted something more, too. She didn't just want people to bow to her because they were afraid. And if she helped the Forsaken, everything would fall into place.

Trust was easy for them. Malachi had thrown their entire plan at her in a moment. Dom was still tense—he would be harder to convince. But all she had to do was go along with them for two more days. Enough to make him fall in love with her, and then she would have both the Scourge and the Forsaken.

"Say that I was inclined to assist you. I would need insurance that you're not going to stab me in the back later." Her eyes burned with fire. Malachi's word was as good as his life, and seeing as she only planned to help minimally, she needed that confirmation.

He looked at her quizzically, as if he could puzzle out everything she wasn't saying. His eyes narrowed, sensing the trick, but still, Malachi nodded.

"Fine. I promise, as Master of the Forsaken, if you help us take down Bronn, I will not move against you."

"Excellent. Shall we get started, then?" She cracked her knuckles.

His eyes were alight with a challenge, or maybe a plea, that she wouldn't go back on her word—if only he knew how deep her lies went.

Dom tensed as they approached one another to shake on it.

"That's it?" Dom asked, incredulous.

"Let her do what she wants. This is a mutually beneficial agreement. If she goes back to the Scourge now, she's giving up her own dream."

Ceylon's chest hitched at his words, a sharp momentary stab through the heart. This deal would cost them everything and her nothing. Well, nothing but her soul, but that had disappeared a long time ago.

She knew the things most people would consider wrong and right, but living in the Underworld taught you differently. The world wasn't cut into perfect little squares of morality, it was a mixing bowl of gray. She had learned to operate in the gray. A fortune here for a meal there. She had survived.

Wasn't that what everyone was trying to do?

The two of them shook hands.

Then she plucked her weapons from the floor and strolled out of the room, hips swaying.

TWENTY

Malachi

Dom and Leo were on him the minute she left the room.

"You can't trust her. She's lying through her teeth," Dom growled.

Leo spoke over him. "What part of you thought this was a good idea? She's using you."

The truth was that Malachi knew she was manipulating him. Deep down, he hoped he was wrong, that Ceylon wanted to help them and change the Underworld for the better. But he had worked with her one too many times to believe she was helping them out of the goodness of her heart.

Still, if he didn't have hope, what else was there?

"Of course she is, but we don't need her to tell the whole truth. Ceylon knows she must give us something or we'll throw her out. From what I can tell, she's yet to retrieve whatever it is she came for. Her best bet is to give us something just damning enough. Once she does, all we have to do is follow the thread a little further until we can get to Bronn. If we play along, she's our in, not our end."

The boys relaxed somewhat, their eyes widening.

"You're playing her?" Leo asked. His fight with Dom had left him with a bruise blooming under his right eye.

Malachi gave one nod, almost imperceptible, as guilt settled deep in his gut.

Dom put a hand on his shoulder. "That's a dangerous game you're playing, Mal. If she figures it out, she might really kill you this time."

Malachi covered Dom's hand with his own, squeezing lightly. "Then we best make sure she doesn't."

He called another meeting—it was a necessity. The Forsaken were never this formal, but Malachi would enforce Wildar's last wish, and he needed everyone there to know it. Malachi leaned back in his chair on the dais, watching the Forsaken file in. A combination of nervous energy and adrenaline filled the room.

Willow took up a post at the back of the sanctuary. She blended into the shadows like no one he had ever met, but he knew where to look for her. Now, she stared at the ceiling, admiring the old wooden beams, her shoulder resting against a pillar, arms crossed. If anyone else were to see her they would say she was bored, but he knew she was vigilant. And likely avoiding his gaze.

The Forsaken took their seats in the ring. Ceylon entered close to the end, taking a position beside Anya who chatted enthusiastically to Riz on her other side. It occurred to him then—Anya hadn't woken him last night when Ceylon snuck out. Neither had Dom. If everyone had been out of commission the whole night, Ceylon must have drugged them, too. A flicker of rage coursed through him at the thought of Anya left helpless. He thought Ceylon had at least some limits.

Dom coughed, loudly, bringing him back to the sanctuary and the many eyes waiting on his announcement. He leaned forward, elbows resting on his knees as he began to speak.

"Wildar had a vision when he opened the abbey to Forsaken from all over Yvelle. He saw what was happening with the Scourge, had witnessed it firsthand, and he knew it needed to be stopped." Malachi couldn't stop his eyes from traveling to Ceylon, but her face was impassive. "As we all know, he passed with his dream unrealized but not abandoned. He left his last wish to me and to you to defeat Bronn, the so-called Lord of the Underworld, and bring about a new age. One that is fair and just, not just for those who can care for themselves."

He paused, taking in the wide eyes and confused stares. Ceylon peered at him through narrowed eyes; it was her father Malachi insulted, no matter how tyrannical he might be.

"We have been given the opportunity to uphold Wildar's last wish." A murmur swept through the crowd. "I know how many of you feel about Ceylon's presence here. Many questioned why I would welcome the enemy into our home. But I can now tell you, friends, this is why. She has agreed to help us defeat the Lord of the Underworld."

The sanctuary erupted with voices. There were some hoots and hollers, a few claps, some slaps on the back. Everyone celebrated, everyone except Willow, who kept a heavy stare on him.

"How are we going to do it? When do we start?" asked one of the younger members, Corrine.

Malachi smiled down at them. "Plans like this take patience. I make no guarantees, but to make sure he doesn't catch wind of any of this, the sooner, the better. I'm trusting all of you to hold onto this secret and this hope. We will soon be living in a new world."

The crowd cheered again, and he let them celebrate. He leaned back in his chair, surveying the pure joy that permeated throughout the sanctuary. Willow had slid out of the room the moment he was finished. Malachi tried not to let the disappointment show on his face.

Ceylon's attention pierced him to the spot. Her demure scrutiny put him off-kilter in a pleasant, heady way. That look was a dangerous one. He had seen it many times, just before she took down a guard or nabbed her take. She was plotting a takedown of her own, and he didn't like where her energy was directed.

TWENTY-ONE

Ceylon

Ceylon draped herself over Malachi's velvet chair, the one closer to the window, and flipped aimlessly through the pages of *Sigils and Signs* by Baromaeus Avery, skimming over the alchemist's circumspection of the future. Across the room, Malachi paced, Dom frowned, and Willow observed. Anya had been sent away, much to her disappointment. The girl had insisted she could handle it, but Malachi wanted her far away from this mess. Ceylon didn't want her involved either, but she had a feeling the girl's presence would be necessary.

She'd just about had it with this crew. They were much too emotional, and they barely thought for themselves. She had no idea how they had managed to make it this far without getting caught.

"What about the sewer?" Malachi suggested.

Ceylon sighed. "He's not an idiot. Stronger, more capable men than you have tried to get to him before. He doesn't leave openings unless he wants to, and if you fall into them, it'll be your sorry rump on the chopping block."

Dom cursed and mumbled out more useless suggestions. He and Malachi went back and forth as Ceylon read her book.

It was Willow's stare that truly bothered her, though. The girl hadn't looked away since entering the room, and Ceylon didn't appreciate the attention.

"Can I help you?" she asked as she slammed the book shut.

Dom jumped at the noise, and the room quieted.

"I'm just wondering why you don't make a suggestion if you know so much," Willow sneered.

Ceylon set the book on the table as she stood. She paced deliberately over to Willow, taking in her dark eyes and darker hair.

"If I knew how to take Bronn down, then someone else would, too, and he wouldn't be Lord of the Underworld anymore. The man is overly cautious for good reason. His backup plans have backup plans, and if those fail, he has himself. Because, while most leaders are probably twiddling their thumbs behind the scenes, Bronn attends to every single one of his problems himself. He trains for hours a day, he never goes out alone, and he always—I mean *always*—triple-checks his security measures."

Willow quirked an eyebrow. "All except one."

Ceylon stared at her. There was no possible way this girl knew Bronn's security measures better than she did.

"And which one is that?" she challenged.

Willow smiled. "You."

Ceylon blinked.

That was only partially true. Bronn kept a tail on her no matter where she went, but she could walk through the front door without a question. If they were strategic about it, she could take anything in with her. And once she was in the manor, she was left alone.

"If we want to be technical, yes, I could go unchecked. But do you know why that is?" Both Dom and Malachi leaned forward. "He can leave the Scourge unchecked when they come and go because if any of them were to double cross him, he will personally pull them apart piece by piece in his dungeons until they bleed out. There's a reason our guild is so loyal."

Willow's smile dipped but remained. Dom looked like he might be sick.

"You're telling me the Daughter of the Underworld is afraid of getting caught by her Daddy?" Willow prodded.

Ceylon knew what Willow was doing, but she had spent enough time in those cages to know *that* fear was justified.

She leaned closer to Willow. "If you're not afraid of that, then you are a fool."

Ceylon backed away, returning to her chair, and picking up the book.

"So that's it. There's still no way to get to Bronn?" Dom asked.

"I didn't say that," Ceylon replied, staring blankly at the pages.

All eyes turned to her, burning with irritation.

"It's easy enough to get to him, it's getting back out that's the problem." She rolled her neck. "I could walk any of you straight through the doors at Scourge Manor, as Willow dearest so kindly pointed out, and you'll have a personal audience with Bronn. But it will be held on a table in the lower levels of the manor, and there will be chains and blood and sharp objects involved. You want to get to Bronn, you'll need some heavy backup to get you back out."

"So why didn't you say that?" Dom said through gritted teeth.

Ceylon shrugged again. "Hearing you talk in circles is much more entertaining. Besides, you have no such backup."

Dom clenched his fists. Malachi's mouth twitched upwards, and she would say he looked amused, although she couldn't say why.

"Here's what you need to do: make friends. Bronn's amalgamated the Black Phantoms and the Untamed. All that's left independent of the Scourge is you and the Iron Clan. He's gunning for them as we speak. But if you can sway them before he does, you might have a chance.

"When Bronn makes his move, he'll bring personal guards with him. One will be Brutus—his loyalty to Bronn runs deep, so you don't have any chance of turning him, and if he catches you, nobody will be able to save you. The other will be randomly selected on the day based on whoever is available and most suited for the job. And that's on top of the army of Scourge that will be there to initiate the takedown.

"Even if you could make it to Bronn with the Iron Clan as your allies, he still won't be an easy target. He didn't rise to his position with smiles and handshakes. You'll have to be ready for the fight of your life. But there's your opportunity," she said.

The Forsaken stared at her. Of course, she wasn't mentioning the most important part: they were probably too late in making that alliance. Bronn already had their ear.

"And that's *if* we have another guild behind us?" Dom asked.

Ceylon nodded, relieved. "You might stand a chance. There's a reason Bronn hasn't hit the Iron Clan until now. They tend to kill first and ask questions later. Bronn needed the extra numbers."

Ceylon folded her hands. The silence in the room grew heavy.

"So we need to find an Iron Clan member, get a solid introduction, and charm our way to an alliance?" Dom asked.

"Yes, that sounds like a good start," she replied.

Dom turned to Malachi. "I know this is what all of us want, but Mal, this is a huge job with a lot of unknowns."

"We're doing it," Willow said. "Bronn cost me everything, and I've waited twelve years already. If we lose the Iron Clan, what other chance are we going to have?"

Ceylon peered through her eyelashes at the girl. There was a lot of history there, she could see it simmering just below the surface.

No matter. They won't succeed. But something in Ceylon drew a heavy weight into her gut. She was likely leading them to ruin—possibly death, and for once, she wasn't sure if that was what she wanted.

"Willow's right," Malachi said. "We exist because Wildar brought us together, but Bronn's the one who put us here in the first place. If we do nothing now, how many more will suffer at his hands?"

"So where do we start?" Dom asked, looking back to Ceylon.

She checked her mental list. "You have three choices: visit their hideout at a pawn shop by the Suri Kulu, take something they want to force their attention, or find a member. If I'm remembering correctly, a few like to hang out at the Stormlock in the evenings."

Malachi blinked. "Those options all sound like suicide."

"Pretty much," Ceylon replied.

"We can't go to their hideout. Hobbes tried to sell them some jewels a few months back and nearly lost his hand."

Ceylon warmed at the memory. She had seen that interaction on one of her own scouting trips. The wolves were a nice touch of the Iron Clan's, hard to train and not for domestic households. But that was the idea. Keep them hungry and they'd guard anything.

"I suggest you find one alone rather than face them head-on," Ceylon said.

"You keep saying that: *you*. Do you not intend to be there?" Willow queried.

"Of course not. The Iron Clan knows exactly who I am, and if I'm there, word will get back to my father. It will put my position in jeopardy if the Daughter of the Underworld is present when the Forsaken make a move against the lord," she replied.

"So, you expect us to pull this off without you? The whole point is for you to help us," Dom growled.

Ceylon glanced around the room. "I'm sorry, is this not helping? Were you aware of these things before we had this conversation? Because if that's the case, I'll be on my way."

Dom rolled his eyes. "No, please. Do continue, Oh Wise One."

"Make no mistake, Domenyk, I'm risking my neck just as much as you are. I can't be seen until after my father has been removed from power and imprisoned, or you'll never be able to lure him out, and we'll all be face down in the river before we can say 'Suri Kulu'."

He shivered.

"All right then, what's the target?" Malachi asked, glancing at his friends.

"The pawn shop is out; I'm opposed to those hounds," Dom said, shaking his head.

Willow nodded. "I don't think we have time to steal anything. Besides, it won't exactly put us in their good graces."

Malachi let out a short breath. "Then I guess we're visiting the Stormlock."

There was very little doubt in her mind this was one of the riskiest jobs the Forsaken would ever attempt. And they were doing it in the name of their dead leader. At the very least, she respected their loyalty—hard to come by in these parts without violence.

But their dedication would be their downfall.

Twenty-Two

Malachi

Two hours.

They needed the schematics for the Stormlock. Ceylon said she knew how to get them. As much as he didn't like sending her out alone, she'd agreed to help, and it was their best chance. He'd given her two hours to get them—a seemingly impossible task—but she came back in one. Apparently, the archivist in Yvelle had a thing for rare poetry, something the Forsaken happened to have in spades.

Now, Malachi watched Ceylon as she leaned over the drawing like he might discover her secrets. When he came up short, he surveyed the prints himself, and his sureness wavered. The tavern took up a whole block, was always lit, and the rooms on the second floor had custom mage locks. There were very few places to hide, and it would be nearly impossible to get an Iron Clan member out without attracting attention. That meant meeting one inside, which added a lot of variables.

Malachi knew Ceylon. There was something she wasn't telling him, and it was driving him crazy thinking through all the possibilities. The one thing he knew for sure: he couldn't trust her, no matter how much he wanted to. He needed her close, to keep an eye on her.

It didn't hurt that he could also make sure she was safe.

"The Stormlock is one of the busiest taverns in Yvelle. Based on what I saw tailing the Iron Clan, that's why they like it. Makes them feel like they can relax because they blend in," Ceylon explained. "But a few keep their tattoos visible. That's what you'll want to look for."

The Stormlock boasted a regular patronage from every unsavory character in Yvelle. Malachi had visited himself, on occasion, but never at peak times and never without a disguise. It was known for getting rowdy, especially when the drinks started flowing, and there was no telling who might be looking for a fight. Just stepping foot inside was a huge risk.

His confidence in Ceylon's abilities slipped.

Dom looked just as unconvinced. "Did you show these to us so we would all agree to give up? Because that's what it looks like."

He swallowed. Malachi knew a thing or two about being a nuisance, but he had never challenged Bronn like this before, not head on. Until now, his whole goal was to keep the Forsaken safe. Now, he was actively walking them into danger to keep that safety.

Ceylon rolled her eyes. They had a glow about them that he only saw when she was on a job.

"If I wanted you to give up, I wouldn't have agreed to help in the first place. It looks impossible, but that's the idea. All security has its weak points; in this case, it happens to be unpredictability."

Three pairs of eyes looked at her.

"If no one can predict it, how is that supposed to help us?" Dom asked.

Ceylon blinked at him. "No one would expect the Forsaken to show up at the Stormlock because they're the elusive thorn in everyone's side. It's harder to find a member of the Forsaken than an honest man in the market. If you appear wanting a truce, they might just listen," she said and leaned back in her chair as though everyone understood. Her smug look diminished as she was met with blank stares.

"You really ought to be more upfront with us. It seems our minds can't possibly keep up with you," Malachi cooed.

Ceylon scrunched her nose. "So unrefined. Fine, here's the plan," she looked at Malachi, "in its *simplest* terms. You walk through the front door, find an Iron Clan, and talk."

"We're *simply* going to walk into a tavern filled with enemies and request an audience with someone who is more likely to kill us *then* wonder why we're there," Malachi clarified.

"Exactly. What fun is a job if the risks aren't high?" She winked at him.

He had to admit, the adrenaline that rushed through him at the prospect of meeting an Iron Clan while surrounded by enemies in the most questionable tavern in the city was quite a high. But, as Ceylon had so kindly pointed out, it was dangerous.

The Forsaken had managed to ruin jobs for more than one guild. Some of the patrons would likely have seen Malachi's face around, and if they happened to make the connection of who he represented, the Forsaken might be finished there and then.

"How many people do we need on the inside?" he asked instead.

"Well, the Stormlock isn't exactly hard to get into. You'll want as much muscle with you as possible, but keep it subtle. You know, just in case," she said.

Willow scoffed. "Just in case someone doesn't want to talk and kills us first, you mean."

Ceylon shrugged like it was obvious.

Malachi didn't want to think about what might happen to those who came with them. Risking his life for the Forsaken was one thing, but asking others to put theirs on the line...

"You realize the majority of the Forsaken are children, right? We're not about to put them up against goons like the Iron Clan." Willow crossed her arms.

Ceylon frowned, and Malachi felt a small sense of satisfaction that there was one thing she hadn't considered.

"Surely you have a handful who can go," she said, looking between the Forsaken.

They all knew the answer. The ones going to the Stormlock were already in the room, for they weren't about to leave Ceylon in the abbey while they went out to challenge her father.

"Let's just say having you there gives us insurance. We have plenty of charcoal to disguise your appearance." Sheer justice radiated from Dom's features.

Ceylon pouted, pulling her hair over her shoulder and stroking it gently. She looked at it longingly but steeled her expression and sat up straighter.

"Fine, I'll go. But just know it's more of a risk for me to go with you than it is to stay behind."

They all nodded in agreement. The evening whittled away as they finalized their plans. Ceylon was right about one thing: jobs were much less fun when the stakes were low.

✀

Malachi adjusted the collar of his shirt and smoothed his dark hair back in the mirror that sat above his fireplace. It had been a long time since he had cared about the way he looked. He knew all the formalities—his mother had made sure of that with all his *kingly* training. But all the training in the world wouldn't change the fact he was an imposter—a drunkard's son in pretty clothes, deep green eyes peering back at him.

There was a light rap at the door, and Willow stepped inside. Her dark hair was piled on top of her head, fringe still brushing her eyebrows. The suit she wore was a special one—designed for things that haunted her dreams. She kept her eyes down, the only sign she was uncomfortable.

They would all be uncomfortable tonight. Actors on a stage in a crowd of strangers. This was what they had worked for, though. They all knew the importance of this meeting.

"Ready?" he asked, turning back to his reflection.

"Are any of us?" she said quietly.

He tucked his amulet into his tunic, hiding it from view.

"Well, shall we?" he asked, sweeping out an arm. Willow nodded, following him into the hall.

Dom and Ceylon bickered. She was clearly unhappy with the charcoal's effect on her hair. He'd tried not to laugh when Willow had doused her with it. The last obstrepat charm had been a bust, so it wasn't as though they had another option. Besides, Willow made it clear she was quite happy to use the charcoal.

It was only temporary, but it felt wrong to see Ceylon with pitch-black hair instead of its usual vibrancy. She had bit her quivering lip but stayed silent as Willow braided it back. When she came out of the privy wearing his clothes, he was sure no one would recognize her. He had to look twice himself.

Now, Malachi shook his head, focusing on the fact that they had exactly four Forsaken heading into the most notorious tavern in Yvelle. Four people potentially walking to their deaths.

"You could have at least gotten me a better shirt," Ceylon complained, pinching the fabric like it was contaminated.

Dom crossed his arms, a small smile crossing his lips. "You can't go in with your stealth suit, it's a dead giveaway. Besides, I thought you'd be thrilled for the chance to ruin something of Malachi's."

For a moment, Malachi wondered if Ceylon might actually stamp her foot. But then her eyes found him, the slightest hint of pink on her cheeks.

"Good, you're here. Let's go," she said and stalked away down the hall.

Dom gave him a look that said tonight would be interesting, one way or another and followed Ceylon. Malachi patted the amulet under his own shirt and hoped it would offer more protection than it had in the past.

They were met by the cool night air. It was never cold in Yvelle, but there was often a chill breeze that came in off the bay. Tonight was a pleasant evening, and the breeze cooled his clammy skin.

It was quiet out, already dark but still early, the dusk masking their cloaked bodies in the shadows. In just a few hours, the streets would be crowded with those looking to drown their day away. But for now, he thanked Magum Makaio there were few prying eyes.

The walk to the Stormlock was short, but it dragged under the weight of their tension. His pounding heart matched the pace of his steps. He couldn't stop looking at the crew with him. Would he be walking back with the same number?

It was just a meeting. Ceylon had assured him, confirmed by her scouting, that the Iron Clan was open to parlays.

Malachi just wasn't sure if he really trusted her word, as much as he might want to.

The commotion of tavern life echoed along the streets of the Underworld as they drew nearer. Dom looked back from under his cloak hood. Malachi gave one nod. Ceylon and Dom went ahead while he and Willow continued at pace.

There was only one entrance—if you didn't count the emergency exit in the back. Malachi didn't want them all going in together. Should the worst happen, there was less chance they'd all be caught.

Malachi took a deep breath as Ceylon and Dom disappeared. She would only be out of sight for a few minutes. How much trouble could she get into in that amount of time?

Malachi held the door open as Willow stepped through, light-footed, onto the stained wooden floors. Malachi followed, but once inside, he was reminded that the Stormlock was more like another world.

The tavern was entirely wood, the ceiling low and close, creating what would be an inviting atmosphere if it were a house. Instead, it was stifling with all the bodies packed in.

The clamor assaulted their ears.

Men fought in a pit off to the right, which most of the patrons crowded around. Mugs of ale sloshed as they shouted and pressed inward. A bar spanned the back wall, one bartender running back and forth, filling orders as they were shouted over the din.

Malachi scanned the room and realized he couldn't see Ceylon at all. It took Dom catching his eye for Malachi to even realize Ceylon was staring right at him from beside the staircase heading up to the second level. Even in a crowd where she was on their side, she was a specter.

Ceylon nodded to a table in the center of the room. He was about to follow her direction when something in Ceylon's eyes caught his attention. He couldn't quite place it; she gave nothing away. Maybe it was the way she pressed closer to the wall, farther from the people, but there was something she wasn't saying—something that set her on edge—and that set him on edge, too.

All he could do was straighten his spine as he looked toward the scariest man he'd ever seen. Tattoos of magical runes curled up his neck and over his bald head. A thick brown beard was braided neatly down his chest. A runed axe rested on the table.

"Is he trying to get jumped?" Willow whispered.

Malachi had to wonder the same. The runes probably wouldn't offer the stranger any protection but might make him feel better. As long as the man didn't step foot over the Suri Kulu to New Town, he supposed most would simply steer clear.

Willow cracked her knuckles and headed for the table where the Iron Clan played cards. She kept her hand near one of her hidden knives—Malachi knew of at least four—and he watched her transform from the tense, timid girl into a guild member as she placed a hand on the table. She kept her head high, eyes bored as she surveyed the men.

The ones playing cards either looked at her with disgust for interrupting their game or let their gazes linger in appreciation. When she had each of their eyes, she slipped out the knife and slammed it onto the table.

"Someone would like to speak with you," she said. The Iron Clan member met her cold stare.

"Scram, wench, we're in the middle of something," the man across from Willow said. He had horrid browning teeth and wiry hair.

Willow dripped congeniality. "I don't think you heard me."

With a leap, she leaned across the table using the same knife to pin the wiry man's shirt to the surface. Blood bloomed but didn't drip. His eyes widened as he glanced down at his sleeve.

"We have business with the Iron Clan. So I suggest *you* scram." She waited a moment longer before plucking back the knife.

The man didn't wait once he was freed. The others loitered but eventually moved on, thankfully deciding this fight wasn't worth it.

The Clan member, on the other hand, grabbed his ax and stood. Malachi stepped forward, but Willow was prepared. She ducked under the Iron Clan's first swing, rolling over the tabletop. Her foot clipped his bearded chin.

The Iron Clan roared, stumbling, and swung again. Willow met his ax with crossed daggers—Malachi hadn't even seen her grab the second.

"I suggest you sit," she said.

The ax pressed closer to Willow. She eyed it, then the Iron Clan with rage in his eyes akin to an erupting volcano. Her blades dropped as she ducked. Two steps had her behind the hulk of a man. With a leap, she wrapped one arm around his neck, the other pressed a dagger to his throat.

"I said: Sit. Down." Willow's feet dangled off the ground, yet she looked fully in control.

Malachi slid into the seat across from where the Iron Clan had been sitting, tense as a metal rod. He wanted to assist Willow, to rip the ax from the Iron Clan's grasp, but he needed to look strong. And not trusting your general was not a strong move.

Malachi waited until the Iron Clan's rage dulled and he dropped into his seat, placing the ax within easy reach. Willow's feet met the floor again. She released the Iron Clan's neck, one dagger still raised as she took a free chair.

The Iron Clan member examined Malachi. Plastering a look of casual nonchalance onto his face, Malachi leaned back in his chair.

"You interrupted a lucrative game," the Iron Clan said, his hand tightening.

"I have a more lucrative proposition. I wish to parlay." Malachi raised an eyebrow.

The Iron Clan laughed. His eyes scanned the master, taking in his outfit. It was clean, but not high-class. Malachi hoped there wasn't anything that looked more valuable than his words. He spread a hand on the table to resist reaching for the amulet under his shirt.

"Seems unlikely. Might get a good price for your buttons if I pry them off your corpse though." The Iron Clan grinned greedily.

Willow cleaned her nails with the tip of her knife.

"There are plenty of ways to kill a man," she began. "One of my personal favorites is hanging them by their toes over a cauldron of boiling water until the pain overwhelms them. Not all of them manage to keep said toes."

The Iron Clan frowned and opened his mouth, but Willow leveled him with a chilling stare. "If you want to talk about death," she leaned in, "I'm sure I know more eloquent ways to end someone. If you want to talk about a future, then listen."

He glowered but leaned back and nodded. "What is it you have to say?"

Malachi rested his elbows on the table. "You know what Bronn is doing. He took the Black Phantoms, then the Untamed; the Iron Clan and the Forsaken are all that's left."

He placed his other palm face down on the table, subtly shifting his hand to reveal the Forsaken token.

A grin began to spread across the Iron Clan's face. "You are here to talk about the Scourge? Ha! You are funny, little man. The Scourge will not overtake the ruthlessness that is the Iron Clan. It cannot fall."

Malachi tried not to snarl. "That's what the Black Phantoms said, too. Look where they are now."

"Enough. We have nothing to fear from the Lord of the Underworld. He will respect the boundaries." The Iron Clan pushed back his chair to stand.

Malachi's heart raced, his only chance slipping away before it even began. But he had prepared as much as he could. Taking a gamble, he recalled the histories Wildar had taught him and said, "Did he respect the boundaries when he took children as hostages?"

The Iron Clan's eyes pinched.

There. That was what Malachi wanted. The Iron Clan had a brutal history, but they had a strong sense of honor when it came to unarmed women and children. They'd lost half their numbers to the Scourge years back and had relied on growing families to swell their clan.

Malachi continued, "Did Bronn respect the boundaries of your peaceful encampment when it was sitting on a rich mine? When he killed entire families simply for being in his path?"

The Iron Clan didn't move. His amusement faded.

"What makes you think you're safer than anyone else?" Malachi asked.

His eyes flicked between Malachi and Willow, and he sank back into his chair. "What are you proposing?"

Malachi tried not to sigh with relief. "An alliance. Just for the time being. Bronn needs to be stopped, and the only way we can both avoid being taken over is to gather as many numbers as we can."

Shouts and exchanging coins rattled from the other end of the tavern. Malachi took the moment to find Dom—tucked into a booth in the corner—and Ceylon—

Where was Ceylon? Dread pooled in his gut.

"And who are you to suggest such an alliance?" the Iron Clan asked suggestively.

"Someone who has the master's ear," Malachi replied, not missing a beat.

The Iron Clan gave a knowing smile but nodded and said, "Say I might be persuaded, I must bring this before our leader."

Malachi signaled to Willow, who casually searched the room, but his eyes focused on the Iron Clan. "Don't worry about that. As long as you can get us an audience, I'll worry about convincing him."

"Her," the Iron Clan said.

Malachi nodded in apology. "Her."

"Well, I must say, little man, you have guts." The Iron Clan shook his head.

Malachi gave a weak chuckle. "Thank you."

"I'll tell you what, we will have drinks to honor the beginning of our new friendship." The Iron Clan lifted a hand to wave the barkeep over, but Willow stood.

"I'll get them," she said as she left the table. Malachi followed her with his eyes as she weaved through the crowd.

Ceylon had to be around somewhere. She said she wouldn't leave—unless she'd recently found what she came for. But he doubted she would disappear without flaunting it.

The Iron Clan mumbled on, but Malachi didn't hear a thing. He just nodded and smiled when it seemed appropriate. Then he spotted her, eyes wide, fighting her way toward him through the crowd. Ceylon mouthed something, then checked over her shoulder toward the door.

She was nowhere near Dom. Willow was too far away. But Ceylon moved with a single-minded purpose directly for his table.

"I'm sorry, but I—" Malachi started as he stood, a frown forming on his brow.

The door burst open—

TWENTY-THREE

Ceylon

Ceylon's gaze flitted about the Stormlock as Malachi and Willow spoke with the Iron Clan member. She'd marked fourteen Clan members upon entering. A few drifted in and out of the rooms above. It was hard to know their total numbers tonight, but she suspected that was on purpose. They were ruthless, not stupid.

A couple stumbled up the stairs beside her, the girl pausing to dry heave over the railing. Cheers sang from a table at the far end of the room. It wouldn't be long before the whole tavern was filled to bursting. It was tight already, but the night was just beginning. For a moment, Ceylon was disappointed she wasn't allowed to join in the fun.

Everything seemed like an average night with the revelers and guilds and ale, but something was off. Ceylon felt eyes on her she couldn't place, and there was a sensation in the air—a pressure—that made her want to leave.

No one paid her any attention as she marked everyone in the room, then the exits—two, really; four if one wished to shove themselves through a window or take their chances on the second story—and who might make the best distraction should she need it. The man stumbling around the hearth looked like a good option.

But she leaned and observed even as her stomach knotted. She tried to convince herself it was excitement.

Something by the barkeep drew Ceylon's attention, and she glanced over. A very drunk woman attempted to convince the barkeep for more ale, which he was less than inclined to offer.

But Ceylon was less interested in the exchange than the discreet chalk mark on the back door to the barkeep's left. She knew that mark—the curved lines that connected at a point at the bottom. It was Bronn's mark, a secret meant only for the Scourge, signifying the time and plan of attack. And it meant he was farther along than she'd suspected.

Her blood chilled, and suspicion gave way to dread. She hadn't noticed any Scourge members thus far, but that didn't mean they weren't on their way.

Ceylon peeked at Dom; he hadn't moved since he sat down, still as a statue. Ceylon dipped toward the bar and purchased herself an ale. A distraction the barkeep seemed welcome to accept as the woman was still on about how unfair he was being, cutting her off like that.

Ceylon stepped to the side, resting by the back door. Without looking, she swiped a hand over the mark as she sipped. Hoping, at least, that if the Scourge showed up tonight it would slow them down. Although Ceylon wasn't exactly sure why. She hoped Bronn did show up to foil Malachi's plan. After all, she was her father's daughter. But something tugged at her stomach at the thought of Bronn getting his hands on the Forsaken. And if everyone was in the same place tonight, he wouldn't waste the opportunity. Especially now that he was aware of who Malachi was.

Ceylon was about to settle into her new post when the flare of a leather coat caught her eye. Instantly, her attention was fully on the stairs the familiar coat had disappeared up. That sip of ale threatened to return to her mouth. Ceylon gave one last look around the room—Dom was still by the windows, Willow was threatening the patrons at the table, and Malachi had his full attention on the Iron Clan.

She slipped up the stairs.

The second floor of the Stormlock hosted guestrooms on either side of the hall. At the far end was a small window letting in lamplight. Shouts and screams sounded from many a room. Hard to determine if those screams were from fear or pleasure. Guests enthralled in each other leaned on walls, drank together, and generally blocked her path as she tried to sneak past.

The swish of the leather coat disappeared through a door at the end of the hall, closing behind. She pressed an ear against the wood, straining to hear anything over the din of the tavern.

Ceylon huffed. She couldn't be sure it was him, but she also couldn't do nothing. The mage lock glowed a light blue, indicating it was unlocked. She rolled her neck, plastering a drunken look on her face as she stumbled through to find the room empty.

There was a bed that looked like it had seen better days, a small dresser, a side table, and a window that would not open, but nothing else. Ceylon frowned. She was sure she'd seen him enter this room.

Ceylon shut the door behind her silently, blocking out the sounds from the hall. She knelt, using the soft light from the hall to find the dust patterns on the floor. Sure enough, there was an irregularity around the dresser.

Running her hands over its surface, she pulled each drawer out, but nothing seemed abnormal. Ceylon sat back, wooden drawers strewn around her, when she realized they weren't deep enough.

With a grin, she pressed her hands to the back of the dresser, discovering that it was not a white plaster wall like it should have been. It was smooth, cool, and wooden, a light draft slipping through it. She shoved the drawers aside and began to push and pull, anything that might open the secret passage.

With a slight tug, the back panel opened toward her, revealing a small door. With a shove, she was stumbling into the open passage. It was short, and she had to crawl through, but on the other side was a ladder that led both up and down.

Ceylon paused, listening. A soft light spilled into the shaft from above, and so she gripped the cool iron bars and hoisted herself upward.

As she approached the attic, voices became audible, and her blood froze in her veins. Ceylon clung closer to the ladder, evening her breath so she didn't make a sound. She'd only had one sip of ale, but already it was making her head spin, her breaths short.

The second voice belonged to a woman whose tone and demeanor she didn't recognize but could only describe as hypnotizing. Something about it left an unsettling feeling within Ceylon, and she tried not to shiver.

The first voice, the one that caused her to stop, was Gideon. Because if Gideon was here, Bronn couldn't be far behind.

"...hope it's to your liking," he said.

A rustling. Hinges squealed. "Oh, now this is just perfect. Kind of the lord to provide me with such splendor."

Feet shuffled against the wood floor. "Then it will work?" Gideon asked.

The woman gave a low chuckle. "Absolutely."

There was silence for a moment. Ceylon pushed herself up, attempting to glance over the top of the ladder. But she didn't know which way the two were facing, and she didn't want to give herself away.

"You're sure you're ready?" Gideon sounded more like he was trying to convince her she wasn't.

Heels clicked. "Of course I'm ready. Really, I find it truly insulting he insists on keeping me hidden away like some pet."

"You're the last thing he would ever call a pet," Gideon said.

Although Ceylon couldn't see anything, she could practically hear the delight as the woman said, "Then he is smarter than most."

Ceylon didn't know which *he* the woman might be referring to. If Gideon was here, it was probably Bronn. But *he* could be anyone. Clearly, there was more Bronn was keeping from her. First the shipments, then her ultimatum, now this woman locked away in the attic and taking the Iron Clan. This was all necessary information for a second-in-command, and yet she was here, in the dark, trying to glean information from a twat.

Although, now that she thought about it, Bronn had mentioned he never sent Gideon to the ship. Which means Gideon was operating on his own. He could have been tailing her, but Gideon seemed just as surprised to see Ceylon there as she was him. Either way, it meant Gideon might be working for someone other than Bronn.

"There was a small hiccup with the latest shipment—"

"What kind of hiccup?" the woman's voice pitched low, dangerous.

"Some gutter rats decided to blow it up. Nothing we can't handle. We've already sent for more; should be here in the next few days."

Ah, so it *was* her father hiding this woman away.

Ceylon couldn't help her curiosity, and she pressed herself up as far as she dared. Warm candlelight filled the attic space. It was all wood, well-maintained but forgotten to time. From her sharp angle, she could just see the tops of their heads—Gideon's dark, unruly locks, and the woman's stark-white hair piled high. Ceylon ducked back down.

The woman *tsked*. "I told him the weaponry was unnecessary. If he's sent for my own shipments, we'll be more than equipped. Really, his style is…direct."

So she knows. Even this hidden woman was aware of Bronn's ultimate plan. Ceylon sucked in a breath. Bronn could be on his way as they spoke, and Malachi was in plain sight, talking to the very guild Bronn was targeting. All possible, thanks to her.

Ceylon's fingers turned to stone around the ladder rung.

Gideon snorted. "You expect a warlord to operate with flair?"

The floorboards groaned. "It wouldn't hurt."

More silence, and for a moment, Ceylon wondered if she should leave. But any movement could cause noise that would direct their attention to her.

"Just wait for the signal. It won't be long now," Gideon growled.

Shoes paced back toward the ladder. Ceylon took her chances and slid down to the guestroom, hurriedly replacing everything as she'd found it.

The slight hum of shoes on iron met her ears as she slipped into the hall. It was just as busy, just as loud, but there was no chance she would make it down the stairs before Gideon saw her.

She grabbed a mug of ale from someone's hand—sloshing some on herself—and tumbled to the floor. There she sat leaning against the wall, head low, mug resting on the floor, as Gideon thumped into the hall.

Her heart pounded in her chest as he drew nearer. He paused at her outstretched leg, scoffed, and kicked her.

And then he was stepping over her as he disappeared down the stairs.

Ceylon gave herself only the briefest moment of relief.

Bronn's mark was on the door, Gideon was here visiting a secret guest, all of which had been withheld from her. If Bronn was here now...something twisted behind her ribs as she remembered giving him Malachi's name. The same Malachi who now sat in the open with a member of the Iron Clan. The only conclusion Bronn would draw from that would be the right one: Malachi was trying to move against him.

She flew off the floor, returning the ale back to the stranger and stopping at the top of the stairs where she could inconspicuously view the room. Malachi was still sitting at the table with the Iron Clan. Willow circled the room. Dom lounged in his booth.

On the surface, everything looked like it was going according to plan, but the feeling came to her like a light breeze. The mood in the room shifted, and she searched frantically for the piece that would help her understand.

And then she saw Brutus.

He was well-hidden for a man of his stature, disguised in a group of gamblers around a far table—the one with the shouts and cheers. But his attention was clearly on the door, not on the game, and as he lifted a hand—index finger crooked just so—she knew she had to move.

Ceylon took the stairs as fast as she could without drawing attention, drunks stumbling into her path. She cursed internally, wishing they'd developed some signal.

It wasn't that she didn't want Bronn bursting through the door and ruining the Forsaken's plan or finding Malachi unawares—she'd never intended for the Forsaken to succeed anyway—but something in her propelled her onward.

She ducked under swinging arms and precarious trays, even dove under a table, but she was still too slow.

The door burst open, shots rang out, and Ceylon stopped caring about who might look her way as she dove the final distance, tackling Malachi to the floor.

TWENTY-FOUR

Malachi

Malachi's lungs refused air. His head pounded as if he had been walloped by a horse. The wood ceiling above him pulsed into view. He tried to move his head, finding a soft hand clamped over his mouth.

Ceylon's body was flush against his, and it would have been comfortable if he could process what was going on. Her eyes were wide, head on a swivel. When she looked back at him, her eye twitched, as if she wanted to leap off him as soon as possible. Yet she didn't. She wouldn't have tackled him if it wasn't important.

Still, he placed his hand gently on her waist as she removed her hand from his mouth. She didn't pull away and was transfixed on his eyes, as if she were concentrating very hard.

"Was there something important you needed to say, or have you always dreamed of tackling me?"

Ceylon's cheeks reddened, biting her lip as she rolled off him. They were still only inches apart. His attempt at sitting up saw him shoved back down.

"Bronn. He's here," she stated.

The chaos of the tavern returned in a rush, assaulting his senses. There were shouts, sword fighting, mugs thrown and smashed against the walls.

The Stormlock was a war zone. He wasn't sure if he'd passed out, but the throbbing in his head told him he must have missed something.

Anger coursed through him, a charging bull. Bronn happened to arrive the very night they met with the Iron Clan? Malachi locked onto Ceylon, gripping her by the arm. "What did you do?"

Genuine pain rippled across her face, and for a moment, he felt guilty for assuming. Had he miscalculated? But she was the only one from the Scourge who knew their plan tonight. It couldn't be a coincidence.

Had she told Bronn everything?

"I didn't know he was coming," she said, her own anger rising like a shield. She looked disgusted.

Malachi couldn't deal with this right now. They needed to get Dom and Willow and—

All the blood drained from Malachi's face, his heart in his stomach. If Willow saw Bronn, she wouldn't hesitate.

"Where's Willow?" he asked, attempting to rise.

Ceylon grabbed his shirt, pulling him back. "Slow down there, hero." She gasped, pushing him away as a boot stamped right where his head had been. They waited until the fighters passed, and then she dragged him under a table.

"I may be able to fool the common folk dressed like this but not Bronn, and neither can you. You've been such a pain over the years he would recognize you anywhere."

He raised his eyebrows. "Then what are you proposing?"

Ceylon huffed, her fist pressing into the wooden floors. "We run."

"I'm not leaving Willow and Dom."

Before she could stop him, Malachi was out from under the table, dodging a fist meant for the Iron Clan whose ax cleaved the air.

Without a thought, Malachi beelined for the bar—the last place he'd seen Willow. He found only a tidal wave of tavern patrons locked in their own battles. He side-stepped a couple as they crashed directly through a table. Willow hadn't left that long ago. Malachi quickened his pace, his eyes flicking past rusty swords, wooden chairs, leather boots, but there was no sign of her.

A shove in his back had him stumbling forward. He spun as Ceylon's dagger clanged against a sword. The man holding it screamed, revealing a set of decaying teeth. A single punch to the gut from Ceylon and he was down.

"At least watch your back." Ceylon kept her knife out, elbows up, as she scanned the room beside him. "She's there, by the hearth."

Malachi blinked, unsure how to process Ceylon saving his life. Twice.

He locked onto Willow, her own fists flying at anyone who came within range, a look of pristine calm on her face. Maybe her past hadn't quite been left behind.

He had to get her out.

And where was Dom?

It was fine. They were going to be fine.

They cut through the fray. Ceylon's knives were drenched in blood by the time they'd made it ten feet. Willow's eyes found them, flashing with familiarity. She looked to Malachi, pointing.

A knife slid into her side. Willow cringed, but she didn't falter, kicking the man with her good leg.

"Willow!" Malachi shoved through the remaining crowd.

"Malachi, no!" Ceylon yelled somewhere behind him, but her voice was drowned out by the noise.

Willow wavered. She clutched a hand to her side, leaving the knife where it was. She kept fighting one-handed, but she was clearly slowing.

His heart slowed with her.

Her eyes locked onto the door behind him. Malachi turned to see Bronn stride in, head high. He surveyed the chaos with a grim bearing.

Willow didn't look back as she sliced her way to Bronn.

"Don't!" Malachi yelled to no avail.

Willow kept going. Her body tensed, her eyes narrowed, as she yanked the knife from her side.

No.

Ceylon doubled her pace, forcing her way through, but Willow's stride was longer.

Malachi threw himself over patrons, ignoring the elbow to his ribs, the blade that tore his pantleg. He focused only on the quickly lessening space between Bronn and Willow and Ceylon.

Bronn's back was toward them. A single strike upwards through the ribcage would incapacitate him.

But Malachi wasn't that naïve. Bronn would never leave his back unguarded, even if it might look that way.

Six steps.

Two steps.

Willow struck, her eyes filled with fire. A hand gripped her wrist as Bronn spun and pulled her into him.

He peered down at her, tilting her chin up with his free hand. He shifted her face this way and that, mumbling something to his companion who laughed.

Willow's face went slack. Bronn had moved so fast.

The Lord of the Underworld lifted his eyes, his gaze freezing Malachi to the bone.

Visions of a dark alley, blood-soaked sheets, and final words flashed through his mind. He was a child again, weak and helpless.

Bronn spun Willow around, her frame looking even smaller against the massive man.

"I suppose this one belongs to you?" Bronn asked.

Malachi swallowed, his lungs hitching.

"She doesn't belong to anyone," he replied, his voice hoarse.

Bronn tutted. "Oh, *master*. Everyone belongs to someone. I knew you were younger than your predecessor, but I didn't think you were more foolish."

The words pierced through Malachi like a blade twisting in his gut, cold realization snaking down Malachi's spine. Bronn had called him master. He'd been betrayed. Malachi clenched his fists, nails biting so hard they drew blood, but he held his ground, letting the fear turn into rage.

"What have you done with my second? If you're here, she must be around somewhere." Bronn glanced casually around the room.

She stumbled over a moment later. Her charcoaled braid flowed free around her waist, followed by a tall man with a scar over his left eye and a self-righteous sneer.

Despite what Malachi knew in his gut, he still wanted to smack that look off the guy's face.

They came to a halt, rounding out the circle. Slowly, the tavern brawls quieted, low moans and the hum of death taking their place. The giant brute beside Bronn frowned at Ceylon's appearance, like he was disappointed to see her there.

"Well, now that we're all here I do believe we have some things to discuss. Shall we go somewhere more private?" Bronn asked. His voice was calm and even, and Malachi couldn't read the tone. But he knew better than to trust that the Lord of the Underworld was in any way pleased.

This night couldn't have gone worse.

Twenty-Five

Ceylon

Damn Willow. The girl should have known better than to attack the Lord of the Underworld in the middle of a takedown. Apparently, her sense of self-preservation wasn't very strong. Ceylon sat in a chair by a window on the second floor of the Stormlock, looking out over the grimy street. Gideon stood beside her, his hand resting precariously on the handle of his knife.

Ceylon had tried to hide. The trouble was the large woman who fell and thrust Ceylon directly into Gideon's path. There was no hiding then. She'd intended to make herself scarce and avoid being implicated, since she couldn't be sure of Malachi's feelings. Confronting Bronn now, when she wasn't certain, put her entire future in jeopardy.

She would have to put on a decent performance.

Bronn sat on the chest at the end of a bed, leaning on his right knee and spinning a dagger in his hands. Brutus secured Willow, holding her in place as she held her side. There was nothing Ceylon could do for her now.

Malachi lounged on the bed, hands bound, feigning nonchalance. But there was a tightness in his mouth, concern in his eyes.

The final guest was the Iron Clan member that Malachi had been dining with. His hands were tied behind his broad back, his face bloodied and swelling so that he was barely recognizable. Looking at him, Ceylon was surprised the man was still breathing.

"Now that we're all acquainted, let's talk business. What shall we address first? The attempted murder or the attempted mutiny?" Bronn's gaze landed on Ceylon like a weight, but she met it nonetheless, keeping her silence.

"Fine. Mutiny it is." Bronn pressed a heavy boot into the Iron Clan's chest. A weak moan left the man's lips. "Your guild is done for, Tomek. If you tell me the names of the Iron Clan who ran and where they went, I'll let them live—so long as they don't resist."

The Iron Clan, Tomek, flicked his eyes open, his voice a mere breath. "You will not have them."

Ceylon clenched a fist. She said nothing as Bronn stood, then knelt over Tomek. His knife glimmered in the candlelight.

"They always choose pain, and yet they always yield to it." Bronn looked directly at Malachi as he sliced the binds free and pinned Tomek's hand to the floor with the knife. The Iron Clan screamed in agony. "The names, Tomek."

The Iron Clan managed to prop an eye open long enough to look at Malachi. Tears spilled onto the large man's cheek. "Kill me. Don't let him take them again."

The statement gained little reaction from Malachi, his mouth drawn into a thin line.

Ceylon bit her tongue to keep herself from speaking. If she was going to make it out of this, she couldn't garner any more wrath from the Lord of the Underworld. She made herself watch.

Bronn's knife slid out of Tomek's hand and plunged it into the other one. "Just a little information, and this can all be over."

The Iron Clan writhed on the floor as blood seeped from his hand. His eyes began to roll back in his head.

It felt like she was seeing her father for the first time. Behind her, Gideon shuffled. For a moment, she wondered if he might be more uncomfortable than she was. The pain went on, the Iron Clan's moans weakening until Bronn finally left the man to his peace. The Lord of the Underworld shook his head.

"Fool. It makes no difference. I'll find them soon enough." Blood dripped from his knife and his hands as he sat back on the chest. "Now, attempted murder?"

Ceylon tried not to shake as he looked at her, bloodlust in his eyes.

"You weren't supposed to be here," she said.

Bronn's lips quirked upwards in amusement. "Wasn't I? Interesting. So, what were you doing then?"

Ceylon's eyes flicked between Malachi and the Iron Clan as she ran through her options. She had been playing Malachi, and the only way to get them out of this was to tell the truth. He would hate her—a thought that made her chest twinge—but at least he'd be alive to do so.

"I told you I could bring you the Forsaken." She shrugged, relaxing in her chair.

Bronn gave her a curious look laced with anger. "We've spoken about this. I didn't ask you to bring me the Forsaken."

Ceylon didn't look at Malachi.

When she didn't respond, Bronn continued, "How was killing me supposed to help me?"

"Like I said, you weren't supposed to be here. I showed them a way to get to you *eventually*. That was supposed to be after I stole what I joined them for. That one had to go rogue and take things into her own hands." She nodded at Willow with a glare.

Willow stared back, death lingering in the depths.

"Stringing them along, were you?" Bronn twisted the bloodied knife in his hands.

The words shouldn't hurt. She was just doing her job—what Bronn had asked—and yet she felt like the world was tipping beneath her, her center of gravity lost in the maelstrom.

"I had to get him to trust me somehow." She avoided looking at Malachi, feeling the heat of his eyes on her neck.

"Then what do I do with this one?" he asked, pointing his dagger at Willow.

Ceylon shrugged again, even as her gut churned. She may not like Willow, but she understood what it was to prove yourself. Based on what Ceylon had seen the past few days, Willow didn't deserve Bronn's condemnation.

Still, she said, "She could be useful if she could be broken. She appears to have a talent as a soldier, but I think she has feelings for Malachi. You'd be hard-pressed to sway her."

Bronn raked his gaze over Willow in consideration. "She could be useful in other ways. I have plenty of clients who would pay handsomely to have someone like her in their household."

Willow snapped at him, but Brutus tightened his grip.

"I will never work for you!" she screamed. Willow looked to Ceylon. "I never liked you, but I believed in you. You will wear this betrayal to your grave."

Those words worked. Ceylon shouldn't feel anything but animosity toward the rivals of the Scourge, and yet here she was feeling sorry and risking her own standing to make sure they didn't end up dead.

She clenched her jaw. "How can you betray someone you were never intending to help?"

Willow's eyes widened, and she sagged.

Ceylon couldn't help it; her eyes flicked to Malachi. His stare was blank, void of emotion, and that hurt more; he had dismissed her completely.

"Well, it seems like we've reached an agreement. That one," Bronn pointed to Willow, "will spend a few days in the cells. What are we to do with the master?"

"We know where the Hollow is and their ranks. They won't be any trouble for us anymore. Let him do what he wants," she replied.

"Did you steal it?" Bronn asked. Ceylon's heart skipped a beat. She didn't know. And if she hadn't, none of it mattered anyway because she would never lead the Scourge in any capacity.

"I don't know," Ceylon said, looking back to Malachi. He scrunched his eyebrows in confusion.

"How do you not know if you stole from me?" he growled. "It seems like you stole everything."

"But does she have your heart?" Bronn asked.

The fire in Malachi's eyes burned her straight to the core. "Not anymore."

Faster than she could have anticipated, Bronn was in front of her. She felt the blow before she saw it. Her gut heaved as she fell to her knees, the shock echoing through her bones.

Bronn yanked her head back by the hair, holding her in place.

"The needles."

Ceylon began to shake. This was what she got for not following through. Bronn said Gideon would be named successor, but she should have known Bronn would kill her.

Brutus took out a small kit. Ceylon's breaths came faster, preparing for the pain. Bronn had taught her; she wouldn't cry out, she wouldn't beg, she wouldn't show weakness. Maybe he would let her go then—if she could prove her strength.

"Hold her," Bronn commanded as he traded Ceylon for the box.

Brutus came around behind her, holding out her arms and splaying her fingers. She had no hope of escaping that grip. As much as she told herself she wasn't afraid, she couldn't stop her eyes from flicking around the room. Like someone might step in to stop Bronn. Like her father wouldn't go through with it.

Her eyes caught on Malachi's, and her stomach plummeted. His stare was blank, vacant like she was nothing to him, and a loneliness took hold of her. Malachi had always been there. She'd thought it an annoyance, but now she realized how much she missed it.

How she would miss *him*.

And how she'd lost him.

The thin shine of the needle caught the light, and then Bronn grabbed Ceylon's hand and forced it under her fingernail.

Her breath came in spurts, stars danced in her eyes. But to her credit, she made no sound.

Bronn stared at her; then he looked at Malachi. "Interesting," he said.

Ceylon clamped her teeth together so hard she thought something would crack.

Her father took her second finger, inserted a second needle.

She felt the tears that stained her cheeks as a distant dream. All she knew was pain.

Bronn clicked his tongue, reaching for a third needle. Ceylon's heart dropped. Maybe she deserved this. She'd failed him, after all. And yet a part of her knew no one deserved to be tortured, not even a gutter rat like herself.

The room spun as the third needle went in. Ceylon had no control over the whimper that left her throat. For a moment, she thought she might be sick. But then the world tipped and darkened, and she imagined Malachi shouting for Bronn to stop.

∞

"Up, up, Second," Gideon sang as he slapped her face.

Ceylon gasped, jerking upright. She was lying on the floor in front of the chair. Her head swam; the room twisted and jerked in dizzying circles. There were no more needles. The distant pain she could manage.

Ceylon looked to Malachi, who stood staring back with a mixture of anger and fear. She found Bronn looming over her.

"What the hell was that for?" Ceylon yelled.

"Seems like you've done your job." Bronn nodded, standing, the box closed in his hands. "Not exactly clean, but done. I suppose I shouldn't have expected more from a stray like you."

A fury like she had never known coursed through her. A test, that's all it was to Bronn —a way to ensure Ceylon could do as told. She knew that. It didn't make his cruelty any easier to bear.

For what was love, really? She couldn't recognize it from the very person who was supposed to nurture and care for her unconditionally. How was she to know if she'd found it in the heart of a thief?

Ceylon looked to Malachi, confusion muddling her thoughts. It couldn't possibly be true. She knew she wasn't the only one playing a role when she was at the Hollow. Those small moments of tenderness were a front. A means to an end. Malachi was as much a fraud as she was. Wasn't he?

Yet his fear for her was real. The way his bound hands twitched, how he stepped toward her, attempting to position himself between her and Bronn.

But in the shine of his eyes, there was sadness, and she didn't know what that meant. She dragged her eyes from him, pushing down her shock.

"Here's how this is going to work," Bronn started. "I will take the girl back to Scourge Manor with me as payment for her treason. You, little master, are welcome to return to your infestation of a home. And I know I don't need to kill you because if you cause any trouble I'll start with your youngest and kill each one until the Forsaken have been purged from Yvelle."

Willow struggled in Brutus's arms. "I won't go with you! I would rather die than go with you," she growled.

Bronn stalked over to her, forcing her to look at him. "I would keep that pretty mouth shut if I were you. There are many things worse than death, and if you keep it up, you will experience all of them."

The chill that swept through the room wasn't in Ceylon's imagination, and she shivered against it.

"Please, Malachi," Willow pleaded. Her eyes teared as Brutus dragged her toward the door. "Kill me, Malachi! Do it!"

But he wouldn't. Ceylon knew he couldn't, and she listened to Willow cry as she was pulled from the room, her pierced fingers throbbing in time.

Bronn and Gideon remained.

"You," he looked to Ceylon. "I have another job, as promised. Do whatever you wish but be back at the manor by noon tomorrow."

Bronn turned to leave.

"Wait!" Ceylon said through gasps. "Am I the successor?"

Bronn met her gaze over his shoulder; the look in his eyes was one of anger, disappointment, regret. She shied away from the sight.

"I'm still deciding."

A pit opened inside Ceylon. She was a fool for not seeing what Bronn thought of her—she was a weapon, like Malachi said. Disposable. He had kept her out of the loop because he never intended to make her successor—the shipments of weapons, the correspondence with the citadel. All this time she hoped he would see her worth...wasted. She was never anything but a tool.

The Scourge left Ceylon behind with Malachi, his bindings cut, fuming by the bed. They were alone, apart from Tomek's body and the pool of blood.

Malachi leaped at her, pulling her to her feet by the collar of his shirt. She let him; she deserved it.

"You did this," he growled. He shook her, and she held his gaze. "You let them take her!"

"It was the only way," she said. Malachi loosened his grip. "If you want to win the game, don't show your hand."

Ceylon smacked his hands away, finding a little bit of heat left within her. Her body trembled with emotions she couldn't even name. Tomek's body lingered at the edge of her vision, but she couldn't bring herself to look.

She paced the room, her thoughts spinning out of control. She'd always believed those who defied Bronn deserved it—they deserved the wrath and pain he inflicted upon them. But Willow didn't. Malachi didn't. She tried to take one breath, then another. Both were shaky.

"I knew exactly what I wanted. I had a plan, Malachi. I spent *years* proving to my father I was the right choice for successor. I was supposed to take over the Scourge and become the next Lord of the Underworld.But you had to march in with your pretty boy face and screw it all up!"

Malachi stared at her, closing the gap. "You think you've had it rough? *I* had everything planned out too. You were supposed to be our saving grace, the thing that changed Yvelle for good. I welcomed you into my family so I could show you exactly what you've been missing. Bronn doesn't care about you, yet you let him lead you along."

The words carved deep within her because she knew he was right.

"Don't you dare accuse me of being weak," Ceylon snarled, stepping forward.

"Weak is the last thing I could ever call you," Malachi replied, voice a deadly low.

They glared at each other, nose to nose. Her chest heaved, fists clenched, fingers aching. And she debated just how much force it would take to smack that look off his face.

But then Malachi's lips were against her own. His arms circled her waist, pulling them chest to chest. Ceylon blinked, fists opening.

Malachi was kissing her, and she was letting him. Her heart thundered against her ribs as she grabbed at his shirt.

Then, it was over. His face panting inches from hers, yet it felt like miles.

Ceylon stared at him. "What was that for?" she breathed. Her stomach fluttered. She didn't pull away.

"I've been waiting to do that for years. When I thought Bronn was going to kill you, my first regret was never kissing you," he said.

Malachi stepped back, looking out the window. Ceylon lifted a cautious hand to her lips. He turned back, and her hand shot to her side.

"What now?" he asked.

"It's not like we're in a relationship," Ceylon mumbled, feeling a short tug in her chest.

"I meant about the fact Bronn has Willow, and the Forsaken can't make a move now that Bronn knows where we are—who we are."

"Oh." Ceylon blushed, irritated Malachi was able to kiss girls heedlessly and then get straight to business. She was better than some lovestruck ninny.

"We need to get Willow back," Ceylon whispered.

Malachi nodded but said nothing, waiting for her to continue.

"It's my fault. I put the Forsaken in the middle of all of this because I thought...I just wanted..." Ceylon's throat tightened. She coughed, straightening. "I should have seen it sooner."

Malachi rested a hand on her cheek. "He raised you that way. It's not your fault for holding out hope."

They stood like that for minutes, hours, she wasn't sure.

Malachi gave her the space to collect herself before he said, "Now that you know, what are you going to do to make it right? That's what matters."

Her eyes flicked to his. "Bronn never intended to make me successor, but he made a mistake in making me an adversary. We get Willow back because it will piss him off, and because I don't want her death on my conscience. Then we figure out his next move."

Malachi gave a grim smile. "For real this time. No lies, no backstabbing. We do what we have to in order to take Bronn down."

There was a bitter taste in her mouth. She was going against a lifetime of ingrained rules.

But Bronn no longer deserved her loyalty.

Malachi did.

She held out a hand. "No more backstabbing."

Malachi took her hand, giving it a firm shake. This deal felt different. She wasn't sure why. But she did know, in the end, either Bronn would be dead or the rest of them would be.

"Bad time?" Dom asked, stepping into the room. His gaze flicked between them, and Ceylon felt her cheeks flush.

"Where were you?" she asked, marching up to him.

"I hid behind the bar as soon as I saw Bronn. I knew Willow would try something, and I couldn't help you if we were all caught." Dom's brow furrowed as he noted the lack of one of their members. "They took Willow, didn't they?"

Malachi nodded solemnly. "We'll fill you in on the way back."

As they fled into the night, leaving the destruction of the Stormlock behind, Ceylon couldn't help but worry about what Bronn had up his sleeves.

Twenty-Six

Malachi

His stomach was in knots. He wanted to march up to Bronn and show him what the Forsaken were made of, but he knew he wouldn't get close. Causing a scene now would only risk Willow's life further. He looked out over the pews in the sanctuary at the sleepy gathering crowd. Ceylon waited to the side, in the shadows. His eyes lingered longer than they needed to, recalling her closeness, her warmth, the feel of her lips against his.

She blinked at him and looked away, as if nothing had happened.

He took it as a reprimand—he needed to be focused, too.

"I apologize for calling you here at this hour," he said.

All eyes weighed on him like iron. He debated not telling them, and figuring out a solution before anyone else knew. But he wasn't positive they could get Willow back, and this development was too dangerous to be kept a secret.

Malachi took a breath. "The Lord of the Underworld is aware of our location," he paused. "He took Willow."

Murmurs and gasps surged through the crowd. Eyes turned to Ceylon, fingers pointing.

"This is all her fault!" Corrine yelled.

"She deserves to die," Venus agreed.

A couple people drew knives in solidarity. Ceylon tensed. She still wore his clothes, but he knew for a fact there were weapons on her. He couldn't afford a brawl right now.

"It's my fault, too. I let her in. I let you down. For that, I'm sorry." Malachi sighed, feeling more tired than he had in a long time. "Accusations won't do us any good. Besides, we need her to get Willow back. Ceylon is the only one who can get us into Scourge Manor."

The crowd quieted begrudgingly.

"I didn't call you here to argue, I came to inform you. We won't let Bronn get away with this, and he will suffer for what he's done," Malachi stated, and a grim cheer rose. A pit grew in his stomach. In the corner, Ceylon tapped a finger against her arm. It was the only way he could tell she was uncomfortable.

"Until further notice, I'm putting a leave ban on the abbey. No one can leave without my say-so, and we are going to reinforce our defenses. Dom has made a schedule, which is located in the dining hall. Report to your stations at the appropriate time."

The Forsaken mumbled their ascent, accepting the dismissal, and dispersed. Malachi pointed to Ceylon and Dom, motioning for them to approach him. Anya had found her way back to Ceylon's side and was clinging to her like a lifeline. She was fighting back tears as Ceylon pushed her toward the door; with a pout, the girl slipped into the hall.

"We need to know everything about the manor. The ins and outs, supply drops, servants…" he trailed off at the look on her face.

"We don't have nearly enough time to go over everything; we only need a silver bullet," she leaned in.

The group waited.

"On a regular day, there would be no chance of making it past Scourge Manor's defenses. They know you're mad, they will anticipate retaliation. That means freeing Willow is going to be even more difficult," Ceylon explained.

Malachi raised an eyebrow.

"So, it's impossible?" Dom asked, voicing everyone's frustration. He gave Malachi a look that said they should just toss her out the door now.

"I didn't say that. Nothing's impossible if you have the right influence, and you have me. I've snuck into Scourge Manor plenty of times—it's all about patience.

"My room is in the attic. It'll be the easiest way in. If Bronn is expecting me tomorrow at noon, they won't be guarding my room because I'll be walking through the front door." She tried to ignore the way the next words caught in her throat. "Granted, Bronn doesn't trust anyone, even me; he'll anticipate me helping you, which means my room is out of the question."

"Is there a point to all this?" Malachi growled, feeling his impatience rising.

Ceylon's jaw set. "The *point* is to show you Bronn will always be one step ahead of you, no matter how well we plan."

Dom sputtered. "So we're back to impossible?"

"No. Anything *we* try to plan will be anticipated. Based on everything he's been keeping from me and my recent treatment at the Stormlock, he's probably changed the security measures since I was there." Her voice wavered. "He doesn't trust me anymore. But if one of *his* men, someone he would never suspect of betraying him, brings her out while I'm in a meeting with him, that's something he would never see coming."

Malachi sighed. This job was getting more difficult by the minute.

"Anya is the key," Ceylon said. "We get Anya to mind-warp a Scourge. They'll take Malachi in as a prisoner. You'll have direct access to the dungeon, and you can walk in and out the front door."

Dom straightened and stared at her blankly. "No. Anya stays out of it, and I'm not sending Malachi in *alone*."

She stared right back. "If you don't want to use Anya, then we will never get Willow back, and you'll all be captured as well."

Malachi pinched his eyes closed.

Dom glanced between them. "You can't be serious about this, Mal. They'll kill Anya."

"She doesn't even have to step foot inside the Manor. She'll be fine," Ceylon shot back.

The two bickered about logistics, the sound a drone in Malachi's mind. If Anya failed, they revealed an innate mage to the Scourge. On the other hand, this would take place far from Scourge eyes, and Malachi was capable of taking on one man. He would much rather be the one taking the biggest risk. If he didn't make it out, well, at least everyone else was safe.

Ceylon glared at Dom as she said, "Anya is coming, whether you like it or not. Or..." the words caught in her throat, "or I'll get Willow out myself."

Malachi's eyes popped open. He studied her. She was fiddling with a coin in her hands, making it disappear and reappear. There was something in the glint of her eyes that made him question her, but not about Anya's safety. He knew the risks of trusting her going into Scourge Manor—she had already planned to double-cross him once—but things were different now. Ceylon had shown as much at the Stormlock, and he knew her well enough to know her feelings for him were genuine.

"I won't let you get her out alone," Malachi said.

Ceylon shrugged. "Then I guess Anya's coming. Aren't we glad we came to that arrangement?" She gave Dom a meaningful look. "If we're going to do this, there's something I need, but I'll go get it myself. I won't risk anyone else."

He didn't like it, leaving her unguarded, but she was right. Any Forsaken that went out might not come back. That's how it had always been, but their secret home had garnered a level of safety that was now gone. Besides, if he was going to leave to get Willow, he should help reinforce the abbey beforehand.

"Wait until first light. If you're not back in two hours, I'm sending someone after you."

She waved a dismissive hand, but her lips were pressed too tight. "Please, what could possibly happen to the Daughter of the Underworld?"

And so, Ceylon took her leave, her bravado the only power keeping his hopes for Willow alive.

TWENTY-SEVEN

Ceylon

Ceylon crept down the alleys of the Underworld as the sun stole over rooftops. There was a knot in her stomach; she had gone against Bronn's wishes before, but they had always been on the same side. She always knew where she stood.

It was different with Malachi. It was as if he'd spun her in a circle and then told her to walk in a straight line. Her feet were planted now, but not on the side of the guild war she was familiar with.

Willow was a pain, but she didn't deserve to be torn apart like so many others Bronn had taken. None of the Forsaken did. They weren't some faceless enemies, and she could no longer believe Bronn when he listed his charges against them.

Voices sounded, and Ceylon ducked into the shadows, back pressed against a wall.

Two women scurried past, heads low, necklines lower. They clutched handfuls of rubits close to them. It was dangerous to be out with that much coin, but not many other options existed in a profession such as theirs.

In the darkness, she brushed a hand against her lips, remembering the feeling of Malachi against her. Her heart sped, but she banished the thoughts. She was a fool, doing this for him.

Ceylon continued on, gut roiling. A week ago, she would have just led Malachi to her father and given him up. She wouldn't have worried about Willow, or Anya, or anyone but herself.

Now she was risking her own life for theirs.

Her thoughts swirled as she neared her destination. Ceylon slipped into the dead-end alley, stone greeting her. She checked her back once more and then heaved herself up the wall. Once on top, she walked over to the drainpipe, and just like at Lord Granvilles' estate, she made her way up to the roof.

The tiles over this particular home were made of clay. A rare sight in the Underworld, but not one large enough to gather interest—except from her. She crawled to the crest, throwing one leg over to straddle the roof line. With careful hands, Ceylon lifted the tile two-thirds down, and there was the white and gold pistol from her father's ship. She picked it up—the weight heavy in her hands—and inspected it. There was no damage, no change, and yet it felt deadlier.

Guns weren't her first weapon of choice, but if she was going up against Bronn, she needed something unexpected.

Ceylon tucked the pistol into her waistband and replaced the tile. She shimmied down the drainpipe, only for her foot to slip when it reached the wall. Gravity betrayed her as she fell.

Her arms flailed, reaching for anything to slow her. Grit from the wall tore through her palms. The ground surged up to meet her. At the last moment, she managed to roll, but the impact still took her breath away, and her ankle shrieked.

Ceylon lay there, back to the earth, face to the red sky. Pain.

Her eyes welled with tears, and in the quiet of the morning, she didn't stop them.

Everything she knew had crashed down around her. Bronn would never name her successor. Perhaps she didn't deserve to be—helping the Forsaken went against everything he had taught her, and even though she was furious with Bronn herself, those years didn't magically disappear. Ceylon had worked her whole life to lead the Scourge, had fought to make her father proud. It was the one thing she always knew she wanted. But now...well, the thought of leading the Scourge at the cost of the lives of the Forsaken left a bad taste in her mouth and a rock in her stomach.

And that was just. It was right. It had to be, if only because she felt it and believed in it. She had to disentangle the truths Bronn had forced into her mind and learn who she was on her own. As Ceylon, not as Daughter of the Underworld. Maybe that meant letting her father go.

She didn't want his Scourge anyway—she wanted her own. She wanted to remake it, like Malachi had suggested.

The pistol was cold against her stomach. An unwelcome reminder. She needed to be at Scourge Manor by noon, and this time, she wasn't sure she'd be walking back out.

Ceylon just had to keep Bronn distracted long enough for Malachi, Dom, and Anya to get Willow out. That was all. And should worst come to worst...she placed a hand on the pistol.

She wasn't certain she'd be able to take the shot if she had to, but she wouldn't let him hurt anyone else again.

Ceylon pushed herself off the ground. Pain shot through her ankle, but she gritted her teeth and stood anyway. She had one chance to make this right.

This time, she wouldn't waste it.

⌇

Ceylon limped back into the abbey. She grimaced as Anya threw her arms around her midsection. Still, she managed to force down the pain enough to hide it.

"All right, I'm not dead. You can let me go." It was another moment before Anya released her. Dom lingered in the doorway. Was that concern lining his features?

"We thought someone had gotten you," Anya sniffled.

"Please, you think anyone could catch me? I own this town." Ceylon winked at the girl.

"Malachi told me about tonight," Anya said, eyes glowing with anticipation.

"Then you know you need to get ready," Ceylon replied and motioned for her to run along. Anya frowned but did so anyway. Dom trailed after her, giving Ceylon a meaningful look over his shoulder.

Malachi stepped out from the shadows.

"Uneventful morning?" Malachi asked. He was a picture of nonchalance, but something in his voice made Ceylon think there was more he wished to say.

His eyes dragged over her, taking in her torn pants, the limp, the raw hands. Her heart stuttered.

"Spying on me?" Ceylon crossed her arms.

"No need when you make it so obvious that you're in trouble."

Ceylon sighed. "I can handle myself."

Malachi scowled. "I shouldn't have let you go alone. I know how reckless you are."

"There is nothing wrong with my decisions." Ceylon lifted her chin.

"You're not invincible, Ceylon," Malachi said, and he tensed. Ceylon clamped her mouth shut. "You're not invincible, and neither is my guild."

"Oh, master," she took a step toward him, "are you worried I might not come back?"

He pinned her with serious eyes and a straight mouth. "That's exactly what I'm worried about."

Ceylon glanced at the ground, feeling suddenly ashamed. Malachi was right. She'd been distracted, and it had cost her. She usually wasn't one to let emotions cloud her judgment.

"I knew what I was doing. I wouldn't have jeopardized things like that—"

Malachi pulled her close, her head resting against his chest. She stood, arms at her sides, and then curled them around him. They stood like that for a while. It was easy—like it had been years ago. She disappeared in his arms, and, for a minute, she wasn't the Daughter of the Underworld. She was just Ceylon.

Malachi stepped back, cupping her face in his hands. "I don't want to lose you, Ceylon."

She couldn't assure him that she'd make it out alive, and she knew the danger of empty promises. So she just placed one raw hand over his.

"I won't let him near the Forsaken any longer."

Hurt flickered over Malachi's face. "Don't do anything reckless; we're in this together now."

Ceylon thought she might be sick. She still wasn't used to having friends. Now that she did, she knew she was willing to sacrifice herself to save them, to save that little bit of light in the world. But she forced a smile to her lips and said, "You won't be rid of me that easily."

The hope in his eyes was a knife to the heart. Then he leaned in, and she felt the slightest brush of his lips against hers.

"I'm holding you to that," he whispered.

Twenty-Eight

Malachi

Malachi rubbed at his eyes as he oversaw the preparations. They had one chance to get Willow out, and the plan hinged on Anya's mage craft. He hadn't slept. It wasn't all that uncommon, but today was too important not to get some kind of rest. Dom and Anya stood in front of him, double-checking their supplies.

"All right. That should be it," Dom stated as he tightened his belt. Malachi nodded, pushing any thoughts of failure to a deep, quiet place within himself.

The three Forsaken left the abbey, attempting to look relaxed and confident. Ceylon had told them there would be a spy from the Scourge watching the Hollow. They could only hope the one who followed them was who they were looking for.

Sure enough, as they twisted down small dark alleys, Malachi felt the presence of a guest behind them. They kept out of sight. Every time he chanced a glance around, there was no one he could see, but he had been followed too many times to think he was just being paranoid.

"Next turn," Malachi mumbled with a smile on his face as if he were sharing a conspiratorial joke with his friends rather than giving orders.

Dom and Anya snickered in response. They had traveled half the distance from the abbey to Scourge Manor using a convoluted route.

As they rounded the next corner, Dom and Malachi slipped into the darkness, leaving Anya in the middle of a deserted street. She stood with her hands behind her back, long blonde hair flowing in the light breeze. She put on the best innocent eyes Malachi had ever seen, wide and full of wonder.

A moment later, a Scourge rounded the corner. He was moving so fast, he almost knocked the girl over. The confusion showed on his face as he towered over her, looking through her.

"Out of my way, runt," he said.

The boy was the same one who had trailed Ceylon at the Storm-lock—Gideon, Ceylon had called him. He held himself proudly and stepped on light feet despite his size. Malachi noted the scar that ran from just above his left eyebrow to his cheekbone. Remembering how he'd treated Ceylon multiple times before, Malachi stayed behind Anya to keep from throttling him.

"What's your name?" Anya asked, stepping into his path every time he tried to get by.

His frustration grew with every motion becoming more brisk and rigid, and Malachi couldn't help but feel satisfaction. The Scourge may be the strongest guild in the Underworld, but they lacked finesse.

After the fourth attempt to pass Anya, he growled, gripped her shoulders, and lifted her aside. Only she gripped back, clinging to his hand. The Scourge member stared down at her soft fingers clutching his, and then his eyes widened as he realized who she was. Gideon tried to pull away, but Anya spoke first.

"Stay still and don't speak unless you are asked a question. You must reply truthfully and honestly," she commanded.

His face twitched, and his hand relaxed as he glared onward. Anya released him, hands at the ready, but he didn't move.

Dom and Malachi stepped forward, each taking up a post beside Anya.

"What's your name?" he asked.

"Gideon Darkthorne," the Scourge snarled, his eyes pits of rage.

Malachi leaned forward. "Is the girl you took from the Stormlock still being held at Scourge Manor?"

"Yes."

"Do you have access to her?"

Gideon hesitated, straining against Anya's magic. His face contorted, turning red. "Yes," he choked.

"Can you help us get her out without detection?" Malachi asked. His heart stilled as he waited for an answer.

"Yes."

Malachi nodded, the tension in his shoulders releasing. "Anya," she took hold of Gideon's hand again, "I need you to repeat exactly this: Gideon Darkthorne, you will enter Scourge Manor immediately to retrieve the prisoner known as Willow from the cells and bring her to the Manor Garden." Anya relayed the demands as Malachi set them. "You will take me with you—pretending to be your prisoner—to access the cells. You will make no motions, signals, or any other indications that you have been influenced by magic to do this against your will. You will be swift and purposeful, and you will not be caught. If you reach resistance, you will make a convincing excuse for why the girl must be moved. Once you have left the manor and brought the girl to Dom, we will disappear. You will have no memory of any of these encounters or who you saw. You will not follow us."

Anya spoke firmly and clearly as if she were commanding a soldier and not puppeteering a member of the deadliest guild. Gideon's eyes grew harder as he took in the words, but he didn't fight them. Dom tied some rope around Malachi's wrists with a special knot that Malachi could release himself. Dom gave it a light tug to check his work and nodded.

As soon as Anya finished relaying the message, Gideon grabbed Malachi by the rope and marched toward Scourge Manor. The Forsaken exchanged a glance and followed them from a distance. He could only hope this was about to be the easiest heist of his career.

Blood pounded in Malachi's ears as Scourge Manor came into view. At his nod, his crew backed off, blending into the scenery.

The street in front of the manor was empty. Dirt blew across the path as if to clear the way ahead of them. Gideon tugged on the ropes and dragged the master forward.

Malachi took a deep, steadying breath as they made their way through the massive double doors. They swung open with a loud creak—if anyone tried to sneak in through the front doors, they would have a hard time.

The manor was terrifying yet awash with splendor. Hand-carved dark wooden stairs and floors greeted him, and gold ceilings painted the entry in a deceptively warm glow. Doors stood sentry to the left and right, leading to a dining room and a sitting room. Everything was large and imposing, and Malachi couldn't help but feel small.

"Move," Gideon growled, breaking Malachi from his trance. They passed four guards with blank stares—two by the entry and two at the base of the grand stairs.

Passages led off the foyer. Gideon shoved him toward the one on the right, and down a long hallway. At the end, there was a window, just peeking out over the garden, but Gideon forced him to stop a few feet before. He kept one hand on Malachi while shoving aside a bookcase. It slid on oiled hinges, revealing an ominous staircase. Although he knew this was where he had to go, everything in Malachi yearned to make a run for it as they started downward.

The stairs grew darker and damper the deeper they climbed. A few moans and howls echoed up the stone walls. Water dripped. The only light came from the sconces, few and far between. Gideon grabbed one as they landed on the basement floor, creating a small ring of light.

A guard leaned against the damp wall, eyes drifting closed. He pushed himself upward as he heard them approach.

"Gideon. I wasn't expecting anyone today," the guard said. He took in Malachi from head to toe, giving him a questioning look.

"Caught this one trying to sift from our cut. A couple days in the cells will teach him better." Gideon shoved Malachi forward so hard he almost fell on his face. Malachi glared back at the Scourge.

The guard gave a deep, belly laugh. "You're in for a rough night, kid."

Malachi kept his expression sour, his posture small. The guard fumbled with the keys at his belt and led them down the row of bars. Gideon shoved him again.

Malachi looked in every cell they passed for a glimpse of Willow, but all he saw were broken bodies huddled in corners. They shied away from the light, making themselves even smaller, if that were possible. A rage he had never known coiled within his gut, but also fear. Where was Willow?

Close to the end of the row, he saw black hair leaking onto the floor, and his heart plummeted into his stomach. It pooled around her slight frame. She lay with her knees to her chest in the middle of the cell, hands gripping her arms, which were nicked with thin red lines that dripped blood. She hissed at the light as Gideon came forward.

Her expression dropped when she realized the guard wasn't alone.

"Let him go," she whispered, her voice dry and hoarse.

Gideon nodded toward the door. There was a pause as the guard looked between her and Gideon curiously. Malachi huffed before launching himself from the floor and throwing his tied hands around the guard's neck, tightening his arms. The other prisoners were in such awful states they didn't even rouse at the attack.

The guard struggled, twisting this way and that. He shoved his whole weight against the wall, crushing Malachi between the two. The air squeezed from his lungs, but he kept his hold.

The guard slowed, labored, and sank to the ground.

Malachi sat on the floor with his arm around the guard's throat for another second, two, then released him. When he was sure the guard wouldn't wake, Gideon grabbed the keys from where they had been dropped and unlocked Willow's door.

"It's okay, Willow. We're getting you out," Malachi said, kneeling at the bars.

Willow tracked Gideon's movements. She kept a wary eye on him as she spoke. "How can you trust him?"

Malachi grinned. "Let's just say he's had the proper *influence*."

She looked at him then, mischief in her eyes.

Together, they rose to their feet. Malachi noted her shoes had been taken. The bars creaked open; Malachi was sure the whole manor must have heard, but no one came. Gideon stepped aside, letting Willow out of the cell. She walked on shaky feet. It had only been a day, but it looked like she had been here for a week.

Malachi pulled her to him and found her freezing to the touch and trembling. He wanted to give her his jacket, but it would look suspicious if they were caught. Gideon closed the cell and locked it, saying nothing. He dropped the keys beside the unconscious guard and placed a hand on both their shoulders, guiding them back toward the stairs.

The light felt too bright as they emerged from the cave-like basement. He blinked against the sunshine coming in through the window, holding up his hands to block the rays. Beside him, Willow didn't flinch. She took in the building with an appraising eye, as if she planned to return later and wanted to remember everything about it.

Malachi clenched his jaw. She wasn't even free and already she was planning another attempt on Bronn's life. Gideon turned them in the opposite direction they had entered, leading them to the south end of the manor.

A hulk of a man rounded the corner from the parlor and paused at the end of the hall. Malachi recognized him as the other henchman from the Stormlock.

"Gideon?" The Scourge inquired, stepping closer.

Gideon continued on their path, his posture calm and relaxed. "Brutus."

The henchman blocked their exit, forcing them to a halt. Beyond the man, Malachi could see a side door just out of reach. He tried not to draw attention to himself.

"Are you going somewhere with…" Brutus eyed the prisoners then, his expression turning even more incredulous. "Why is she out of the cells? And what is he doing here?"

"Bronn's orders. He said she needed one last glimpse of fresh air before she was forced underground forever or something like that. This one," he shook Malachi, "I just caught trying to sneak in, probably to break her out. Figured I'd take him to the cells on my return."

Malachi tried to shrug him off. Brutus didn't look convinced.

"It looks like you've got your hands full there. I can take the boy to the cells," Brutus said. He reached for Malachi, but Gideon pulled him back.

"Thanks for the offer, but I have some lessons of my own I'd like to teach this one. If you know what I mean?" Gideon whispered conspiratorially.

Brutus flicked between them, skepticism lingering, but he nodded. "As long as you know what you're doing. You know what Bronn will do if they get the better of you."

"They're not going anywhere," Gideon said.

Brutus stepped aside, but his mass filled the hall, forcing them to walk single file. Malachi squeezed his hands together like he might hold their plan in place. Eyes pressed into his back as they left through the side door.

It opened into a garden. Green and lush, the contrast between the soft flora and harsh manor was obvious. He took in purple elesarry and orange drop. Many of these were rare and poisonous, disguised as beautiful house plants. He kept his hands to himself.

A flash of light greeted them from across the street. Malachi turned to Gideon and nodded to the alley.

Gideon flicked his gaze to it and smirked. "Run, and my job is done."

Willow and Malachi stared at him. They exchanged a glance.

"Go," Malachi whispered.

Willow didn't move. Her eyes narrowed as she examined Malachi.

"Not without you." Willow moved for Malachi's hand, but he pulled away.

"Get a move on." Gideon shoved Willow forward.

She stumbled but righted herself. Malachi could see the conflict in her, but he wouldn't be going with her. That had never been his plan.

"Go," he urged.

With a heartbroken look, Willow turned and broke into a sprint. She leaped over bushes and around the fountain, taking the most direct path to freedom. Beside Malachi, Gideon squinted and shook his head, his eyes clearing as if a fog had been lifted from his mind. He hollered at Willow to stop. His hand reached to his side where a pistol sat, ready.

Malachi ripped the binds from his hands and grabbed for the pistol. Gideon managed to aim and fire once before Malachi forced his hand down.

The two grappled for purchase. Malachi twisted, trapping Gideon's arm.

The Scourge grunted. He threw a punch that hit Malachi square in the jaw.

Malachi stumbled back.

Gideon aimed and shot once more.

Willow cried out but didn't slow. Thirty feet between her and freedom.

Malachi tackled Gideon to the ground. A third shot rang out, but he had no idea where it went. He managed to pin Gideon beneath his weight, slamming the Scourge's hand against the ground until he released the pistol. Malachi was on offense now. He threw blow after blow, finally grabbing Gideon's skull and smacking it back against the ground.

Gideon's head lolled. Unconscious, but not dead.

Malachi sighed as he slipped off.

Shouting and footsteps sounded in the house. There would be guards on him soon. He needed to get back into the manor if he had any hope of completing his mission.

Dom and Anya stood in the shadows across the street. Their faces were frantic, arms swinging for Malachi to join them. Dom had an arm under Willow's, helping her stand. Malachi noted the blood dripping down her calf.

"Come on!" Dom pleaded.

Malachi just shook his head. "Get her home."

Willow huffed but convinced the others to move. Tears sparkled in Anya's eyes as she resisted. She cried for him.

Dom's glare was stone cold. This was better though. This way, Malachi was only risking one person.

And he would kill Bronn.

The three Forsaken hobbled away. The shouts drew nearer, and Malachi pushed himself off the ground, keeping low as he made his way to the side door. He waited, back to the wall, until three Scourge ran out. They found Gideon and went to him. With the distraction, Malachi slipped back inside.

Ceylon had explained the layout just in case things didn't go as planned. So instead of heading back to the lobby, he headed for the servants' stairwell at the back of the manor. More shoes pounded on the floor. Malachi ducked behind a shelf as two Scourge ran past. When the coast was clear, he continued.

The servants' stairs were through the kitchens. A few workers glanced at the door as he walked in, but he kept his head high, walking as if he was supposed to be there, and no one gave him a second look. At the back of the room, a small door opened to the stairwell. He took the stairs two at a time, heading for the second floor and Bronn's office. Malachi paused on the second level, listening for any signs of movement before cracking the door open.

The hall in front of him mirrored the floor below. Malachi didn't linger any longer than necessary as he stepped out. His hands twitched as he wished for any kind of weapon. He moved slowly, walking on his toes, ready for anything. As he neared the bend, he could feel the sweat drip down his back.

One chance. That's all he would have.

Malachi stepped around the corner.

More Scourge poured down the main stairs, but no one looked down the hall at him. Malachi crept on as fast as he dared. Ceylon had told him Bronn's office was in the middle of the manor across from the main stairs on the second story. He was so close.

Malachi slowed his breath as the closed doors came into view. He reached for the handle.

A shot cracked in the room.

Malachi jumped. His heart skipped.

Ceylon.

His hand encircled the knob.

Something hit him in the head, and he stumbled into the wood of the door. A giant hand around his arm stopped him from sinking to the floor. His skull ached, sending the hall into throbbing waves.

"Going somewhere?" Gideon asked as he grinned down.

"You shouldn't be here," Malachi stated. He thought Gideon would be out for longer.

"I think that's my line," Gideon sneered.

Brutus hauled Malachi to standing, and his face cinched with annoyance—or maybe confusion.

Malachi struggled against Brutus' hold, but his plan was drifting farther and farther from his mind. All he could think about now was how he might save Ceylon. How he might still get one shot.

But Gideon threw the doors open, and Malachi knew the odds. They were done for.

TWENTY-NINE

Ceylon

Earlier that day...

Ceylon rubbed a hand over her arm. The absence of Malachi's touch left her feeling cold as she stood in the deserted abbey hall.

She'd lost so much. Everything she thought she wanted. And yet there was so much to replace it—this chance at a home, a family, at real love. She could see that now. What she'd thought was Bronn showing his approval was nothing. He treated her like a stranger, and she created a fantasy about their family because she wanted to believe it, because she couldn't accept that cruelty was in his nature.

Ceylon would never be anything to him but another member of his guild.

The more she thought about it, the angrier she felt. Bronn had forced her to prove herself over and over. His little torture stunt at the Stormlock showed his true colors. Brutus looked at her like an older brother would, but his loyalties lay with Bronn. And Gideon was a prick.

The Forsaken may not be blood, but she didn't really know a better way to be a family.

Ceylon stalked down the halls of the abbey to her dorm. It was nearing late morning, and she was surprised there were no guild members in the vicinity. All the better. She didn't really want to think about them right now.

Anya was waiting for her in their room, splayed out on the ground. Ceylon stared at the girl for a long moment before Anya realized she was there.

The girl sat up with a lopsided grin. She was trying not to be afraid, but her care for Willow was evident, and she wouldn't be happy until she was back at the abbey.

Ceylon couldn't blame her. "Are you ready?"

Anya nodded. "Malachi told me the plan."

"Good, then you know everything that could go wrong, too."

She frowned, her child-like face turning to a pout. "I'm not going to mess up. Willow's life depends on this."

"Not just Willow's. Yours, Malachi's, everyone here is at risk," Ceylon stated. Anya gave her a pointed look. "It wasn't my intention to expose the Hollow."

But it was her fault, and she couldn't live with herself if she lost Anya, that one pure piece of innocence. Her plan would work because it had to.

There was one thing Dom had been right about from the start. Malachi never should have let her out of that cell. What a mess she had made.

Ceylon took a moment to change into her stealth suit. It would be noticeable in the day, so she threw a cloak back over it.

Subtly, she tucked the pistol she'd retrieved into a holster in the suit, hidden by the folds of the cloak. She didn't like the feel of it, the weight and the power that came with it.

Malachi and Dom were sporting similar changes in wardrobe, only theirs looked less stealthy and more common. Anya wore tight-fitted pants; Dom looked like he always did, only now he carried a satchel at his hip.

"Good luck," Ceylon said. She never wished anyone luck before a job, but something told her they might need it today.

Malachi looked like he might say something. But then he nodded and turned with the other Forsaken, disappearing down the hall. She watched them go, secretly hoping they would all return. If things went wrong, she would probably never see them again. Bronn would never let her live for working against him this way.

Ceylon only went into a job if she knew it would work. If today didn't go to plan, she didn't know what she would do. She wasn't sure if she would even have anywhere left to go...

She took the most direct route to the manor, hopping over rooftops instead of back alleys, every step taking her further from her old life.

It was odd, seeing it again. It was just over a day since she had been there, but it felt like an eternity. Staring at the old bricks and shiny windows, it no longer felt like coming home. For the first time, she was seeing the manor as everyone else must—ancient, intimidating, cold.

Ceylon let the thoughts tumble from her mind. She scanned the gardens, what she could see inside the sitting room, and the streets below. Three men outside, as expected. Ceylon knew a fourth lurked around the back of the building. Inside, Brutus would be wandering. He made it his duty to oversee all the guards and checked on their posts regularly. Her father was likely in his study.

There was no sign of Gideon. It was nearing midday. The more time they wasted, the more people would occupy the manor.

With a final deep breath, she hopped down from the roof. Her landing was graceful, a cat from a windowsill.

The commanding oak doors creaked on their hinges as she forced them open. She paused in the foyer, taking in the grand staircase and tall ceilings. Everything about it was dark. She had become so desensitized to her own home that she'd failed to notice how grim it was, as though wandering into the castle of some cruel mage.

Ceylon shuddered as she made her way upstairs; something was wrong. There were no guards on this floor; Bronn would never allow such lax security. She kept her hands ready.

The doors to her father's office were open, another abnormality. Ceylon tried to comfort herself in the knowledge that this was her father. She was prepared for the unpredictable.

Ceylon stepped in front of the doors to find Bronn sat in his chair, eyes locked on the world beyond the window. The street below was empty. Ceylon's uneasiness intensified.

"You're early." Bronn didn't turn to face her. He had always had a knack for knowing when she was near.

"I know how punctuality matters to you. Didn't want to be late," she said.

Her eyes scanned the study for a trap. She couldn't see any, and she set her jaw at the realization.

"There's nothing to be afraid of. I was expecting you to be later, but I did train you well." Bronn spun a knife in his hand, the blade caressing his fingers. It was black from tip to hilt with edges that could slice a feather mid-fall—a wicked thing. Ceylon had never seen anything like it. They didn't make black blades in Yvelle. In fact, it reminded her of

Sobravar. There was every chance it was enchanted, infused with a dark magic.

"Where are the guards?" Ceylon crossed the room boldly, sprawling into the guest chair as if she didn't have a care in the world.

Her hands tingled, palms slick. She had never gone up against Bronn before. It was thrilling and entirely terrifying.

"They're busy." He tossed a glance over his shoulder. "You see, I'm expecting guests. Some of your new friends, perhaps?"

Three shots cracked outside. Shouts echoed off the old walls of the Underworld. Ceylon tried not to react, fighting not to rush to the window.

Her hands began to tremble. Her father was being incredibly calm which generally meant he was furious. She tried to focus on the room, running the plays in her mind, but she was doing exactly the opposite of anything she would normally do.

"Nothing to say to your lord?" His eyes returned to the window.

"They're not my friends. Whatever they do is on their own terms."

Amusement crept across Bronn's face. "My dear, Ceylon. I do believe you're lying."

Ice coated her veins. Very few times had Bronn used that tone with her, but it never meant anything good. Its cadence would fall, often resigning its victims to a day without sun. Only this time, something was different. He was smiling.

Bronn stood. Sometimes she forgot how truly enormous her father was. This was not one of those times.

He reached into his coat. Ceylon held her breath.

The locket, her mother's locket, dropped onto his desk.

She stared at it, wanting nothing more than to snatch it up and keep it forever. It was the only piece of her mother she had left. But she couldn't let Bronn know that.

Ceylon glanced to Bronn. "What is that?"

He smirked. "I must admit, I've raised an excellent liar. It was a natural talent, easily cultivated. Unfortunately for you, I'm better. I know all your tricks, Ceylon, and no matter how stealthy you think you are, you always forget that I'm the one who trained you," Bronn said. He rounded the desk, leaning heavily against it.

"Perhaps that training made you soft," she replied.

"That was never going to be an issue." His eyes grew colder. "You see, I only ever needed you for your mother."

Ceylon glanced around the room. "Is this a trick?"

"Hardly. But you can think of it what you will."

"But my mother is dead."

Bronn winced, but it passed quickly. As if missing Ceylon's words completely, he said, "I met your mother in the royal gardens. She was a lovely thing, kind-hearted and gentle. She spoke to me like I was just...a man. She didn't care for my position."

Ceylon's fingernails dug into her palms, and she kept them hidden under her cloak. She knew better than to interrupt. Bronn had never shared anything of his life before Ceylon, anything of her mother—though it hadn't stopped her from asking. It felt cruel to be getting it at such a vital time.

She shifted in her seat.

Bronn ran a hand absently over the desk. It stopped atop the envelope, the one with the king's seal, crumpling the parchment.

"I loved her with all my heart." His face darkened. "I could have everything, anything I wanted, but not her."

"What does—" Ceylon started.

Bronn's knife slammed into the desk, piercing the envelope. Ceylon jumped, then straightened.

"Did I say you could speak?" Bronn asked.

Ceylon didn't respond, eyeing the blade instead.

"Pay. Attention."

Bronn plucked the dagger from the wood, his eyes pinning Ceylon in place. "I killed for her. I made the world better *for her*. And what did the king and queen do? They stripped me of my title and right to rule and gave it all to Owynn. They hid Adelaide away."

A deep chill sank into Ceylon's bones. The king and queen? What did they have to do with any of this? Everything sounded wrong. His love sounded like ownership, nothing like what Malachi had shown her. And his lineage. Could he be related to King Owynn?

"It took years, but eventually I found her. She was living in a small hut on the outskirts of Yvelle, and she was married."

Ceylon kept her face neutral as the words washed over her. Adelaide, married to someone who wasn't Bronn. A weight pulled her downwards.

"He was wrong for her." Bronn's jaw clenched. "He was weak, ill-suited to such a kind soul. I was going to show her. But the night I went to get her, the man attacked me. There was a fight and confusion and because of *that man*, Adelaide died as well."

Ceylon studied the flicker of hurt that flashed across his eyes. Bronn didn't love. He didn't hurt. She didn't like this story, and she didn't like where it was going.

"He'd used Adelaide for protection, and they both fell at my blade. It was the worst day of my life. But as I planned to leave, there was a baby. Cooing. The baby was now an orphan, alone in the world, just like me. And so I took the child." His gaze swung to her. "You created a perfect opportunity."

No. The word clanged through her head over and over as his words speared her directly through the heart. Ceylon hoped she was wrong. Her hand inched closer to the pistol.

"Do you know why I built the Underworld?"

Her throat was dry. She said nothing, but then, Bronn didn't want her to.

"Revenge. As soon as I saw you, I knew. I built myself an empire so that, one day, I'd show my family what they wrought, and I would use you to do it. Granted, the king and queen took care of themselves. But Owynn, well, he took my birthright."

The air ripped from her lungs. The missing prince, lost to time and memory. Erased from the annals of recent history, a small fact that inspired only an ember of thought in the lives of a commoner.

Somewhere, deep down, she had known. It was obvious now. But she could no longer deny it, hearing the words aloud.

He had killed her parents. He had killed her parents, and she'd spent her whole life striving to impress him. She'd wanted him to love her, to be proud of her.

But Bronn didn't love.

Ceylon leaped from the chair, aiming and firing the pistol in one swift motion.

She felt a knife whiz by her left shoulder. She hadn't seen him move, but Bronn had nearly skewered her with the blade that had been in his hand.

The bullet smoked hot in the wood behind him. The knife hummed. Two warning shots.

"If there was anything you taught me, it was to only trust myself," she hissed, holding the pistol steady.

He glanced at it. "That's really not your style," Bronn said.

Ceylon cocked the gun. "That's the point," she replied. "Step down and leave me the Scourge."

Bronn chuckled. "Or what? You'll shoot me?"

"You've already tempted me."

"Kill me, and they will never follow you. Besides, you're not strong enough. You were always too much like your mother."

Ceylon held in a sob, the words an arrow through the heart. The discarded locket lay on the desk between them. But her focus remained on the gun. Where she trembled before, now she was steady, trigger finger poised.

"Why did you send me to the Forsaken? I gave you what you asked, and you never even used it."

"No matter how much I teach you, you're still a disappointment. I should have killed you when I had the chance." Bronn glanced upwards, like the explanation was beneath him. "I never cared what happened to their little scrap of a guild. I needed you distracted while I put my final pieces in place."

He never meant to make her heir. She was a pawn, disposable. And she'd fallen for all his talk.

"So you kept me around to fulfill your vengeful fantasy? What are you going to do, kill your brother and take back the throne?" she asked.

Bronn strode around the room, her pistol following his movements, but it was like her hand wouldn't listen. She knew she would miss when she pulled the trigger earlier, now she wasn't sure she would get a second shot out.

"That was always your problem. You're too short-sighted. This is the long game," he said. "I couldn't care less about the throne of Yvelle, but as it happens, there's someone I know who needs it. In exchange, I'll get Adelaide back."

Ceylon blinked. Adelaide couldn't come back.

A *thump* sounded from the hall, then voices, and her veins chilled further. Malachi shouted, his feet dragging along wood and carpet.

"I thought you might like to see your *friend* one last time."

Gideon threw the doors open. Behind him, Brutus pulled Malachi along.

The lump in Ceylon's throat grew.

Malachi's fiery eyes flicked around the room, his struggle fading as he took everything in. Ceylon could do nothing but stare.

"Under regular circumstances, I would have you whipped for turning on me," Bronn said.

Malachi's head snapped to attention, genuine terror coating his features. He glanced between the Lord of the Underworld and his daughter, silently pleading with him not to kill her.

"Don't let him—"

Brutus punched Malachi in the throat, cutting off the words with coughs and sputters. Ceylon shifted, moving an inch toward him. There weren't many times in her life where she would have said she was terrified, but this was one of them.

Bronn's gaze shifted between the two. "Well, this is an interesting development." Ceylon couldn't stop the tears that welled. She told herself it was her anger. "I asked you to gain the boy's affection, and you've given yours in return."

Ceylon gritted her teeth. She knew she was in love with Malachi. She'd known it from the moment Bronn showed up at the Stormlock. But Bronn knowing it was a dangerous thing.

"How pathetic. Falling for a weak prince with no kingdom," Gideon sneered.

Ceylon's fist tightened around the pistol in her hand, shifting her aim to Gideon, and this time she did fire.

Gideon screamed as the bullet pierced his shoulder. It was all the distraction Bronn needed. His hand closed around the pistol. Ceylon gasped, wrenching it back. She threw a left hook, connecting with Bronn's jaw, but he barely reacted. They grappled for the gun.

She was no match. Even on her best days, she would never have beaten the Lord of the Underworld in a fight, but she had a lot more to lose now.

Still, Bronn grabbed her free wrist and slammed his forehead into her own. Stars danced as Ceylon stumbled into something solid. When her vision cleared, Bronn was handing the gun to Brutus, and she was leaning against the bookshelves behind her.

Gideon's howling broke her daze. He gripped his shoulder, attempting to hold the blood in by sheer will. At least she'd managed to do some kind of damage.

"Enough, Gideon." Bronn's voice cut through her thoughts. "Put the house on alert for the rest. I want the little witch. And do something about that shoulder." The Lord of the Underworld's words were final, a hint of ire peeking through.

Gideon reluctantly nodded, pale, and marched out the doors with a murderous look at Ceylon.

Part of Ceylon was grateful—at least they hadn't gotten anyone else. The other part of her was horrified. She knew how ruthless Bronn could be, and Anya would never follow his orders. Death would be a mercy compared to the pain she was sure to endure if they caught her.

"Please, leave the Forsaken alone." Ceylon's voice felt far too small. Nothing she said would change his mind, of that she had little doubt, but she had to try.

Bronn waved a dismissive hand.

Had he always been this cruel?

Malachi had tried to warn her. She refused to listen because she wanted to believe there was some part of him that loved her. Some part that wasn't overwhelmed with a desire for power.

Bronn dismissed Brutus with a nod. The mountain of a man hesitated, looking to Ceylon. She minutely shook her head. She would take whatever was coming as she always had—alone and with her head held high.

At last, it was only the three of them in the room.

Ceylon didn't know where to move. She wanted to check on Malachi, but she couldn't without weakening her position. She wanted to attack Bronn, but that would only get her and Malachi killed. Instead, she remained suspended between the two, a balanced scale. Her hands were entirely too empty.

"Isn't this quaint?" Bronn pulled out a new dagger, delicately running a finger along its serrated edged.

Malachi stepped toward Ceylon. "Quaint isn't the word I would use," he growled at the Lord of the Underworld.

"While I don't condone letting your feelings cloud your judgement, Ceylon, at least you managed to fall for someone with bite." If Ceylon could have clawed Bronn's face in, she would have. "Tell me little lordling, what hurts more? Finding out that Ceylon was working for me all along? Or that she really does love you, but she still can't save you?"

Malachi's hatred crackled across the room. Bronn's smirk remained.

Malachi brushed past Ceylon, scoffing.

"You're just an old man who's too scared of love to see it as valuable."

Bronn was across the room in a bound, and he thrust the knife into Malachi's thigh.

Malachi let out a howl of pain but quickly schooled his features. There was sweat on his brow and his breathing came quickly, but he did not cry out again.

"Do not speak to me of love, boy. You know nothing of it. You think you can turn Ceylon against me? She will always return to her family."

"Maybe. But you're not family anymore."

Ceylon gasped as Malachi lurched, realizing the familiar weight of the dagger she kept at her hip was gone.

Malachi thrust Ceylon's dagger at Bronn.

The blade met Bronn's flesh, but he was too fast, the warlord stepping back and avoiding any real damage. Yet blood bloomed beneath the hand Bronn held to his chest.

Bronn's face contorted into something wild as he let out a roar of frustration. But then that roar turned to laughter.

Ceylon didn't think as she ripped a piece of cloth from her cloak. She tied it around Malachi's upper thigh, ripping a second piece to put pressure on the wound.

"What the hell are you doing here?" she whispered while she worked. She was supposed to be the only one in the manor, the Forsaken miles away.

"Thought you might try something reckless. I wanted to be here to bail you out." He attempted his signature cocky grin, but it came out more like a grimace.

Bronn's laughter subsided, and Ceylon spun, her body a shield between Malachi and the lord.

"I must say, I am mildly impressed. That may be the closest anyone has come to killing me." Bronn's smile turned to a sneer. "Try again, and your breath will leave you faster than the east winds."

Malachi squeezed Ceylon's hand, so hard her fingers numbed, but she didn't move.

"Here's the thing, Ceylon," Bronn continued, "you completed the task I gave you, whether by your knowledge or not. Now I have another for you."

"What makes you think I even want to be a part of it after all this?"

Bronn raised his eyebrows. "Do you have somewhere else to be?"

Ceylon couldn't answer. She knew he was right when he said the Scourge would never follow her, not now. She'd shown weakness in their eyes.

She stared at the man she'd thought was her father.

"If you truly wanted to leave, there would be...consequences." Bronn leveled her with a vicious stare. "Are you interested in the job or not?"

It didn't seem like she had much of a choice. Ceylon gave a small nod.

"Good. You will kill King Owynn."

Ceylon was sure she stopped breathing, or maybe she had just heard incorrectly.

"I'm not going to kill the king." She sincerely hoped Bronn would correct her. She was disappointed.

"If you don't, Malachi won't live long enough to see the sunset." Bronn shrugged at the casual treason.

"I'm a thief, not an assassin. Get Alfie to do it, he's sycophantic enough to try."

"A thief you may be, but an assassin is your potential. I had you trained by the best. You can do anything you put your mind to. You intended to kill *me* just a moment ago."

"Don't, Ceylon," Malachi choked out, his face growing a concerning shade of white.

"How charming. He would rather die than let you become a murderer. Tell me, lordling, how many Forsaken do you leave behind if she lets you die? Do you think I will allow them to undermine my authority now I know where to find them? Ceylon is the only thing keeping your precious little family together."

Malachi uttered some response. Ceylon had stopped listening.

Bronn was placing the weight of dozens of lives on her shoulders. There was little choice involved. It was sacrificing one life or many. She would choose the one, even if that one was a king.

"I'll do it, but I want my own crew."

Bronn's eyes pierced her.

"No, you do this alone, and you do it tomorrow." Ceylon's stomach heaved. She only had one day to figure out how to break into the citadel and kill a monarch? "The king is hosting a gala tomorrow evening. I've already made the arrangements. Your name is on the list."

The letter on his desk, the one with the seal from the citadel; he had been planning this all along. And if he planned to have her kill the king, he never intended to make her successor because there was no way she was making it out of the citadel alive.

"A gala is far too public—my noble name is already known in Wellborn. You expect me to commit treason in front of the entire kingdom?"

"Hardly. You're much more resourceful than that. I trained you better."

Ceylon gnawed at the inside of her cheek.

"Of course," Bronn sneered, "I'll be there to supervise. I'll bring along your pet for extra incentive. And just in case you get any ideas, Gideon will be your date."

She risked a glance at Malachi. He stared back with sad eyes.

"At least patch up his leg. It'll draw too much attention if he's limping into a royal party." Ceylon tore her gaze from Malachi's.

"Fine. He needs to live long enough to be useful anyway."

That was the best she was going to get.

"And I want insurance. If I do this, I'll be charged with treason. I'll need to leave Yvelle. I want your promise that when I'm gone, you'll leave Malachi and the Forsaken alone." It indulged the fantasy that she could kill a king and live, but she had to stand her ground.

"All right, I'm a man of my word. So long as they stay out of my way, I promise to leave the lordling and his band of hooligans alone. *If* you kill King Owynn."

Ceylon nodded her agreement.

She knelt beside Malachi one last time, brushing a strand of hair from his face. She stared into his eyes, memorizing the flecks of yellow amongst the green.

And then she forced herself away.

Ceylon had an assassination to plan.

THIRTY

Ceylon

As Ceylon delved into the heart of Yvelle, cutting through the smog and haze of city life, she found herself unexpectedly meeting dead ends and unfamiliar alleyways. The streets whirled and bled together in her mind; she was lost in her own home.

This was to be expected. So much of what she was once certain of was false; there were very few things she knew to be true. She held onto those truths, hoping they would guide her.

One, she could no longer deny her feelings for Malachi. Two, in order to save him, she had to kill the king. And three, her father was not her father, and she had spent many years fighting for the wrong side.

It was this third point she focused on to keep her mind from spinning entirely out of control. She had fought her whole life for Bronn's attention, for his approval. Now, it was never going to happen. Malachi was right—she was Bronn's weapon, that was all. Whatever title or relation they had as family was simply a means to an end.

At least she knew where she stood as she threw her life away.

The citadel was a vast expanse that could be seen from anywhere in Yvelle. It taunted Ceylon as she made her way through town, hoping an idea might fall into her lap.

She was so distracted she didn't even notice Domenyk step out of the shadows directly into her path. Ceylon bounced off him, stumbling into the alley.

"Where is Malachi?" he asked, eyes aflame.

She couldn't muster anything more than a whisper. "Bronn has him."

"We have to get him back. The Lord of the Underworld won't keep him alive for long. Come with me."

Ceylon held her ground as Domenyk pulled on her wrist. Her arm was limp in his hand. He gave her an incredulous look, eyes widening at the blood that still stained her.

"We need to help him."

"He's safe for now. You need to gather the Forsaken and leave Yvelle, especially Anya." Ceylon's eyes stayed riveted to the ground. She had placed her trust in an evil man. Every life Bronn took prior to her time with the Forsaken had been but a symptom of her acquiescence. She could not bear the thought of facing Dom with this news.

"What do you mean he's safe for now? If he's with the Lord of the Underworld, he's not safe at all." Domenyk dropped her wrist; it flopped to her side.

"A deal has been made. You should go before we're seen together, it could compromise everything." Ceylon made to leave.

Domenyk stepped in her path. "Malachi sacrificed himself today to save you. Don't you feel any kind of responsibility to save him?"

"You think I don't know that? As soon as I saw him with Bronn, I knew what he had done. I have the situation under control, and you need to trust I'll take care of it."

"How am I supposed to trust you? You're the reason we're even in this mess! If you had just stayed in your pretty tower with your father none of this would have happened."

An ember of anger welled, and her chest hitched as she fought for breath.

"That man is *not* my father," she yelled. "I don't know who he is."

Ceylon's shoulders slumped forward as the truth of the words settled over her, a shroud from which she could not escape. Bronn had raised her, trained her, had misguidedly taught her what family meant. It wasn't so easy to discount eighteen years of her life.

All of it was spoiled, rotted fruits withering before her eyes. Her parents were dead, and her guardian was a stranger, a madman holding the only people she truly cared about hostage.

Sometimes the title of family needed to be earned.

Domenyk was quiet for a long while. "What do we do?"

"*We* do nothing. *I* am going to kill the king. In exchange, Bronn will release the Forsaken and Malachi."

"You can't kill the king, that's treason." Domenyk's eyes were as big as saucers.

"What choice do I have? The options are to kill one man or be responsible for the deaths of many. What would you choose?"

He did not speak. Ceylon turned to leave again.

"Wait," Domenyk whispered.

Her feet stilled on the cobblestones. Ceylon didn't know what she hoped to hear, but her heart stuttered.

"At least come get cleaned up. You won't get anywhere covered in blood like that."

Ceylon glanced down at her cloak, Malachi's blood splotched and splattered across the torn fabric.

Ceylon didn't fight as Dom placed a gentle hand on her shoulder, leading her toward the Hollow. She was probably being watched. She knew she should turn around and head in the opposite direction, but she couldn't muster the strength.

Before long, the familiar abbey façade came into view. They tucked inside, and Dom led her to the washing rooms. He helped her out of her cloak, discarding it on the floor. For a moment, she thought he might clean her off, too, but he just pressed a damp cloth into her hand.

Her fingers clenched around it, but she didn't move.

"Come on, Ceylon, you can't give up now."

They sat in silence another moment, and then she whispered, "He killed my parents."

"What?" Dom froze, brow furrowing.

Ceylon stared at the worn stones beneath her feet. "Bronn killed my parents, and now he's going to kill Malachi."

Dom leaned in to see her face. "You said earlier Bronn wasn't your father…"

The words caught in her throat. It was one thing to be told the truth, it was another to share it. Saying the words aloud made it real. It meant she could no longer deny what was right in front of her.

"He stole me when I was a child. He killed my family and raised me as an act of revenge."

Dom absorbed her words, holding them in.

Ceylon realized she had more in common with the Forsaken than she'd even realized; Willow, Anya, and countless other guild members, bound together by the violence Bronn had inflicted upon them. Now that she knew that hurt, she could finally understand their kinship.

No wonder they felt like family.

"What are you going to do?" Dom asked.

"The only thing I can." She raised her head, meeting his gaze even as she felt hollowed out on the inside. "I'm going to kill the king at tomorrow night's gala to save Malachi. Bronn made a promise: he leaves you all alone if I kill King Owynn."

Dom crossed his arms. After a moment he said, "That's still a selfish choice. What happens to the rest of Yvelle if the king dies?"

Ceylon's jaw clenched. "I didn't say you had to agree."

"I'm just saying, we still don't know why Bronn wants the king dead, not really. I want to save Mal probably more than you, but I also know he wouldn't sacrifice a whole kingdom for his own life."

"If you're not going to be of use, you can just go." Ceylon turned her back to Dom, facing the pool of water.

"I just—" Dom sighed. "I didn't say I wouldn't make the same choice."

Something lightened in Ceylon's chest at the words. She knew what Dom meant. She knew he was right.

"One problem at a time," Ceylon breathed. "First, I save Malachi. I save the Forsaken. Anything after is tomorrow's problem."

The quiet in the room stretched to discomfort.

"You know you'll never make it out," Dom said.

Ceylon couldn't help the dark chuckle that burst from her. Malachi had mentioned once how logical Dom was, how it wasn't always the most welcome, but it was necessary. She never imagined Dom would use it against her.

Still, she didn't respond.

"Have you ever killed someone before?" Willow's voice echoed off the walls.

Ceylon turned to see her leaning against the doorframe. A bandage bound her calf, and thin scars covered her arms, but otherwise she looked no less like herself.

Ceylon shrunk as Willow limped closer; the girl set herself down on the edge of the baths. The familiar glint of ire, held in reserve for Ceylon, was missing from Willow's eyes.

"I take it you have?" Ceylon wasn't sure what else to say.

"I've been many things to many people, but my blades sing their own songs." Her eyes darkened. "I don't wish to go back there, but I would, for Malachi. Would you?"

Ceylon wanted to disappear. She didn't want to think about any of this, but she knew the truth, even before she answered. "For Malachi."

Willow's eyes shuttered closed. Dom watched them intently, bracing as though waiting for a fight.

"I'll help you," Willow said. "I still don't like you. I think you deserve everything that's come your way. But Malachi doesn't, and for whatever stupid reason, he seems to trust you."

Ceylon clenched her teeth together to keep from responding.

"What do you know?" Willow asked.

Ceylon didn't have a choice in allies, so she would take what she could get. Dom settled in, pulling up a wooden stool, interested to hear her plan.

She relayed what little information Bronn had given her. She had never stepped foot inside the citadel, though, and so her notes were rather short.

"And I need to do it alone. Bronn will know if anyone is helping me. I'm not willing to put Malachi at risk like that again, not anymore."

Dom scrubbed a hand over his face as Willow sighed.

"Well, two things are certain: the king has to make an appearance, and he has to leave," Willow said, considering.

They flew through bad ideas, crossing them off one by one, in a world of their own. Ceylon's mind grew distant as two new ideas came to her.

There was a possibility Ceylon could catch the king's attention at the gala—Ceylon of Townsend was a well-known name in Wellborn. She would only need a second to kill him. But that would mean leaving a dead body in a crowd full of witnesses and guards. If she were to choose that method, she would need to frame someone else for the murder in order to leave the citadel as a free woman. Poison would be the best bet for that choice. She could spend a second with the king and leave him before he reacted. With the right compound, she may not need to frame anyone at all—even if he had a taster.

Her second choice was to wait until he retired for the night. It would be a much simpler process if he were alone, as there was less chance of being caught. The king was unmarried with no children, much to the chagrin of his advisors, so there was no worry about being caught ahead of time.

The risk was the guards. She had no chance to observe their patterns. They were likely to check his chamber before he entered. Ceylon would not have a chance to examine the room thoroughly enough to pick a hiding place. Plus, there was no telling how long the king would stay at the gala. If Bronn got tired or restless, he may kill Malachi before she had the chance to make a move.

Willow and Dom continued their chatter, but they stopped short as Ceylon said, "I need to poison him."

"It does seem like the best choice to escape implication. But very few have access to such toxins," Willow agreed.

"I know someone," Ceylon whispered.

Poison meant a trip to the healer's cabin. Ceylon debated heading there immediately but decided it could wait until the morning. She had never used it before, but she had retrieved some for Bronn. It could be made in a few hours.

"Well, then I guess we should all get some rest," Dom said as he stood.

Willow nodded, glancing down to the blood still staining Ceylon's hands. "We'll be along in a minute."

Dom hesitated, but ultimately left the room. Willow took the cold cloth from Ceylon's hands, guiding her into the water, clothes and all. Willow's hands were gentle as she began wiping away the trace of what Bronn had done, and then she started in on the charcoal, still a patchy coating on Ceylon's hair. Slowly, the water around her turned black, then diluted into a cloud of gray.

Ceylon swished a hand through the murky water.

They didn't speak as Willow worked, and somehow, it was a comfortable silence.

Once dried, Ceylon let Willow lead her to an empty dorm. Willow didn't stay to stand guard over Ceylon as she might once have done.

Alone in the waning light, Ceylon curled into a ball on the cot. Loneliness taunted her as she watched the sun paint the walls in oranges and yellows. A hollowness spread through her, starting from her chest. It was as though she was nothing, just the essence of a being floating in time and space. She had let her world come crashing down around her and had been too blind to see it happening.

She missed Malachi.

This would be the only time she permitted herself to feel these emotions. She had a job to do, and it would only hinder her progress. Besides, she was not completely lost yet. She had a family to protect—one she had chosen for herself.

In the cool air of early morning, Ceylon crept out of the abbey before anyone else woke, tracking back through the streets to the best healer in town. The sky flashed a vibrant red as the sun peeked over the horizon. Red skies at morning were rare in Yvelle—it meant there was a storm coming.

The healer had no name, and no one ever saw his face. He worked his magic in potions and brews for those who could afford them. He did not pry as to where they ended up.

His small hut lurked on the edge of the Underworld. Once inside, the healer faced her, head shrouded by his dark hood. He did not speak, waiting for Ceylon. The few words she had gotten out of him over the years were short in a deep, calming voice.

"I require a brew, one that will be undetectable and appear as a natural death."

The healer gave a slight nod of his head, motioning for Ceylon to make herself comfortable in whatever way she could.

Ceylon paced about the shop. All the herbs were neatly labelled, and the place smelled of a fragrant valley. She wondered how one learned about all the plants Yvelle had to offer and how they could be used. Watching him work was similar to watching a clockmaker fit each small cog into its place. The only real difference was the glitter of light that surged from his cauldron every so often.

She tapped her foot against the old wood floors. Dried lavender crackled under her fingers. If she hadn't become a thief, maybe she would have been a botanist. Maybe she would have joined with Malachi and moved to a tiny hut at the edge of New Town. Maybe she would have had a real home, a place that was a home because it held family, not because it relied on some transaction.

Sooner than she would have liked, the healer was thrusting the poison into her hands. Ceylon held it at a distance, not wanting to accept the task she had to accomplish, clinging instead to the fast-fading dream life. The vial contained a cloudy white liquid, but there was barely any inside. Still, it roiled back and forth in whispering tendrils. One could tell just by looking at it that it was not for consumption.

The healer teetered back to his station, dismissing her without another word. The concoction added to the Lord of the Underworld's tab.

Ceylon pocketed the vial, feeling the weight against her thigh. She tried to push the thought from her mind as she made her way back to the abbey, unsure where else to go.

Her trip to the healer had felt like a blink, but the sun sat high in the sky now, revealing she had spent a couple hours in the shop. Ceylon needed to pick up her pace.

THIRTY-ONE

Malachi

They didn't put him in the dungeons. Malachi wasn't quite sure why. Instead, he had a view of the Suri Kulu through a window gilded with metal bars. The only piece of furniture was a bed. Simple, unlike the four-poster one Wildar had left behind. But in some strange way, this empty wooden room felt comfortable and familiar.

Maybe because he was indulging his sorry state.

Blood still leaked from the wound on his leg. Bronn had said they'd send someone to patch him up, but Malachi was beginning to suspect that was a lie. Sweat dripped down his back and his hands shook, his skin paler than it should have been.

Well, nothing he could do about that now.

His mind wandered to Ceylon, to the Forsaken. He had failed to kill Bronn, and now Ceylon was about to commit treason. For him. In a way, he was thrilled. He had finally managed to show her Bronn's true colors, that they were on the same side, and yet, he wouldn't be with her to share in the victory.

He didn't think he could accept the possibility of defeat.

But maybe, should the worst come to pass and Bronn get away with his plans, Ceylon would be there to continue to fight. Maybe she believed strongly enough to take up the helm once Malachi was gone.

The door of his jail snapped open. Malachi straightened from his position on the floor as he readied for whatever came next. Gideon shouldered through the door, carrying an armful of glass vials and bottles.

Malachi gave the Scourge a thorough—but subtle—once over. Aside from whatever was in his arms, Gideon didn't appear to have any weapons. His shoulder injury seemingly healed as well.

The Scourge knelt beside Malachi, setting everything on the ground except one vial, which he thrust toward Malachi.

"Drink this," he said as he perused the rest of his trove.

Malachi took the bottle, but he did not open it. After a moment, Gideon looked up.

"That wasn't a request. If Bronn wanted you dead, you wouldn't have made it out of his office."

Malachi's jaw twitched. Gideon was right. Bronn gained nothing from killing Malachi now. He was smart enough to know Malachi was a good bargaining piece.

Malachi unstoppered the bottle and sniffed. There was no scent; the liquid was a gloomy pink. He couldn't place the concoction, but he also wasn't a healer. As far as potions went, he only studied what he needed.

He tossed the liquid back. It burned on the way down, like whisky, but the pleasant warming that followed was not one of a buzz. It was definitely magic, his body awakening to his injury and marching to heal. Instantly, Malachi was alert.

With a deep breath, he pushed off the floor, tackling Gideon to the ground. The Scourge, startled, throwing his hands up, and grunting as his back hit the floor. Malachi placed all his weight on Gideon, clutching at his throat. But his leg was still weak, and he couldn't hold the position long. Gideon bucked, threw punches, and managed to shove Malachi off.

"Stop," Gideon ordered hoarsely.

"I know what you did to her," Malachi growled.

His legs shook beneath his own weight. Whatever that pink liquid was gave him some strength, but not enough.

"You know nothing." Gideon glanced at the scattered bottles. "Just let me help you."

"I don't need help from the Scourge." But as Malachi said it, his knees buckled.

"Seems like you might, mate."

Malachi's breaths became heaves. His head spun, or maybe the room was really tilting. Before he knew it, the floor surged to meet him. Only he didn't land. Gideon's arms wrapped around Malachi's torso and dragged him onto the bed.

"Believe me, I'd rather you be far from here, too," Gideon mumbled.

Gideon returned to his bottles. He picked a few, along with some clean linens, and sat on the edge of the bed beside Malachi.

Malachi wanted to run, but Gideon was right—he'd never make it far in this state. That didn't mean he was helpless, though.

"You know Ceylon will die," Malachi said, hoping at least some part of the Scourge might care. Some small piece that might not have been shredded like the rest of his soul.

Gideon's face hardened as he ripped away Malachi's pant leg. "She wasn't supposed to."

It wasn't the answer Malachi had expected. Gideon rolled his eyes. "But it's all the better for me."

Gideon smeared something on Malachi's wound. Malachi hissed at it sting, a burning sensation like someone was cauterizing it. When he glanced down, that's exactly what it looked like, too. The gash bubbled, reddened, and began to close.

"Now, drink this." Gideon handed Malachi a different vial.

Malachi didn't hesitate with this one but was disappointed to find it didn't return any strength to him.

Gideon started wrapping Malachi's leg in clean linens.

"Why are you helping me?" Malachi asked.

"Boss' orders."

But Malachi wasn't so sure. Bronn could have sent anyone. Gideon seemed smart but was clearly not a healer. Ayleth knew the body inside and out. Charms and potions helped heal people, but she didn't rely on them. Gideon, on the other hand, seemed to use them exclusively.

"You need to be able to walk for the gala," Gideon said as he stood.

"I won't go." Malachi's head swam.

"You won't have a choice. You're not that strong."

The Scourge began to pick up the remaining contents he'd brought in.

"Someone will bring you a suit later. Don't try anything with them either—you don't stand a chance in the Manor." Gideon paused and stared until Malachi felt uncomfortable.

He didn't stand a chance *in the Manor*. Did that mean he might outside of it?

"Try not to die," Gideon said as he turned and left.

Malachi's head swam in a different way. Bronn would be at the gala, so would Ceylon. The king, too. There would be plenty of eyes, but the truth remained: if Bronn was dead, Ceylon wouldn't have to kill the king, and the Forsaken would be safe.

He might not make it out, but he didn't have to. All Malachi needed was a moment to get close to Bronn. Malachi lay back down, thinking through everything he knew of royal galas. It wasn't much of a plan—waiting for the right moment—but it was all he had.

Thirty-Two

Ceylon

Ceylon breathed in the verdant scent of the Hollow's airy courtyard, taking in all the beautiful plants, savoring them. She might not have another opportunity to do so.

The moment was crushed as Willow limped into the gardens.

"There you are, I've been looking all over," the girl said.

She grasped Ceylon's arm and dragged her back inside. For someone with a pretty serious leg injury, Willow moved quickly.

"Where are we going?" Ceylon asked.

"You can't go to a gala looking like death, now can you?"

Ceylon considered the implication—she wasn't sure she'd make it out alive anyway.

Forsaken ran to and fro with weapons of all kinds. Children carried guns. Her gut twisted.

"I don't have anything else to wear," Ceylon mumbled as she stepped around a cannon. She couldn't imagine where they'd been hiding it for her not to notice.

"I do," Willow said.

They came to stop outside a locked door on the top floor. Willow took out three keys, turning them in the mage locks to reveal a dusty trove of Wellborn treasure. Ceylon stepped inside, running a finger over a dust-laden chest.

"Is all this yours?" Ceylon asked.

Willow stood in the doorway, staring. "It was."

Ceylon had always thought Willow looked like she belonged in another world. One with galas and dances and princes. She'd mentioned Bronn killed her whole family.

Willow was a noble.

Ceylon swallowed the lump in her throat.

Willow didn't look around as she walked to the chest and unlatched it. Fabrics from various lands were neatly folded, pristine despite the dust in the room. Protected from the years locked inside the wood.

Willow picked up the one on top, bringing it to her nose. Eyes closed, she inhaled. Ceylon wasn't sure where to look. It felt like intruding on a private moment, and for once, a room full of priceless treasures felt like the wrong place to be. But then Willow opened her eyes and continued her search.

"This one," Willow said, thrusting a gown at Ceylon.

Ceylon wanted to say no. She wanted to say she wasn't comfortable wearing something of Willow's. But then Willow was back outside, leaving Ceylon to change alone.

The dress was made of a silk in such a pale blue it was almost white. It was simple—a high neck with long sleeves that fastened around her middle fingers and no embellishments. It was fitted to the waist, flaring out just slightly to mimic womanly curves. What surprised Ceylon the most was the back seemed to be absent.

She turned the dress this way and that to see if she was missing something. The harder she looked the more confused she became.

"Willow, I think the moths got to this one..." Ceylon hollered through the door. Willow *tsked* back and told her to just "put it on". So, she did.

It fit Ceylon perfectly—which was a surprise considering it belonged to someone else. The neck buttoned at the top, but the back of the dress was entirely open until just above her tailbone. Of course, Ceylon had worn questionable things before, but this was a different kind of event where drawing attention was not necessarily a benefit.

When Ceylon emerged, Willow shoved Ceylon's shoulders back, forcing her to stand upright. Ceylon frowned before she realized it wasn't an attack, just a critique.

"It'll work." Willow nodded, but her eyes were haunted.

"Don't you think it's a little...much?"

Willow glared. "The women at these affairs wear wilder things than this. You'll blend in."

Ceylon bit back a response. This was the dress Ceylon was getting, and she had to admit it was rather beautiful. For any other occasion, she would have been swooning to wear such a masterpiece.

"Now we need to do something about that hair." Willow grabbed Ceylon's hand and paused. "And your face. You do look a little dead."

Ceylon raised a protective hand to her cheek. She didn't think she needed makeup, but she also hadn't looked in a mirror in a while. If Willow had been to galas like these before, Ceylon's best bet to make it out was to follow her instruction.

Willow dragged her back through the halls to a make-shift powder room.

"Sit." Willow pushed Ceylon onto a settee and set to work, brushing and braiding and pinning hair all over, inserting pearls and wildflowers that seemingly appeared from nowhere. Ceylon didn't argue with the woman's fashion sense—as much as she may have wanted to.

By the time Willow was finished with her, the sun was hanging low in the sky. Ceylon had run out of time to scout anything; she would barely have time to make it across the Suri Kulu. Her fingers began to tap along her thigh as anxiety spiked.

What if she didn't make it in time? What would happen to Malachi?

Willow shook Ceylon from her thoughts by placing a mirror in front of her face. Ceylon was taken aback by the style. Her eyes were lined with kohl, her lashes impressively long, and her hair had never looked so wonderful. There wasn't a bruise or scratch in sight. Ceylon would never know how Willow had placed so much hair atop her head.

Willow finished the look with a dark lip stain that matched the color of her hair. Ceylon was radiant. There was no way she would blend in as much as Willow suggested.

Ceylon stood, glancing down at the full ensemble. She felt like a different person, and for once, she wasn't sure if that was a good thing.

Then Willow handed over two knives.

Ceylon looked at the woman, the slight downward tilt of her lips. "I can't take these from you."

"Consider it a loan." Willow placed them in Ceylon's free hand. "There are hidden compartments in the dress. They won't find anything if they search you."

Ceylon nodded, tucking everything away as her stomach gave a twist. With a dress as tight as this one, no one would question whether or not she was dangerous. She wished they were right.

The spent obstrepat charm from Malachi still hung around her neck. And though it didn't match her current splendor, she didn't take it off, brushing her hand over it for comfort. A reminder of what she stood to lose.

"Good." Willow almost smiled. Ceylon was glad to have her help.

"I guess I should be going." Ceylon couldn't convince herself to move from her spot.

"Take the coach." Willow pointed to the far end of the abbey, where there may once have been a stable.

"You have a coach?" Ceylon asked.

"For emergencies only." Willow shrugged. "I'd say this counts."

Dom jogged into the hall, panting. "Good, I thought I'd miss you."

Ceylon gave him a weak smile.

"I'll get the Forsaken out of Yvelle. And if you're not out of the citadel by midnight, I'll come find you," he said.

Ceylon didn't know how to express the hope that welled within her. She just nodded, turning to leave.

"And Ceylon," Willow started. Ceylon looked back over her shoulder. "Make him pay."

There was fire in Willow's eyes even the dying sun couldn't dim. Ceylon pressed a palm to the poison hidden in her dress.

"I will," she said.

Gideon sat across from Ceylon in the carriage. Leo, who'd offered to drive, had paused to pick him up where they had originally intended to meet. Gideon's eyes lingered uncomfortably long, holding a secret she couldn't quite read, and she decided to teach him a lesson about propriety later. For now, she ignored his leers and walked through her plan.

As she watched the citadel loom into sight, she wished she had more time to study it. Her situation weighed on her. There were layers upon layers of stone walls that would be easy to lose yourself in if one didn't know the way around. The actual structure was built into a small mountain, the center of the building standing stories above the rest of Yvelle. It looked like the most extravagant layer cake Ceylon had ever seen.

She was not one to get nervous before a job, yet she couldn't stop her pulse from racing as the carriage rolled down the gravel path, through stone arches to the bottom of the grand staircase. Leo leaped down from his seat to open the door. He held out his hand to help her down the step. She took it gracefully, telling herself she had been raised noble and knew the customs inside and out.

She took a deep breath, noting the scent of lilacs from the garden. Stars hung in the sky far above her, and she hoped they remembered her after tonight, if no one else. Ceylon burned the image into her memory, determined to see it again.

Gideon stepped out beside her, and for the first time she fully witnessed the atrocity that was his outfit. He wore a garish green suit, and he pulled on a mask. It was made of snakeskin and covered the top half of his face leaving his mouth exposed. Two small fangs sat just over his lips.

How fitting.

All around her, guests filed up the stairs wearing exotic clothing in vibrant, eye-catching colors. Willow had been right when she said Ceylon's dress was modest. What Bronn failed to mention was this was a costume ball. While Ceylon *felt* as though she was wearing a costume, she did not appear to be.

Gideon held out his arm. With a final deep breath, she gathered her skirts and placed her arm in his. The line ahead of them moved quickly with each noble being announced upon arrival. Ceylon was sure the names listed would be easily recognizable by those attending. While the Daughter of the Underworld was well known in the Underworld, her name in New Town and Wellborn was a different one.

All too fast she was at the front of the line with the herald waiting on them. She whispered to the man who gave her a vaguely impressed look but announced it to the room all the same.

"Lord Gideon and Lady Ceylon of Townsend," he boomed across the room. A slow murmur rustled through the crowd as they stepped forward to descend the staircase.

Ceylon took her time on the stairs, scanning the room for every guard, noble, and beverage cart.

"If you stand on the stairs much longer, you're going to turn into a statue," Gideon hissed through a smile.

She elbowed him in the ribs, and he grunted.

There were guards on the balcony that ran the length of the ballroom one story up, fourteen of them not failing to make themselves known. On the floor, more guards milled about, trying to blend in. Ten in total. Then another two at each door and four among the crowd in costumes instead of uniforms. That meant forty in total. Forty guards and at least a hundred guests.

"Care to dance?" Gideon asked as they reached the ballroom floor.

"No. Goodbye." Ceylon stomped on his foot and disappeared into the crowd. She knew Gideon wouldn't take his eyes off her, but that didn't mean she needed to hang about.

She had been mingling for only a short while, measuring her breaths to even her heartbeat, staying within sight of those two guards so as not to raise suspicions, when the herald's staff thumped against the marble floors. All eyes turned to the two large doors with complex designs at the far end of the hall. The herald announced His Royal Highness King Owynn Regimount Vaire the Third, and the doors sprang open.

The king was not what she had been expecting. He was younger, for one, looking only slightly younger than Bronn himself. He was well dressed but not nearly as exotic as the rest of his guests. The king had a kind face, one that had seen many difficult things and grown softer because of it.

She stopped her thoughts there. She could not feel for the man she was tasked to kill.

Once the king was on the ballroom floor, the crowd resumed the revelry. The music sang from a corner of the room and guests danced in circles in the center. The king made his way calmly through the crowd, pausing at every introduction, offering genuine concern for his subjects. Ceylon tracked him.

The two guards tailing him would need to be distracted.

A movement caught her eye. Her heart skipped a beat as she saw Bronn enter, Malachi close behind. Bronn wore a silver mask covering the top half of his face. It looked like a cross between a soldier's helmet and a masculine crown.

Subtle.

Bronn gave her a sharp look, prompting her to action. She risked only one glance at Malachi. He was trying to put on a brave face, but she knew he would rather die than have her commit treason. Ceylon would not let the Forsaken fall because of her mistakes.

She held two drinks in her hand, carefully placing a single drop of the brew into one. Once certain that no one had seen, she made her way toward the king. Ceylon reviewed her plan over and over in her mind as she walked, head high.

A sound on her right caught her attention, and she glanced to the left just as the king's sentry stepped in front of her. One of the glasses doused the sentry's uniform. Ceylon stared, mouth open, at the disaster in front of her. The sentry looked visibly jostled.

King Owynn's gaze landed on her. She could not tell what his stare conveyed but hoped it wasn't anger.

"My deepest apologies, Your Majesty, I meant no disrespect." She kept her head bowed and sank into a deep curtsy. His small chuckle caught her off guard.

"Please, child. Do not trouble yourself." He motioned for her to stand and looked at his soggy sentry. "Jerald, go clean yourself up. Pearson can handle my watch tonight."

The sentry bowed at the waist and left the king's side.

"I have not seen you at these functions before, what is your name?" The king's eyes traveled over her dress, taking in the simplicity amongst the many gaudy outfits.

"Lady Ceylon of Townsend, Your Majesty."

He rolled his eyes. "You may call me, Owynn. No need for formality at such a frivolous event."

Ceylon was taken aback. The king was much less pretentious than she expected. She held out her remaining beverage to him.

"Please."

"Thank you, but I do not drink." He gave a small smile. "I still have some duties to attend to, even at a function such as this."

Ceylon gave a small curse in her head. If the king did not drink, this was going to be a much more difficult task. Something she would have been able to discern had she more time to study her mark. The second sentry stepped forward to take the glass from her. He set it on the closest table.

She stared at the glass, trying to think of any other option.

Curse Bronn and his timelines.

If she'd had another day, a chance to scout the grounds, anything, she might have been able to get out unscathed. But as the liquid taunted her from the table, the truth settled like a stone within her. Killing the king would probably kill her too.

"Would you like to dance?" The king held out a hand. His sentry stepped forward, eyes wide, as if to oppose, but the king waved a dismissive hand.

Ceylon body grew numb, empty, as she forced her face to display the exact opposite. The secret knives pressed against her skin like unwelcome reminders.

"You're too kind," she replied as she placed her fingers against his palm.

The music swelled and the dance floor cleared as he led her to the center of the room. He hadn't been there long, meaning she was receiving the first dance. Her hands began to tremble, and she took a deep breath.

One step, two, and they were twirling around the room. She let herself relax.

"Your costume, it's like water. Simple and pure," the king stated. Ceylon stumbled, glancing down at her dress. "Did you not pick it out yourself?"

"No, Your Ma—" he gave her a pointed look, "Owynn," she amended. "A friend of mine loaned it to me. She's a visionary."

"I can see that. I may have to invite her to the citadel and have her pick something for me. Can't be outdone as the king, you see." The genuine warmth in his face solidified that pit of rock in her gut.

He was just a man, like any other. Yvelle could survive without him.

As they twirled, Ceylon considered her arsenal. She had a knife tucked into her sleeve. A single flick of the wrist, and it would be over before either of them knew it. He swung her out, and she prepared her strike. But she paused as he pulled her back in.

The king sighed. "I'm sorry, I can't keep pretending, it's not in my nature. I didn't expect to see you here tonight."

They didn't stop dancing. He kept her close, as if having a private conversation. The patrons would have suspected nothing, but Ceylon tensed, readying to defend herself. She had never met the king before—she would have remembered that.

The weight of hundreds of eyes fell heavy on her.

"You speak like you know me," she said, gauging the king's reaction.

His eyes met hers, and they were filled with sadness. "I do not know you, but I knew your mother, and the man you call father."

Ceylon held in her gasp. "Then it's true," she whispered. She had hoped it wasn't, that Bronn had made it up.

Owynn nodded. "You look very much like her."

"He claims everything was taken from him," Ceylon stated, her hand gripping tighter. The king winced but said nothing.

"He's not entirely wrong, but it was his own actions that led him there. He may say he loved your mother, but I believe he was obsessed. He was prepared to murder everyone in the kingdom on her behalf. He killed dozens of innocent people, convinced they were the scum of the earth. That's why the crown was taken, why Adelaide was hidden away," Owynn explained. His face grew graver with each word.

"He said he killed her accidentally, that my real father used her as a shield." Ceylon held her breath, hoping there was some kind of explanation. That he hadn't ruthlessly killed the woman he claimed to love and taken Ceylon only for the sake of revenge.

"He may tell himself that, but it was no accident. She died defending *you* from his blade."

As Ceylon's heart stuttered, she paused in the middle of the dance floor. Another couple skidded to a halt just before slamming into them. Words were exchanged, and Owynn led Ceylon off the floor, toward a bench along the edge of the room. Gazes followed, curious about her identity, but she ignored them. The roaring in her ears was too loud to make anything clear.

"How do you know all this?" Ceylon asked.

Owynn hesitated. He shifted on his feet before sitting beside her. "I had spies on my brother, Zorynn. I still do. I didn't know what kind of man he would become when he left, and I needed to make sure he wasn't going to become a threat to the kingdom," he said.

Ceylon was hyperventilating. The shallow breaths caused her head to spin. Ceylon glanced up, ignoring the leering partygoers. Her eyes locked onto Bronn—Zorynn—who headed straight for them.

Her mind cleared, her focus sharpened, until the disgraced prince was the only thing in her vision. She palmed the knife from her sleeve, a small, subtle thing, and rose from the bench.

There were no doubts in her now. She would kill the Lord of the Underworld.

THIRTY-THREE

Malachi

"Having a little heart-to-heart are we, brother?" Bronn eyed the king.

Malachi glanced between the king and Bronn. Surely, he wasn't implying he was the lost prince, Zorynn? As he looked between the two men, however, his doubts began to fade. They had the same nose, the same crease between their brows, the same stance. The similarities were undeniable.

Zorynn tightened his grip on Malachi's shirt, the collar biting into his neck. He tried not to grimace in front of the onlookers.

King Owynn took a step forward, all his attention focused on Malachi.

"Son?" Owynn asked, confusion filling his eyes. He blinked it away and straightened, steeling his expression as he looked back at his brother. "Perhaps we should go somewhere more private."

Ceylon looked like she was ready for the murder she came here for. Her hand shook, but her face remained casual. She didn't draw attention to herself as she slowly moved toward Zorynn.

"I think this is as fine a place as any, don't you, little brother?"

A few partygoers approached the king, unaware of the silent war brewing in the room. They fawned over him. He turned and smiled, greeting them without any of the tension that settled on the Lord of the Underworld.

Malachi stared at the king. *Son*, he had said. Maybe his mother really had been telling the truth. But if that were the case, he had been disowned. The king had denied him the chance at a relationship and caused his mother to spin out of control.

The king had denied him a family.

A flurry of emotions tore through Malachi, too numerous to name, but the one he felt, the one he could grasp onto, was rage.

At the king? At himself for not believing? At his mother for not telling him the truth? For giving up?

His life would have been different had the king accepted him. His mother would have been there when he needed her most. He would have had a true family.

The thought made his rage simmer—the Forsaken were more than he could have asked for. This stranger had no right to steal that from him.

All he could focus on was that anger as he watched the scene before him.

"Can we help you, Majesty?" A few of the sentries had joined their gathering, eyeing Zorynn attentively.

Zorynn tightened his grip on Malachi and raised his eyebrows to his brother as if to ask, *can they*?

"No, gentlemen. We're just fine as we are, thank you," he responded. The sentries wandered off, but not far, less than convinced their king was okay.

"What does he mean 'son'?" Ceylon asked, glancing between brothers.

Zorynn's eyes bore into Owynn's. The king returned the stare with a look of disappointment and wariness.

"Has he been telling you all about my past, dear Ceylon? All the truths you've been denied for so many years? Did he happen to mention his own faults?" Zorynn looked to Ceylon; there was obvious uncertainty in her eyes. "Really, Owynn, does that seem fair? Malachi, here, is the bastard son of the king."

Malachi's heart dropped into his stomach. Hearing someone say the words made it real, but it also made him an even more valuable bargaining chip. Ceylon's eyes widened. She looked at him, likely recalling a conversation in a hall with a boy who had believed he was going to be king.

"She deserved the truth. It wasn't going to come from you," Owynn growled.

Zorynn's eyes locked on Ceylon. "Tell me, *daughter*, what do you have to say to dear, old dad?"

Ceylon's hand tightened around something, and Malachi could only guess what it was. Her eyes burned with a fire he had never seen before.

"You're no family of mine," she breathed.

Zorynn glared at her. "I hardly think that's fair. After all, I did raise you."

"You did no such thing. You trained me. You did *not* love me. All you've ever done is take my family from me."

"Ah, but I made you. I made you strong and smart and loyal to a fault. Everything you are, standing before me today, is because *I* wanted you to be that way. If you had taken a single moment to truly look at yourself, you may not have been so easily fooled."

Fooled? What was he talking about? Malachi wracked his brain for anything he could do, any way he could escape Zorynn's grasp. He wriggled, and the Lord of the Underworld gave him a disapproving stare.

Ceylon lashed out with the tiny blade in her hand. Zorynn caught it with his own palm, leaking blood onto the marble floors. He shoved Malachi backwards, and he landed in someone else's arms. He struggled against the grip, about to yell, when his captor leaned close to his ear.

"Be quiet, and everyone might live," Gideon hissed.

Malachi thrust his head backwards, hoping to hit the Scourge in the nose, but missed.

"Just stay still," Gideon whispered.

He didn't have many other options.

Ceylon fought against Zorynn's strength, but she was no match for him. She slipped out a second knife, slicing him across the leg. He frowned but showed no pain.

"You've been nothing but a disappointment," Zorynn breathed.

Their fight was invisible. To anyone looking on they could be dancing as they grappled for purchase. Both of Ceylon's hands were now trapped in Zorynn's grip. He spun, making Ceylon stumble. She righted herself, thrusting her knife once more, but he stepped out of the way.

Her blade landed, hitting King Owynn in the chest. Both Ceylon and the king stared at each other in unbelieving shock. Zorynn pushed her into Owynn, and the two fell to the ground. Ceylon tried to remove her hand, but it was the only thing keeping her steady. She landed on top of the king, knife sinking further and cutting wider.

"No!" Malachi shouted.

The ballroom went silent. Every guest turned toward his scream, and he sincerely wished he had kept his mouth shut.

Ceylon was covered in the king's blood. Her stunning gown now a mess of pale blue and crimson. She attempted to push the blood back into his chest, her eyes empty and glazed. Malachi wrestled himself free from Gideon in his surprise and knelt beside the king.

Owynn turned to him. "I'm sorry, son," he choked. "I tried to protect you from all this."

Blood gurgled from the king's mouth. His eyes went cold, and his head fell back.

"Sentries! Help! The king has been stabbed!" Zorynn yelled.

Malachi barely registered the words as a numbness crept through him. All those emotions disappearing in an empty wave.

The ballroom exploded into chaos.

Guests screamed and shoved, forcing their way to the exits. Some pressed in on the scene like vultures hoping to pick at the gossip the king's dead body would inspire. Sentries fought valiantly to enact order as they ushered everyone out. Guards gathered around their king, taking in the gruesome scene. Ceylon stood, slowly, blood swiped on her face and dripping from her hands. She took one step back, her eyes now clear and calculating.

"Who are you?" the sentry in the middle asked the group.

"My name is Zorynn Raymond Thaddeus Vaire, first born of King Henryk and Queen Rania of Yvelle. This is Prince Malachi Vaire, lost son of King Owynn. That girl is an assassin. She has just murdered the king and attacked me." He held up his hands, revealing the blood dripping from where he had grabbed her blade. One knife lay on the floor beside the king, the other in his chest.

The sentries in the room tensed. The crowd looked between the two men. Even in death, Owynn had an uncanny resemblance to Zorynn.

"I know you. You have your mother's eyes. You used to play in the gardens when you were small." One of the older looking sentries spoke as he stared at Zorynn. His words sounded so genuine and loving, as though it was his own son who had returned.

Malachi recognized him from Scourge Manor. He had been there the day they went to get Willow. He doubted very much the sentry worked for the king. The rest of the sentries remained undecided, their weapons raised.

"You, girl. What do you have to say for yourself?"

Ceylon raised her hands.

"She didn't do it, he did," Malachi stated, pointing at Zorynn.

Zorynn sighed. "Oh, you poor thing. Nobody should have to witness the death of his own father."

Zorynn peered down at Malachi and gave an intentional look to the room. To the hidden soldiers, dressed as partygoers, now all holding weapons trained on Ceylon. Weapons like the ones they had destroyed on that ship.

Malachi clamped his mouth shut. No matter what, Bronn was leaving this room as a king.

The sentries shuffled and waited, unsure how to proceed. The older guard—the one who claimed to recognize Zorynn—stepped forward. "Take them all into custody; we'll verify their claims. But that one," he pointed at Ceylon, "lock her in the dungeons."

Guards stepped toward Ceylon; for once, her face was entirely an open book. Tears pooled in her eyes. She looked tired, empty. But through all that, he saw the apology in her eyes just before she turned and ran.

She side-stepped the first sentry that reached for her. Twenty paces across the ballroom floor and more sentries descended.

Ceylon twisted and turned, slipping out of their reach.

But there were so many sentries and only one of her. He knew how good she was, but even Ceylon couldn't outrun them.

Malachi's eyes found the knife, still lying beside the king's body. His father's body.

Zorynn didn't look Malachi's way as he leaped for the small dagger. With two swift movements, the blade was in his hand, and he surged for Zorynn.

"Hey!" Gideon yelled as he attempted to jump between the two.

Zorynn turned.

Malachi screamed as the knife slashed downward, connecting with Zorynn's shoulder. But not deep enough.

"I told you not to try that again," Zorynn growled, trapping Malachi's arms and pulling him in.

Across the room, a fist caught Ceylon in the stomach. She folded, sucking in a breath. Her fists were up, fighting back. She swung, and they grabbed her wrist.

With one hand trapped, she ducked and twisted out of the way.

Six guards surrounded her, trying to avoid her flailing arms. A second sentry managed to grab her other wrist. The others moved in, dodging her kicks. She let out a guttural scream as they lifted her off the ground.

They dragged her back across the dance floor, passing in front of Malachi and Zorynn. Her stare was fire and murder and hatred, all trained on the soon-to-be king. Malachi shivered. That look lias a promise.

"I'm going to kill you," she growled as the sentries led her past.

Zorynn shrugged. "You can try."

All Malachi could do was watch as she disappeared. He would get her out, he had to. Struggling against Bronn's hold, an idea began to form, and he stilled. If he was to be a prince, he would use his power to the best of his ability.

Guards separated Zorynn from Malachi as the warlord was ushered away, and the dead king's body was lifted from the ground. Malachi only had one thought, one motivation, one focus.

Ceylon had killed a king. Now it was Malachi's turn.

Thirty-Four

Ceylon

Ceylon was led through the citadel halls to the dungeons. They tossed her inside a damp cell smelling of musty stone and waste. She stumbled, bouncing off the back wall, all her fight lost.

"Sleep tight, murderous scum," the sentries taunted as they locked the door. The cell had a chill, and Willow's ruined dress did little to keep her warm. All she had was her own body heat.

Ceylon examined the floor, searching for the driest place to set herself down—an exercise in futility, as slick with the king's blood as she was. She settled for a corner, pulling her knees up to her chest and wrapping her arms around them.

The distant crash of waves from the bay lapping against the shore gave her some sense of space. She closed her eyes, trying to picture the shores beyond the dungeon's walls.

She didn't want to think about everything that had happened. About how she finally understood what love was, and how she would never get to experience it to the fullest. About how she was leaving Malachi in the hands of pure evil. About Zorynn's betrayal and Owynn's death. Death by her hand, no matter how it happened. She had stabbed the king. And now, there was a murderous tyrant who was about to become ruler over an entire kingdom.

At least she wouldn't live to see it.

Ceylon was unsure if she felt better or worse after hearing the truth about her parents. She had sought that knowledge for so many years. Now she had it, and she wished she didn't—it blurred the lines. She had lived in the grey for so long it was seeping into the only parts of her life that were clear.

The weight of consciousness was too much. She managed to drift to sleep, dreaming of a different life. One in a small cottage at the edge of town with a father who was a baker and a mother who loved plants. One where she hadn't been raised to assassinate a king.

Ceylon didn't know how many days had passed. They hadn't fed her but had brought a cup of water that was supposed to last her until whenever they returned. She made it work; it wasn't the first time she'd been placed in such a position. At the Scourge, she had been trained to withstand many interrogation measures. As far as she was concerned, this was one of the milder options.

She'd used a small amount of the precious water to clean the blood off her hands. It made her feel somewhat human again, allowing her to set her mind to other things—like all the ways she could go back in time and kill Zorynn.

She kept herself busy doing what little exercise she could in such a confined space. Sometimes she would hold herself up to the small window that overlooked the bay far below and daydream about the warmth of the sun.

The sentries had relieved her of any weapons. At the time, she had been recovering from shock and hadn't registered it. When they found everything she had, she cursed herself for not being more vigilant.

Ceylon tore off the bottom half of her dress not long into her stay. It made movement easier, but it also proved useful. When she was freezing, it could be used as a blanket, and during the warmer nights it served as a pillow or something to sleep on that wasn't the rocky floor.

She was just contemplating a second round of push-ups when the metal door leading into the dungeon creaked open. She assumed it was a sentry bringing her a new glass of water but was surprised to see Zorynn emerge from the stone staircase.

She rushed the bars. Thrusting her hand through, she grabbed at anything within reach. Zorynn was faster, deftly stepping out of reach. Ceylon slapped the bars in anger.

"Still have some fight left in you, I see. Well, I wouldn't have expected anything less from a daughter of mine."

"Do not call me that. You are nothing to me," Ceylon growled. She retreated, settling into a seated position in the middle of the chamber.

Zorynn watched her closely. He had no sentries with him, so it was safe to assume she wasn't going to die today. If he planned to hang her for the king's murder, he would have brought more men. He didn't underestimate anyone.

His hair had been smoothed back, his beard was combed into place, his clothes were extravagant, and a gold crown with deadly pointed spires rested on his brow. But his skin was paler, a sheen of sweat lined his forehead. And just for a moment, hope surged within her once more.

"Feeling okay, *Your Majesty?*" she asked, her heart speeding.

Zorynn gave a slight cough, and his eyes narrowed. "I'm fine. Kind of you to inquire after my health."

Ceylon hid her smile as she changed the subject. "That's a nice cloak. Did you steal that, too?"

"No need to steal something that's rightfully mine." Zorynn brushed a thread from his shoulder.

"The throne belongs to you as much as it does to me. Your own parents didn't think you deserved it."

The muscle at Zorynn's temple twitched.

"If the king and queen hadn't been so simpleminded, we could have ruled the whole continent, not just this kingdom. They were fools who deserved to die. My brother was no different." Zorynn paced, his movements purposeful. This seemed like a topic he did not care to discuss. It made Ceylon want to press the issue further. She opened her mouth to ask another question, but Zorynn interrupted.

"Don't you care what's become of your beloved Forsaken?"

Ceylon knew this game. If she spoke before Zorynn was ready, he wouldn't tell her a single thing. She sat with growing impatience, focusing on her breathing instead of the need to throttle the new king.

"They're safe, for now. Or at least, that's what they think. They left the abbey as soon as you entered the citadel. I've had each one marked and tailed as a contingency, should you or that little twat, Malachi, become a problem. I also had the abbey destroyed. No point in hoarding a disease when it could be so easily extinguished." He spoke in facts, as though that made it easier to swallow. It was clear what he was saying: As long as both of them played by Zorynn's rules, the Forsaken wouldn't be harmed.

Her fingers dug into her shins. "You promised they would be left alone."

"And I delivered. You did not specify the terms. The Forsaken are alone, free from the home they squandered. And your little Malachi is more alone than he's ever been—he's a prince."

"That wasn't the deal, they're still under your thumb." Ceylon leveled him with a glare she imagined could melt flesh.

Zorynn leaned closer to the bars, relishing his power. "Funny how that works."

Ceylon closed her eyes and focused on her breaths. There was no convincing him, nothing she could say would let any of them go, but she could still make him talk.

"Why do you even need Malachi? How does having him around benefit you?"

"Bringing in a lost prince paints me in a better light. Whatever Yvelle remembers of me, it wouldn't be someone who would save another, who would choose a successor." The word made Ceylon cringe. "Besides, I need both of you in different ways. As long as you're both here and alive, you'll do whatever I ask. Keep your enemies close." He gave Ceylon a wicked grin that made her skin crawl. She wanted to hide herself in the walls just to escape that look.

"And what do you want from me?" she asked, hesitantly.

"That's a more interesting question. At first, I wanted you to suffer. After all, you are the reason I was unable to convince Adelaide to run away with me."

"That was your own fault. If you had taken a single moment to realize how unhinged you really were, maybe things would have gone differently." Ceylon kept her eyes on Zorynn's.

The cell's bars rang with the impact of his hand; Ceylon jumped.

"Don't you tell me how things could have gone. You insolent little—"

"Now Zorynn, we don't want to harm the child. Do we?" A woman's voice whispered from the shadows, low and melodic. She was firm in her words but soft in her delivery; the hypnotic notes came back to Ceylon, the same voice from the Stormlock.

The woman stepped forward with a grace and ease that unnerved Ceylon. She hadn't even realized the woman was there. Her white hair, more stunning than Ceylon had ever seen before, was pulled back low. Sharp features only accentuated her beauty. Eyes, such a pale blue they were almost white, emphasized the dark shadows and sharp black kohl. Her lips were bow-shaped with a dark stain, and she wore a black gown with a collar that covered her neck entirely, curving out just below her ears.

But what stood out to Ceylon most of all was the small silver crown tucked into her hair, resting on her forehead.

"How lovely to finally meet you, my child." The woman placed her hand gently in the crook of Zorynn's arm. He had a tight-lipped expression on his face that said he wasn't pleased to be told what to do, but for some reason he had no choice with this woman.

"Who are you?" Ceylon asked, pushing herself to her feet.

The woman laughed, a light, beautiful sound. "How rude of me. My name is Magdaleana, but most know me simply as the Necromancer."

A chill crept over the dungeons, as though she controlled the shadows and whatever hid inside them. It couldn't be true. She couldn't be real. The Necromancer was a story told to keep children away from the forest. And yet, here she stood.

But if the stories *were* true, what business did Zorynn have with this woman?

Ceylon's eyes flitted between the two, hoping to see some answer they were not saying. Then it dawned on her.

"Adelaide," Ceylon breathed. Magdaleana smiled.

"Quite right. Zorynn and I have struck a simple deal. He would get me the throne, and I would return his lost love to him. It really is a tragic story, how she passed, isn't it?" Magdaleana put on a pouty face to feign her sadness. It only irked Ceylon more.

"Tragic doesn't begin to describe it."

Magdaleana laughed again with the clarity of a struck bell. Zorynn stood stoic beside her, eyes locked on Ceylon.

"Why did you come here? To gloat about having my mother all to yourself? If that's the case, feel free to leave. You've done what you came to do."

Magdaleana's eyes traveled back and forth between Ceylon and Zorynn.

"You didn't tell her? What's the fun in that?"

Zorynn gave a side-glance to the Necromancer.

"Tell me what?" Ceylon growled.

"Well, as it turns out, there is a small limit to my power. You see, in order to bring someone back from the dead, I require a living soul. Something to build their own soul around—a foundation, if you would."

The cell seemed to close in around her. Ceylon's fingers scratched against stone. A small time ago, she had believed today would not be the day she died. She was beginning to second guess that assumption.

"What does that have to do with me?" she asked cautiously.

"Ceylon, dear, you're the foundation."

It was poetic, in a way. Ceylon would die in order to give her mother life. That was how it was supposed to be the first time, wasn't it? Maybe this was just the universe's way of righting what had been wronged.

But maybe this is what she deserved. She'd caused so many people so much pain. She'd brought Zorynn to the Forsaken's doorstep. And now, all of Yvelle would be under his control. This was her mess. They were better off without her.

Ceylon couldn't find it in herself to feel much of anything at the realization. If she had to die, at least she was giving life to another. She barely noticed the tears spilling over her cheeks.

"Just do it," Ceylon whispered after a while.

"Excellent! The spell works so much better when the participants are willing. Zorynn, would you be so kind as to open the door?"

Zorynn glanced at Ceylon, then at the door, then at Magdaleana.

"You want me to let you inside with her? She'll kill you." Zorynn spoke matter-of-factly.

Ceylon would be lying if she said she wasn't tempted, but violence now would only ensure Malachi and the Forsaken's doom. She would not risk their lives to save her own. It was the life of one over the lives of many.

"I won't, I promise."

Magdaleana gave Zorynn a pointed look. "You see? She won't be any trouble." She held out her hand for the key to the cell, and Zorynn handed it over begrudgingly.

The sound of the door opening made Ceylon's heart pound. Zorynn locked the door behind Magdaleana, leaving the two in the already-cramped cell.

Magdaleana placed a perfectly polished hand on her cheek. The Necromancer's nails scratched at Ceylon's skin; they were filed to points and the color of blood.

"It is a noble thing you are doing for your mother. Please, lie down." She motioned to the center of the cell, the exact spot Ceylon had been sitting not moments before.

The rock was cold beneath her dress. It sapped any of her remaining warmth. Ceylon brushed her hands along the floor, feeling each bump and crack.

Magdaleana's skirts bunched around her waist as she knelt beside Ceylon. She made a couple motions in the air, depicting some magical rune lost to time, and whispered in a language Ceylon did not recognize.

The cell began to glow luminescent green, the floor around her echoing the symbols traced in the air. How few could say they'd seen the Necromancer's magics at work? A soft breeze blew through the dungeons. Ceylon closed her eyes, readying herself for whatever was to come. The energy hummed within her, resonating somewhere deep in her soul.

She felt the Necromancer's hand hovering over her chest. Ceylon expected to feel something more, a pull or a dash of ice, but nothing came. Instead, the winds subsided, and the glow of the room quieted. Ceylon risked opening her eyes. Magdaleana was glaring at her hands, at the diminishing circle on the floor, and then finally, at Ceylon.

"What are you? I can feel your soul, and yet, I cannot reach it," the Necromancer probed. Her voice was different this time, harsher, more frightening.

"What's happened? Why isn't it working?" Zorynn stood just outside the cell, his arms crossed.

Magdaleana gripped Ceylon's face, pointed nails digging into her cheek and jaw. Ceylon felt blood slip down her face. The Necromancer's eyes bored into her, searching for answers.

"Tell me what you are," Magdaleana whispered in a low growl. It was a threatening sound.

"What do you mean?" Ceylon asked. She glanced to Zorynn like he might have the answer, like this was just another thing he was keeping from her, but he looked just as lost as she felt.

"You did not tell me the child was an innate mage," Magdaleana's voice grew dark and accusing. She stood from the floor of the cell, dropping Ceylon's face. Zorynn unlocked the door, releasing Magdaleana and leaving Ceylon sitting alone.

"What do you mean she's a mage? She's shown no sign of innate magic. The child is human."

Magdaleana slapped Zorynn across the face. He stumbled, clutching his cheek, eyes alight with rage. A small piece of Ceylon was satisfied at his pain; he deserved a lot more than that. But he dropped his hand, clenching his fist, and said nothing.

"Obviously that is not the case as my magic did not work on her." Magdaleana took a deep breath, smoothed her skirts, and righted her tiara. "No matter, we can still use her. It will just take some time to figure out what she is and how to dampen her magic."

"I'm telling you, there is no way this girl has magic." Zorynn looked bewildered.

Magdaleana gave him a hard look. "Surely you are not suggesting I am so incompetent I cannot handle one child?"

Zorynn seemed to remember himself. "Of course not. I just didn't think it was possible."

Magdaleana placed a reassuring hand on Zorynn's shoulder. "Fear not, my king. We will find a way to bring your beloved back to you. And when we do, there will be nothing holding us back from all we desire. Patience."

The Necromancer lifted her skirts and ascended the stairs of the dungeon, leaving Zorynn alone with Ceylon. He did not speak, only stared at her for a very long time. After what felt like ages, Zorynn wiped the back of his hand across his brow and left.

Ceylon looked at her hands. She was a mage? She had no idea what her power might be, or how long she'd had it. The only other time someone used magic on her was Anya, and it hadn't worked either. Ceylon had thought it was a fluke, that Anya wasn't focusing enough.

Now pieces came back to her. The way she could never see the effects of obstrepat charms—or how they sometimes didn't work, and how the charm on the abbey felt blocked, like there was a wall between them. Whenever magic was trying to influence her, it was like there was something in the way.

She let out an angry cry. If she was so magical, why hadn't it ever showed up to help her before?

She wasn't sure how long she sat there thinking through all the possibilities.

The door at the top of the stairs sounded again. Ceylon barely registered it this time.

"You look pathetic," Gideon stated.

She glared at him. He held a single glass of water in his hands.

"What do you want? Come to gloat about your new standing?" Ceylon growled.

He placed the glass of water at the edge of the cell, just within reach.

"While I can't say I'm disappointed with it," he looked down at his fancy velvet coat, brushing the sleeve lovingly, "that's not why I'm here. Just remember Ceylon, some things aren't as black and white as you think they are."

She didn't say anything, just burned all her hatred for the boy through her stare.

After a moment he turned and paused. "Goodbye, Ceylon." Then he disappeared up the stairs and out the dungeon door.

Her brow crinkled. He wasn't one for sentimentality.

Ceylon crawled forward, retrieving the cup. There was barely anything in it today, another of Gideon's pranks. She didn't have it in her to ration it and downed the measly sips in a single gulp.

As her thoughts turned to the Forsaken, to Anya and Malachi, anger rose within her. She had to go along with whatever Zorynn had planned or her friends would pay the price.

Ceylon threw the cup across the room. It hit the back wall with a loud clang, rolling onto its side on the floor. She was about to dismiss it when something on the side of the glass caught her eye.

She crawled over to it, lifting it into the little light that peeked through the small window. There was something stuck to the side.

Carefully, she peeled away a small piece of paper. She unrolled it, her lock picks clinking to the ground. Ceylon snatched them up, hiding them in the collar of her dress and listening for any sounds of movement above her. Nothing came.

She glanced at the paper. Messy handwriting she recognized as Malachi's scrawl said, "*We'll need you on the outside.*"

Ceylon tucked the piece of paper into her dress. If she stayed and sacrificed herself for her mother, there were no guarantees Zorynn wouldn't kill the Forsaken anyway. Malachi was at the greatest risk for retaliation with his proximity, but he was the one telling her to go.

If Ceylon made it out, she could find a way to hide the Forsaken and get Malachi out. All she needed was a head start. She blinked, recalling Gideon's goodbye. Did he know what he'd just given her?

She didn't let the thought linger. She perked her ears to the dungeon door—nothing sounded behind it. Once her daily water was dropped off, no one bothered her until the next day.

Ceylon only needed to wait until dark.

THIRTY-FIVE

Ceylon

Night came slowly and all at once. Ceylon paused, listening for any sound of movement. They hadn't left a guard down here with her, and in this moment, she was all the more thankful.

The lock was more challenging than the one on Malachi's room—her heart gave a precarious *thump*—but it was still no match for her practiced hand. Before her panic could rise, she was greeted by the click of the bolt sliding back.

Ceylon wanted to squeal, but she kept her head level. She tied the extra fabric around her waist, slipping the lock picks in tight. It wasn't much for a weapon, but it was better than nothing.

The damp of the dungeons weighed on her as she cracked the door open. The hinges didn't squeak. Her shoulders loosened the slightest fraction. Outside of the bars, she bounded up the stairs, pausing at the top and pressing her ear to the door. There were the soft breaths of one guard, two. Two against one.

She'd seen worse odds.

Ceylon turned the knob slowly, testing if it was locked—it wasn't. She only let herself ponder for a moment what that might mean—someone was indeed helping her. Then she took a clarifying breath and thrust the wooden door open.

A punch to the throat had the first guard floundering on his knees, her arm already wrapped around the other's neck. She clung for dear life as they struggled, gasping for breath, slowly sinking to the ground. She dealt another swift kick to the side of the first guard's head. Ceylon leaped forward on silent feet, laying him on the floor. She took the dagger from his belt and listened. No movement, no alarms. She was clear to proceed.

The halls by the dungeon were simple grey stone, a stark contrast to the golden opulence of the ballroom. She rushed on—her knowledge of the citadel was weak at best, and she had no time to waste.

Heart thrumming in her ears, she took the hallways at a sprint, pausing at corners to check for guards. The farther she went, the more she was convinced someone had cleared the way for her. She'd traveled from the dingy stone halls to plastered and painted walls. The scent of warm stews filled her, and she realized she was getting close to the servants' quarters and kitchens.

Ceylon slowed as she drew closer. Her chest heaved, but she kept her breaths quiet. The door to the kitchens was open, the clanging of pots and pans resounding in a symphony. She debated snagging some food for her escape, but as she peeked around the door, there were at least twenty staff. Too many eyes. She waited until no one was looking and skirted past.

At the end of the hall was a small set of servants' stairs. From where she was in the lower levels, she gathered that going upward meant she'd be close to the foyer and her escape. Ceylon took the stairs two at a time, the worn stone soft against her feet.

Three levels up, she paused before the staircase door, but she heard nothing. Slipping into the hall beyond was a change in worlds. The corridor spanned wide before her. To the right, it continued; to the left, it opened to the foyer. Ceylon didn't allow herself the time to admire the luxury.

She scurried along the wall and across an opening, tucking in behind a white, gilded pillar. She was on a balcony, looking down to the wide-open main doors. A grand staircase led to the silver and azure double doors. She counted eight guards, four by the doors, two at the bottom of the stairs, and two by the adjoining corridors.

A coach was just about to leave.

Ceylon gripped the stolen dagger tight. She had a chance if she maintained the element of surprise. But eight guards in the middle of such an open area—easily within shouting range—the odds weren't good. She was about to backtrack when she turned to find a servant. The man took one look at Ceylon, at the dried blood and bruising, and dropped the silver tray to the floor with a crash. She sighed. No time like the present.

The servant screamed and bolted down the corridor leaving the tray and silver tea set leaking out on the carpets. The sentries spun, searching for the noise. She was still hidden behind the pillar, and a plan began to form.

She tucked the knife into her dress, picking up the teapot and tray. With her back to the pillar, she counted the footsteps. Two guards. A brief peek around the pillar—the two from the staircase.

A moment longer.

Ceylon swung the teapot out, scalding water hitting the first guard in the face. He screamed and backed away, blinded. With another swing she caught the second sentry in the head. The weight of the silver smashed into his skull, and he crumpled to the ground.

Six to go.

She ran for the stairs and threw herself over the banister, sliding to the main level. The sentries from the corridors shouted for reinforcements. Ceylon chucked the teapot as hard as she could at the closest one. It caught him in the gut, and he buckled.

Her feet smacked into the marble floors, and she ran. Four guards dashed for her, drawing weapons. But she didn't need to fight and win, she needed to make it through those doors.

The sentries converged, and Ceylon held the tray in her arms. With a dive, she pushed off the floor and landed on the tray, sliding through one sentry's legs and past the others. The impact knocked the wind out of her, but her eyes were already on the footman climbing onto the coach.

The last sentry desperately tried to pull the doors shut, but they were much too heavy for one man. She was on her feet and through the doors before they could blink. Down the stairs she pounded, a hand on the footman's shoulder. She didn't ask, simply pulled and threw him to the ground. Ceylon thrust herself into the seat, whipping the reins.

Two horses whinnied and took off down the laneway. Shouts surrounded, alarm bells sang, but Ceylon focused on the portcullis that was lowering much too fast. There was an open field to her left, a straight shot through, but the coach would drag too much. With a grunt, Ceylon stood, wobbled, and leaped for the horse on the left. It cried out, tossing her left and right, but she held on for dear life.

With a few slashes of the stolen knife, the horse was free of the coach, and she yanked left. Over bushes and grass she fled, leaving the rest behind. Wind whipped her hair, and water streamed from her eyes. She narrowly dodged an arrow.

Only a few feet left. The spikes of the portcullis loomed dangerously low.

It would be tight.

"Halt!" the sentries yelled. Their voices grew clearer as she got closer.

She ignored them. A couple bounds, and she would be out. The portcullis wailed before her. It was too low. It would take her head off.

She gasped as her horse took her through, throwing herself backward. Sweat dripped down her brow.

She stared up at the thick metal as they squeezed under.

And in a breath, it passed.

Ceylon righted herself. She led the horse away from the citadel, the alarms, and the shouts of angry men. Her heart was a storm, but she felt suddenly lighter.

Free.

She risked a single glance back over her shoulder. The gates of the portcullis now fully closed. The citadel, a place she had once fantasized about. Now she wasn't sure she ever wanted to go back, but as she stared, the silhouette of a boy in the window made her pause. He was too far to really make out, but she felt it. Him.

Malachi stared down at her from a fourth story window.

It felt like leaving her heart behind, but Ceylon turned forward in her seat, pushing the horse faster down the winding roads away from the citadel until she was sure she wasn't being followed. Then she curved to the east, toward the immense forest.

Only to meet a lone traveler on a horse in the middle of the road.

Ceylon grabbed for the knife, but the stranger removed his cloak.

Domenyk.

"What are you doing here?" she asked.

He came closer, eyes taking in the mess she was with concern. "I told you. If you didn't get Malachi out, I would find you."

Ceylon's heart flopped in her chest. This was a new feeling—pure gratitude. Some might even call it friendship. She nearly sobbed with relief. Before she could stop herself, Ceylon's hand whipped out, gripping Dom's arm in a grateful gesture. Dom stiffened, but after a moment, placed one of his own over hers.

"Come on, I know a place we can rest."

Dom led her further down the road and into an alcove that was far enough out of the way not to be seen. She welcomed the reprieve. Her muscles ached as she dismounted, the horse whinnying softly. She ran a hand over its snout. A moment of calm.

From this altitude, she could see Laoryf Bae in the distance, the ships docked and moored for the night. She hoped Bronn was lying, that the Forsaken were well hidden or long gone by now.

Dom came to rest beside her, staring out at the night. "So, what now?"

Ceylon let a killing calm wash over her. She glanced upward, where she knew the citadel hid just beyond the mountain bend.

"First, we regroup. We make sure everyone is safe."

Dom nodded in agreeance.

A deep wrath settled in Ceylon's gut as the image of Bronn—*Zorynn*—flashed into her mind.

"Then, we kill the king."

Acknowledgements

I should have kept track of everyone who read this book for me over the years. I know I've forgotten many (because, let's face it, this book was five-to-six years in the making). When I started writing this story, I thought it was just a fun little jaunt about a thief stealing something intangible. Instead, I realized I was writing about my own sad love story and what I thought love was supposed to look like.

So, to those who have read, thank you so much. You helped get this book right. A special thanks to Aspen Stafford and Lauren Searson-Patrick who were forced through multiple iterations of this story. Thanks also to Loie Dunn and Esther Weatherall for beta reading. To Laura Ross and Megan Wald for being my super-encouragers. To Max, Cass, and Angelina who assisted through many queries of, "What's a word for...?" To Aurora Rae who read this and loved it when I, once again, thought it was trash. And if I've forgot you in writing, please know that I have not forgotten the impact you had on getting this story to print.

Where would I be without my fabulous editor, Henry Sinclair? You took this fledgling story and made it shine, gave it life. Or my cover designer, Miriam Schwardt? (I would pick this book off of shelves because of you.) Or Emma Smith, for combing to catch all the mistakes that slipped through?

But the biggest thanks goes to the one who sat with me while I cried at yet another query letter rejection and offered to copy edit and proofread and be my whole team just to get this book into the hands of readers. Thank you for seeing how much this book means to me. Thank you for believing in me when I couldn't.

I also have to thank myself for being vulnerable enough to explore these feelings and pushing through over years to complete this story. So thanks to me for trusting the process.

And last, but not least at all, thank you for sharing this little square of the world with me.

About the Author

Erin (E.A.) Whyte has been devouring books since she could read. Though she never imagined the path of authorship, she's glad it found her in the end.

With certificates in Developmental Editing, Grammar, and more, she loves spending her days trapped between pages—of her works or others.

Erin enjoys a good café, corgi butts, and exploring the world, and she can't wait to get her next books into your hands.

Follow Erin on Instagram @eawhyte

For future book news, head on over to www.eawhyte.com